THE GOOD
POLICEMAN

Books by Jerome Charyn

THE GOOD POLICEMAN
MOVIELAND
THE MAGICIAN'S WIFE
   (Illustrated by François Boucq)
PARADISE MAN
METROPOLIS
WAR CRIES OVER AVENUE C
PINOCCHIO'S NOSE
PANNA MARIA
DARLIN' BILL
THE CATFISH MAN
THE SEVENTH BABE
SECRET ISAAC
THE FRANKLIN SCARE
THE EDUCATION OF PATRICK SILVER
MARILYN THE WILD
BLUE EYES
THE TAR BABY
EISENHOWER, MY EISENHOWER
AMERICAN SCRAPBOOK
GOING TO JERUSALEM
THE MAN WHO GREW YOUNGER
ON THE DARKENING GREEN
ONCE UPON A DROSHKY

THE GOOD POLICEMAN

JEROME CHARYN

THE MYSTERIOUS PRESS

New York • London
Tokyo • Sweden • Milan

The Mysterious Press, 129 West 56th Street, New York, N.Y. 10019

Printed in the United States of America
First Printing: July 1990

10 9 8 7 6 5 4 3 2 1

Library of Congress Cataloging-in-Publication Data

Charyn, Jerome.
    The good policeman : a novel / by Jerome Charyn.
        p.   cm.
    ISBN 0-89296-360-3
    I. Title.
    PS3553.H33G6   1990
    813'.54—dc20   89-39574
                                            CIP

THE GOOD
POLICEMAN

Part One

She was the little darling of
Pushkin Street. She would arrive at the Opera with Prince
Finkelshtein and Uncle Ferdinand. It was 1942. The Opera
House had lost part of its roof, but no one seemed to care. The
German tenor Minos Schmidt was Don Giovanni that night.
She could see the spittle flying from his mouth. Finkelshtein
wept. Magda thought it was unbecoming of a prince. But she
couldn't understand why a member of the Russian nobility
had to slave for Ferdinand in his own house. And she'd never
heard of a prince called Finkelshtein.

"Ma jolie," the prince said, holding her hand.

Ferdinand would taunt him. "Finkelshtein, you don't have
much longer to live . . . would you like to sleep with the
child?"

"No, Your Excellency."

"Then please let go of her hand."

She couldn't quite grasp the curious talk between them—
French, German, English, Roumanian, and Greek. They
were like Berlitz professors on the prowl. Ferdinand had once

3

slapped the prince in public. Finkelshtein. He'd been the most powerful man in Odessa until the war. It had something to do with olive oil. He'd created his own school for violinists. He'd lured opera companies from all over the world to Lastochkina Street. And now he was a kitchen drudge.

Ferdinand wanted to rename every street in Odessa. He put up new signs. Pushkin became Danube Street. Red Alley was Fortune Road. The Deribasovka was Little Angel Street. But the signs only angered people. No one would ever admit where Little Angel Street was, no matter what the signs said.

It embittered Ferdinand. He blamed the prince. "These are your lackeys, Monsieur."

"But I can't control their eyes."

"Of course you can. They're nothing but Odessa Jews."

"The Jews have fled, Your Excellency."

"No. They're hiding in the Catacombs."

The Catacombs was where the bad people were. The bad people hated Ferdinand. They lived in long tunnels under the town. It was 1942, and only some of the people were starving. Uncle Ferdinand had his Opera and a circus and bits of Finkelshtein's music school.

Magda was twelve years old. She lived with Uncle in a mansion on Little Angel Street. One night the Nazis came for Finkelshtein. Uncle could have stopped them. His signature was gold. The Nazis grabbed Finkelshtein by his feet. He managed to smile at her.

"Au revoir, ma jolie."

"Au revoir, Monsieur le prince."

And when Ferdinand made love to her that night, his great bulk above her, Magda moved like stone. How else could she punish him for not saving the prince?

She wouldn't cry. Ferdinand would only have shouted at her, and it couldn't have helped Finkelshtein. He wore his gun to bed, because no one could tell when the bad people might come, the partisans who lived like bats in their tunnels and caves. One of the cooks told her there was a second Odessa, under the ground, with an opera and palaces and a Pushkin Street for the partisans, because they couldn't bear to be without the city they adored. What did Magda know about people who were crazy enough to build their own Odessa in the dark?

She had two or three nights with Ferdinand, and then he buckled up his uniform and said, "Come."

"Where are we going, Uncle?"

"Come."

They got into Ferdinand's limousine and rode three blocks. The emperor of Odessa didn't like to walk. They arrived at Gestapo Headquarters on Gogol Street. Uncle danced her over to the little corporal at the gate.

"Major König, bitte."

"He's occupied, Mein Herr."

"He's always occupied," Ferdinand said. "My niece doesn't have time to wait. She has her dancing lessons, Herr Korporal."

And they flew into the major's office unannounced.

His tunic was draped over the chair. All his medals blinked at Magda. He was with a lady.

"Countess Leskov," he said, "this is our Roumanian friend. Herr Ferdinand, finance minister of the Odessa region . . . and his niece."

The Countess Leskov was naked under her coat. Her lipstick had bled onto her chin. She was the fattest countess Magda had ever seen.

The major put on his tunic. The countess took some of his money and left.

"How are you, Mademoiselle Magda?" the major asked. He had a beautiful blond face, with a tiny scar on his lip.

"Leave her alone," Ferdinand barked. "She's mourning the prince."

"I don't understand."

"Finkelshtein. She misses that man."

"But he's a Reichskriminal," the major said. "He's been

shipping guns to those dogs in the Catacombs. And he's not an authentic prince."

"Ah, but I think he is," Ferdinand said. "The czars liked to elevate a few of their moneylenders. And the Finkelshteins go back years and years in Odessa."

"An old wives' tale."

"Perhaps, but I need him back."

"I told you, Herr Ferdinand. He's a Reichskriminal. He's being processed this minute."

"I'm glad. But unprocess him. You'll have to lend me the prince."

"That's impossible."

"Then I will resign, Herr Major. Or perhaps you'd rather arrest me and the mademoiselle . . . I won't leave the building without Herr Finkelshtein."

"You'll end up paying a very bitter price."

"Yes, but my domestic situation will improve. That's what matters to me at the moment."

It took half an hour to produce the prince. He must have been lost somewhere in Gestapo Headquarters. His mouth was black-and-blue. His ears had tiny rings of blood. His eyes sat deep in his skull. Ferdinand found him a German private's coat to wear.

Finkelshtein wouldn't talk on his way home to Little Angel Street. He was Magda's soldier-prince. His face was much too swollen to laugh or cry. Magda wanted to ask him about that Odessa of the dark, where Gestapo majors didn't grab Gogol Street for themselves. But she couldn't say a word while Ferdinand was in the car. Finkelshtein muttered to her from the side of his mouth. "Merci, ma petite," he said, "merci," before he wandered up Ferdinand's steps to the house that was no longer his.

1

It could have been St. Louis. There was a metal rainbow in the sky, an arc that loomed over the city like a gigantic toy. And Isaac didn't feel like testing himself against toys. He wasn't little David out on a picnic with his lyre. He was a police chief who'd been riding across the country as a guest of the Justice Department. The great American detective out on a tour. Justice was sending him to meet with the country's other detectives, to share his information with them, his expertise, and to discover how police departments in Seattle or St. Louis dealt with the same pathology that Isaac found in New York. He'd captured Henry Armstrong Lee, the FBI's Most Wanted Man, a bank robber who liked to dress in women's clothes. And now Isaac was the first Alexander Hamilton Fellow, lecturing to men and women who had more sophisticated gadgets than Isaac had ever seen, who could reconstruct whole bloodlines from a speck of hair, identify serial killers with one spot of semen, but couldn't make the pathology disappear any better than Isaac.

The arc was bloodred this morning.

What other town had a metal rainbow right on the levee? He'd arrived with ten other chiefs from Missouri and Kansas who'd heard him lecture about social disease. Poverty and decay. The no-man's-land of certain housing projects where citizens had to form posses to leave their apartments. The biggest deterrent to crime, Isaac had said, was an alphabet book. "Teach a kid how to read and his curiosity goes inward. He'll dream about Sinbad the Sailor and he won't steal cigarettes from the old man down the hall."

And then the chief of some border town in Kansas asked Isaac if alphabet books could cure New York of the Mafia. Isaac said no. "There's nothing to cure. The Mafia's big business. But it's not on the board. It doesn't need a stock exchange. All it needs are citizens who can't get what they want from city government because it's too involved with feeling its own belly, and tickling its own back."

The chiefs smiled to themselves and wondered how long this Alexander Hamilton Fellow was going to survive in the same bed with the Justice Department, talking like the Mafia was only another city agency. But they liked his gruff manner and his graying sideburns, Isaac Sidel, police commissioner and big-city boy. He belonged in the funny papers, with Dick Tracy. But Dick Tracy didn't carry a bottle of milk in his coat, the way Isaac did. Isaac always carried a bottle of milk. He had a tapeworm, and when it got hungry and mashed his insides, he fed it with a swallow of milk.

He rode out with the chiefs along the Daniel Boone Expressway, across Gravois Avenue, to visit a "juvenile facility," because that's what Isaac wanted to see. And it broke his heart. Not because the jailers seemed cruel. They were as enlightened as he could expect from a city shelter. The nurses didn't even have an institutional smile. It was the children. Isaac knew that half of them were a little retarded. And the other half were already beyond repair. They had that maimed look Isaac had met in a hundred other classrooms and shelters, kids with uncurious eyes.

He traveled from room to room with his delegation of chiefs. He visited the soup kitchen, drank the minestrone that was offered him, and sucked on his bottle of milk. But he couldn't get away from those uncurious eyes. The walls were ocean-green in the recreation room. The shuffleboard sticks were all new. But the children seemed to play in slow motion, as if they didn't have an attitude toward the wooden discs they shoved into the scoring zones.

Isaac joined the game. The chiefs could do nothing but watch as Isaac gripped his long wooden cue and scored a perfect seven. The disc had its own strange music, like a flattened planet sliding on a painted floor. But not even Isaac and his cue stick could bring those children out of their slumber.

He left the shuffleboard field, the chiefs right behind him, most of them in uniform, like a little army of many coats. Isaac wanted to get out of this children's jail. He wanted to give up his fellowship and remind Justice to go to hell. He had nothing to teach. He wasn't Dick Tracy. He was more like a commissioning agent who gathered detectives and stoolies around him, some kind of clever spider. And while he prepared himself to make his exit with the chiefs, to run from this jail and that metal rainbow over St. Louis, he was trapped by a face. It belonged to a boy who was as runty as the rest, a boy in the same brown jumpsuit that was standard issue in this jail. A uniform with many pockets.

"Hello," the boy said, singling Isaac out from the other chiefs. His mouth was crooked and there was a mockery in his voice, a form of play that Isaac hadn't found in the shuffleboard room. The boy had lots of wrinkles. His face was used up, but he wasn't a little sleepwalker. He was like a wizened old man of six, with an old man's eyes.

"How old are you, son?"

"Twelve," the boy said.

Isaac didn't believe the kid. Where were his shoulders?

"What's your name?"

"Kingsley McCardle."

"And how long have you been living here?"

"Half my life."

The chiefs pulled at Isaac's elbow. They didn't like this colloquy. He wasn't supposed to engage the children in a heart-to-heart talk. These were wards of St. Louis, a city with its own unusual life, because it belonged to no other county in America. It was like a landbound island named after Louis IX, the crusader king who watched over this old French village on the Mississippi. But the boy wouldn't stay silent.

"Who are you, grandpa?"

"Isaac Sidel . . . police commissioner of New York."

"Heck, that ain't much of a living," the boy said, and the cops continued to pull at Isaac.

"Loren," Isaac said to the city's chief of detectives, who'd brought him out of Kansas and into that little country under the metal rainbow. "I'd like to sit with the boy."

"No time, Isaac. We're having lunch at Catfish and Crystal. The mayor'll be there."

"Loren, I've had too many mayors for lunch. Let me talk to the kid."

And Loren Cole, who ran the detective bureau like a crusader king, who was as incorruptible as Isaac, and decided where justice fell in St. Louis, took Isaac aside.

"Kingsley's not for public consumption."

"I'm not going to write about him, Loren."

Captain Cole stood belly to belly with that cop from New York. He was bigger than Isaac. He could have dragged Isaac to Catfish & Crystal, but Isaac would only have haunted him in the restaurant, haunted him about Kingsley. "He's one of our invisibles, Isaac. Supposed to be lost. We didn't want him running through the courts. So we stuck him in this crevice, if you know what I mean?"

"What the hell did he do?"

"Do? He lived with an uncle in a goddamn shack behind Busch Stadium. The uncle tossed him around. I'm not sure. There weren't no other kin. Kingsley took a Coke bottle, sharpened the lip, and while the old man was sleeping, he dug him in the neck. I saw the shack. I saw that old man's river of blood. We brought Kingsley in, tested him, had a team of child psychologists studying the color of his piss. The kid had an IQ that was taller than a church. He knew all the Cardinal greats. He'd read the Bible, Isaac, every verse. He talked about the stars and how things were dying everywhere. I can't say that uncle needed a Coke bottle in his neck. But I didn't want reporters interviewing the boy. I didn't want him on the six o'clock news like a freak. I took him to a friendly judge and had him remanded here. The case is still sitting in my drawer. Don't spoil it, Isaac."

"I'm not keeping a journal, Loren. I don't work for Justice. Let me talk to him."

"No."

But Isaac was stubborn and explosive, like the boy, and Loren knew the kind of day he'd have to endure if Isaac didn't get a couple of words with McCardle. Dick Tracy would destroy Catfish & Crystal, bring that restaurant down.

"Two minutes, Isaac. And if you bring up unpleasant matters, I swear to Jesus I'll put my cuffs on you and lock you in the toilet."

"Anything you say, Loren."

And while the other chiefs waited, Loren put Isaac together with McCardle in a pantry between the kitchen and the nurses' station.

"I'd gut him again, old Uncle Sol," the boy said without a bit of provocation from Isaac. "He was mean as a tit."

"I didn't ask you about family business."

McCardle laughed. "I know what's on your mind, grandpa. How old are you?"

Isaac sucked on his milk bottle.

"Forget it. What would you like to be when you grow up?"

"Grandpa, are you dumb?" McCardle said, wrinkling his eyes. "I can't afford to grow. I got to stay here with the children. Ask the cop. I teach them arithmetic."

"It's not much of a future," Isaac said.

"Depends on what you mean, grandpa. I have a future. I can be the oldest kid in St. Louis. I get to see the Cards every summer on Stan Musial Day. I hear Enos Slaughter had a better arm than Stan. Is that true?"

"Slaughter had the best arm in baseball."

"How would you know that?" McCardle asked with his old man's eyes looking at Isaac's milk bottle.

"I grew up with the New York Giants."

"What was Slaughter like?"

"He was bald and had big ears and he ran like an donkey and threw like a knife."

"That's Slaughter all right. I read about him in *Guffy's Guide to St. Louis* . . ."

Loren peeked into the pantry. "Time's up," he said.

"Wait a minute," McCardle said. "I'm talking to the man."

"Time's up."

Isaac walked out of the closet and returned Kingsley to his jailers. He didn't even say good-bye to the boy. An anger was building in Isaac. He sat next to Loren in the limousine.

"What are you going to do with the boy?" Isaac whispered.

"There's no secrets here," Loren said. "Everybody knows McCardle."

"Well, what are you going to do? You can't let him rot inside that little jail."

"Rot?" Loren said. "He's doing high school in there."

"And then?"

"We sneak him through the back door at Washington U."

"What if the back door is closed?"

"This isn't Moscow, Isaac. We can always try another college. We'll get him in."

"He's dying in that little jail, Loren, can't you tell? His face is all wrinkled."

"He was like that when we found him."

"Well, maybe he could use another environment."

"We're not stage designers, Isaac. We gave him what we've got."

"But you could lend him to me."

Loren lowered his head and whistled into his hands. "Don't even dream of it, Isaac. The boy is ours. And if you make a stink, if you cry to some judge, I'll have to shorten the life of your fellowship . . . we don't lend out orphans in St. Louis."

The chiefs all sat with sour faces. They arrived at Catfish & Crystal. Isaac romanced the mayor, charmed him with stories of how he'd captured Henry Armstrong Lee, the Most Wanted Man in America. "We had our best stoolies on the case. Henry Armstrong didn't have a chance."

He devoured a dozen crab cakes. And when Loren went to the john, Isaac followed him. "I apologize, Captain Cole. I was getting a little greedy. But I thought I could help the kid. He wouldn't have a past history in New York. He could start all over again. I could get him into a decent school, find him a place to live."

"It wouldn't solve a thing. That uncle of his was the only kin he had. We don't believe in forgettin' kin . . . thanks for the pitch, Isaac. But Kingsley would die of loneliness in Manhattan."

"I guess you're right." Isaac didn't believe it. His head whirled with kidnapping schemes. But he couldn't make war on the city of St. Louis. He didn't have any stoolies in town.

He said good-bye to the mayor and went to his suite at the Breckenridge. He could see right into Busch Stadium from his bedroom window. It was a windy afternoon, and Isaac imagined ol' "Country" Slaughter throwing bullets, forty years back in time. Why had that runt upset him so? Did Isaac read his own sadness in McCardle's eyes? They could have been a pair of orphans together. Isaac's dad had abandoned him to become a painter in Paris, his mother had started to pick rags, and Isaac ran around with murder in his brain. That's why he was such a good policeman. He liked to dance at the very edge of violence.

He'd had one semester at Columbia College, had devoured all of James Joyce like a detective prowling for clues in a sea of words. He'd read Durkheim and Veblen and Harry Stack Sullivan and hundreds of books on the criminal mind. He'd lectured at police academies, lunched with the best pathologists in the world. But he wasn't sure what kind of social pathology could explain McCardle. Was that uncle a demon or a violent drunk who slept a little too long one morning?

The telephone rang around midnight. Isaac woke out of a fever. He'd fallen asleep in front of the tube, watching Steve McQueen as a stone-faced cop. "Hello?" he growled into the phone. "Loren, is that you?"

"No, grandpa. What was Slaughter's last year with the Cards?"

"How'd you get my number, kid? Did Captain Cole tell you to call me?"

"Ah, all the big cops stay at the Breckenridge. What was Slaughter's last year with the Cards?"

"'Fifty-three." Isaac had the memory of a bat. It was metal rainbows that confused him, not "Country" Slaughter. "Anything else I can tell you?"

"Drink your milk, grandpa. Good-bye."

Isaac slept like a baby. The worm didn't bother him once.

He got up at seven, ate toast and tea in his room, scribbled a note to the Justice Department, and hopped on a plane to New York. Justice could find a new singing policeman. He was only Isaac Sidel. He didn't want to go to bed in Seattle and think he was in St. Louis. He sat in the sky and didn't have to worry about bumping into metal rainbows or being startled by a boy like Kingsley McCardle. He read *Newsweek* and *Time*, took a suck of milk, and arrived in New York as the former Hamilton Fellow.

2

There was the usual fury around him, all the fury of the fourteenth floor, where the commissioners presided at One Police Plaza. Isaac missed the old Police Headquarters, a crumbling palazzo on Centre Street, which was being converted into condominiums. He would sit in Teddy Roosevelt's office, with marble all around him, like a wayward prince, some Renaissance man who recognized the maddening colors of crime. He'd felt needed at the palazzo. He'd dance up the marble stairs that led to his office, chat with reporters who followed his every move, drink cups of coffee crowned with hot milk, brought to him from the Caffè Roma with cupcakes of ricotta cheese. Isaac was adored in Little Italy. He was Don Isacco, who happened to be the *commandante di polizia*. He was called *dottore*, like any other man of substance with a high-school diploma.

But the new headquarters was a brick tomb. It had no cafes or stone lions or the private terraces of a palazzo, gifts of a nobler time, when a policeman was like a *consiglieri* who settled arguments and delivered babies and whacked burglars over the head. Now Isaac's band of cops were remote functionaries who worked out of a bunker in the sky.

He'd been gone two weeks, and it was as if he hadn't been away at all. His deputies thrived without Don Isacco. They had their little territories to protect. They formed their own alliances while the PC was in San Diego somewhere, singing for his supper. He had to ask two of his sergeants to comb the building for the first deputy commissioner, who ran the Department whether Isaac was away or not. Isaac spoke at banquets. Isaac sat with the widow of a dead cop. He attended press conferences with Her Honor, Rebecca Karp, the mayor of New York, but he couldn't have told you how many cops were in the field on a particular day.

His First Dep was a black man who stood six feet six. Carlton Montgomery III. He'd come out of the black bourgeoisie. His dad had been a dentist. But no one called him Carlton on the commissioners' floor. He was Sweets, after Sweetwater Clifton, the first black basketball player on the New York Knicks. But this Sweets had never played professional ball. He'd heard Isaac lecture at the John Jay College of Criminal Justice, watched him tremble like some Jeremiah chanting about the brutalities of city life, and Sweets had decided to become a cop. He was Isaac's heir apparent, perhaps the next PC.

Sweets arrived after the third or fourth summons. There was a crisis in Williamsburg. The Hasidim were in the middle of a new war with the blacks. Children had been hurt. And Sweets had to bring rabbis and ministers and activists together, sit them down in the same room. Three years ago Isaac would have gone to Williamsburg himself. But he was more and more remote. He lectured and disappeared, like some cardinal or chief of state.

"Sweets," he said, "is there anything I ought to know?"

"Like what, Isaac? The morale in Manhattan North is fucking low. The Academy is shoving kids at us who can't fire a gun. We have sergeants who are dying on their feet.

Internal Affairs is busting up my best precinct. Reports of police brutality are up nine percent. We still can't get enough Latinos to pass the sergeants' test. You have a goddamn Irish hierarchy that keeps bitching about their nigger First Dep, and their Pink Commish, who talks about Stalin to the Knights of Columbus."

"Yeah," Isaac said, "but what's new?"

"The Rastafarians are controlling more and more of the drug traffic."

"Jesus, I'm not Rip Van Winkle. I don't sleep at my desk. The Rasties were banging up Brooklyn when I was the First Dep."

"Goodstein hasn't surfaced for a month."

"Ah," Isaac said. "A whole month." Maurice Goodstein was the best mob lawyer New York ever had. He'd started out as a young assistant district attorney in the forests of Brooklyn. He'd sent half a dozen mafiosi to jail. His papa had died on the bench. He had all the best rabbis in town. He should have been the new federal attorney for the Southern District of New York. That might have brought him a seat in the U.S. Senate. But he fell out of grace in Brooklyn and began his own law practice. In a year's time every important don from Syracuse to Staten Island was offering him a permanent retainer. The Feds sneezed and cried and called him the nation's number one menace, the Al Capone of the courts. But he still had lunch at The Four Seasons and went to parties with ambassadors and former secretaries of state.

"Is he alive?" Isaac mused, half to himself.

"The statistics are against that, but I'd still say yes. Maurice is a cunning boy."

"But what the hell is the word out on the street?"

"There is no word, Isaac. That's the trouble. You mention Maurie Goodstein, and every little mother closes his eyes and plays dead."

"No fucking don has that kind of power. Sweets, it's something else."

"Isaac, I've got work to do. I'll consider Maurie's fate next time I'm on the can."

Carlton Montgomery III started out the door. Isaac wondered who the real commissioner was. He felt like a boarder in this brick tomb. But he knew that Sweets wouldn't politick behind his back. The First Dep was as loyal to Isaac as one "Commish" could be to another. There was a slight barrier of skin. But Isaac was too wild to be considered much of a white man. And Sweets didn't play the nigger on the commissioners' floor. He ran the Department. He cracked his own whip.

He stopped outside the PC's door. "Isaac, one thing. Why'd you come home?"

"I was sick of having lunch with police captains."

"You have a contract with Justice. You should have finished the tour. LeComte is going to come down on our ass. No more favors from the FBI. No more special treatment. No more hard cash."

"I'll handle LeComte," Isaac said, and Sweets was gone.

But five minutes later LeComte was on the phone from D.C. Isaac had to decide like some rabbinical student whether he should take the call, or leave LeComte hanging for a week, play sick or dumb, or the harried commissioner who couldn't speak to the number-three man at Justice. He took the call.

Frederic LeComte was the cultural commissar of the Justice Department. Treasury was frightened of him. The IRS sent him Christmas cards. The CIA invited him to Langley for their Monday brunches. He had all the resources of the FBI in his pocket. He'd come out of Salt Lake City, a poet turned policeman. He was an ex–Rhodes Scholar. He could have become a diplomat. But he preferred Justice. The Hamilton Fellows had been his idea. He wanted cops around the country to meet and shake each other out of their usual sloth. And Frederic LeComte had chosen Isaac because Isaac was the most unorthodox PC in America, a Hebraic scholar of crime who didn't believe in the magic of software. But Isaac wasn't loved at the Justice Department. He meddled too much in FBI business, and LeComte had to convince Justice to accept Isaac as the first Hamilton Fellow. And now Isaac had betrayed LeComte's trust.

"You prick," LeComte said, "you miserable, ungrateful prick."

"I hope you're taping this conversation," Isaac said. "I'd be disappointed if you didn't."

"I can get the governor on the horn, Isaac. One phone call, that's all it takes. We control half your budget. I want you on the plane to Wichita by six."

"Can't," Isaac said.

"Why not?"

"My tapeworm."

"Tapeworm? I'll cut out your fucking heart. I'll pull on that worm and strangle you with it. You owe me, Isaac."

"Yes. That's true. But I can't go on the road, LeComte. I can't. I met a kid in St. Louis, an orphan, and I realized all my talking was a waste of time."

"Don't tell me about orphans," LeComte said. "I want you on that plane."

"All right, LeComte, get me fired. Go into my files at the Bureau and find out how many ladies I kissed and the false arrests I made."

"I could do worse than that, much worse."

"I know," Isaac said. "But you won't. You prefer a son of a bitch like me in this chair, instead of some crusader you couldn't work with . . . I need a rest. I'll pick up the tour. Maybe. Next month."

"Ten days, Isaac. That's all you have."

"I'll decide when the vacation is over. Now tell me about Maurice."

Isaac could feel that tick of silence. He'd caught LeComte, no matter what the commissar said.

"You mean little Maurie Goodstein? He's probably at the bottom of some lake where he belongs."

"I hear different," Isaac said. "I hear he's alive."

"Well, you're close to the action, Isaac. I'm in D.C. We don't talk much about Maurie at Justice."

"I'll bet," Isaac said. "What kind of deal did you make to keep Maurie out of business? He's been clobbering all your prosecutors. You can't get a conviction with Maurie around. Where is he, LeComte?"

"You're the wizard, Isaac. You're Sherlock Holmes. You tell me."

And LeComte got off the line. Isaac had no jurisdiction over Goodstein's life or death. He wasn't even fond of Maurice. But he admired Maurice's cunning in the courtroom. Maurie was five feet four. But he could puff himself up like a baby bull and wound any government witness.

LeComte was right. Isaac was a little like Sherlock Holmes, without the fiddle or the cocaine or a bumbling doctor to tell his tales. He'd become an "amateur" of crime.

He marched out of headquarters, sucking on his bottle of milk. He zigzagged across the city like a soldier, losing whatever tail LeComte might have on him. He walked in and out of buildings, taking rear entrances not even a native would have known. Isaac had a map of every little corridor and alley in the five boroughs. He landed in an old shirt factory near the edge of Chinatown, climbed a flight of stairs, and Isaac was in his own "waters," the special department of the PC. It functioned like a secret service. It sought out radical groups, mad bombers, the safe houses of other countries' secret agents.

LeComte supplied the cash. LeComte needed a liaison in New York. But Justice didn't know the depths of Isaac's pursuits. The PC spied on all the spiers. He couldn't have a hundred different agencies carousing in his city under the protection of a hundred different flags. Isaac didn't have the resources of the Justice Department. He didn't even have one authentic spy on his payroll. But he'd cultivated his contacts with "sleepwalkers" from Bulgaria's counterintel or the KGB, disgruntled men and women who liked to sit in some corner with Isaac and chat about philosophy, religion, or winters in New York. Isaac never asked these sleepwalkers to compromise themselves, but from a word here and there he made his own "quilt" and could tell if the KGB was going to be involved in some heavy traffic. Isaac couldn't pounce. But he could provide a shadow detail and capture some of that crazy dance between the different spiers. At least he wouldn't be ignorant of all those armies that worked his village.

But his own sleepwalkers had nothing new for Isaac. They weren't official policemen. They had no existence outside the special department, no pension plan, and nowhere to retire to. But the department did have a code name: Ivanhoe. And these were Isaac's renegade cops, former mercenaries, jailbirds whom the PC had to trust with his life. Isaac's Ivanhoes. It was curiously medieval. Outcasts with their own secret affiliation. Fallen knights who lived in an old shirt factory.

Burton Bortelsman was their commandant. He was a refugee from Capetown. He'd been the captain of his own criminal brigade, with a hundred detectives under his wing. But he'd killed a man in a drunken fury, the former lover of a wife he pretended not to care about. And Bortelsman had to leave the country. He'd found his way to Isaac. And he was one more Ivanhoe.

"Are the Russkies mounting something?" Isaac had to ask.

"Nothing out of the ordinary. They had to put one of their decoders on a plane to Moscow."

"A bit of extracurricular romance?"

"Exactly. Fell in love with the genuine article. She came right out of some cradle at British intelligence. I feel sorry for the man. She's a classic, Isaac. Believe me."

"And the Syrians?"

"They're asleep."

"Then do me a favor, Burt. There's a mob lawyer who's been missing for a month. I don't think it was a Mafia kill. He's too valuable an item."

"Maurice Goodstein."

Isaac smiled. "I'd like to know what happened to Maurice."

"I'd say he's sitting on some high wire, between oblivion and the witness protection program."

"Then Justice has copped him. And he's going to squeal on a few of the dons. But that doesn't sound like Maurice. He's a fighter."

"But LeComte could have taken all the fight out of him. He fucks people—constantly. Why not Maurice?"

"Then have a look, Burt."

"It could bring LeComte to our door. I can't run down Maurice and stay invisible."

"All right," Isaac said. "Don't break too many backs. It bothers me that Maurice could disappear like that. And I don't like LeComte entering my territories. Find Maurice."

And Isaac left the old shirt factory with its band of Ivanhoes. He wasn't thinking of Maurice. He had Kingsley McCardle in his head, that orphan boy from St. Louis.

Isaac shivered in the street. "Enos Slaughter," he muttered to himself, before he started on his own crooked path to One Police Plaza.

3

Fuck the FBI. Someone else would have to play Alexander Hamilton for Frederic Le-Comte. Isaac wasn't in the mood to travel. He spent afternoons in his office contemplating young McCardle's brown jumpsuit. It brought him back to his own days as a truant on the Lower East Side, when he was the terror of P.S. 88, a school that looked like a French cathedral, with gargoyles that crouched from the window ledges and spat blue rain on your head. No one could account for that blue rain. Perhaps the gargoyles had a chalky substance in their stone mouths. Isaac's dad had abandoned the Sidels, had gone to Paris to paint. And Isaac was left with a baby brother, Leo, and his mom, who'd opened a junk shop. He grew into a terrible thief. He stole to keep alive, and to burn out some of the anger against his dad. He felt orphaned, like McCardle. The boy wore Isaac's own internal weather. Isaac's dad came back after a while. But he was no longer part of the family. He was like a man in a haunted house. He left for Paris again when

23

Isaac was eighteen. And Isaac abandoned college to get married and become a supercop.

He'd been invited to address the Christy Mathewson Club, a brotherhood of addicts who collected notes and memorabilia on baseball as it was played before World War II. The Christys were antiquarians. Joe DiMaggio was almost too modern for them. History stopped after the decline of Babe Ruth. Baseball had been Isaac's passion, baseball and chess. He'd steal into the Polo Grounds twice a week, burrowing under a fence to watch his beloved Giants. And he'd become his own encyclopedist. His knowledge wouldn't have meant much to the Christys if Isaac had been some lone wolf living in a closet. But the police commissioner was a catch. The club could capitalize on Isaac's fame.

Isaac understood the club's particular code. The Christys believed in an America without Jackie Robinson, when baseball was a white man's province, and black men lived and died in their own little league. But the Christys weren't the Ku Klux Klan. They were racist in their own odd fashion. They had black members who listened to white men's fables about Ty Cobb and Tris Speaker and the shame of Shoeless Joe. Isaac could have boycotted the club. But he wanted to talk to those antiquarians. The Christys knew there had been black players in the big leagues long before Jackie Robinson. Like Bones McClintlick, who was advertised as an Indian while he was with Louisville a hundred years ago. And the Emery brothers, Slats and Charles, who ate up the National League at the start of this century. There had been others, who were blessed (or cursed) with blue eyes, men and boys who came out of some farm country and took a convenient nickname, like Tadpoles or Mad Tom. Isaac himself had fallen in love with the names of catchers and pitchers and first basemen who belonged to an era when every village could field its own team. Isaac was a hillbilly at heart. He never lectured for the money. He'd donate whatever loot he got to the Police Athletic League.

And so he arrived at the club, a blue sandstone building on East Twenty-ninth. The Christys had their own house. They were as rich as some Byzantine king. The club owned several banks and an entire block of brownstones. Isaac saw his own face on a placard outside the club. He looked like a grandfather, with gray sideburns and thick lines in his forehead. It startled him how much he'd aged. He was still that boy who burrowed under the fence.

He had his lecture prepared. He meant to talk about the litany of names that had formed Isaac's America. He was forgetful now and had to remind himself of his own commissioners and their wives, but he could recite the names and statistics of men who'd played before he was born. Baby Doll Jacobson. Sad Sam Jones. Roger Peckinpaugh.

The auditorium was packed. And Isaac was welcomed by the president of the Christy Mathewson Club, Schyler Knott. Schyler's granddad had once been captain of the Princeton baseball team. And Schyler himself was a second baseman at Swarthmore or Hamilton or another school Isaac couldn't keep in his head. He was an investment banker in his grandfather's firm. A curious man of thirty-six or -seven. He didn't seem like much of an antiquarian. He wore banker's clothes, but he didn't have that "old boy's" presence of the other Christys. Schyler would have celebrated Jackie Robinson. But he presided over a club that couldn't even mention Willie Mays.

He pumped Isaac's hand. He was blonder than a movie star. He didn't bother to ask Isaac about his speech. And Isaac began to feel wicked. I'm going to get away with murder tonight.

"Where's Maurie Goodstein?" Schyler asked.

And Isaac forced himself to smile. There were photographs of Mathewson and Babe Ruth and Three Finger Brown on the wall. Little Maurice didn't seem to belong in their company.

"I went to Colgate with him," Schyler said. "He was a

friend. He's also a member of this club. I'm sure he would have wanted to hear you speak."

"He never mentioned the Christys to me."

"You know Maurice," Schyler said. "Didn't want to give the club a bad name. But he sat on our board. He was our biggest fund-raiser."

All of a sudden the Christys didn't seem so antiquarian to Isaac. Had the club been laundering money for some Staten Island don under Maurie's own umbrella? Isaac had an itch to flee the antiquarians, to run away from this house of the dead.

"Schyler, there hasn't been a clue about Maurice."

"But you must have some theories."

"Of course. But it's police business. I couldn't compromise my own detectives out in the field."

"That's the trouble," Schyler said. "I was the last one to see Maurie. And none of your detectives ever bothered to knock on our door. Maurie was having lunch with me at the club."

"Was he agitated?"

"Not at all."

"Think, Schyler," Isaac said, the policeman again, not the baseball fanatic.

"He was happy . . . for Maurice. Had a new boyfriend, I gather."

"Did he give you a name?"

"No."

"What about a line of work? What did the boyfriend do?"

"I'm not sure. He might have been a male nurse. Maurie mentioned some hospital."

"Which hospital?"

"I can't remember. And this isn't the time for an inquisition, Isaac. You're our guest."

Most of Schyler's blondness was gone. He'd lost that lithe, youthful look. He was one more antiquarian. And Isaac began to mingle with other members of the club. He traveled from face to face until he stopped in front of another old man. Isaac felt a brutal pull.

"The Bomber," he said. "Harry Lieberman."

The old man laughed. "Yes," he said. "I'm Harry. I've wanted to tell you for ages how much I admire the stances you've taken. You're the best commissioner we have."

"Not everyone would agree. But you should have written . . . or telephoned me."

"I'm too shy," the old man said, and Isaac recognized the Bomber's big, unmistakable hands.

"You were my hero," Isaac said. "I watched you from the bleachers for two whole seasons. You hit twenty-five homers in 1944."

"Mr. Commissioner, half the talent was overseas. I couldn't even get near the team when the regulars got back. That's why I jumped to the Mexican League. I'd spent most of my life in the minors. If there hadn't been a war, I'd still be with the Jersey Giants."

Yes, that was the rabbinical side of the story. The Second World War had depleted the majors. And all of baseball had become one big farm team, without DiMaggio or Greenberg or Ted Williams. But the bomber wasn't a bush-league kid. He had the bat and those big mitts. He'd ripened during the war. Isaac remembered his catlike moves, the way he'd taunt the entire Cardinal infield. He could have been the Joe DiMaggio of the New York Giants. But he succumbed to that myth of the secondhand ballplayer, and those garbage teams the war had bred. The Bomber shouldn't have vanished in 1946. He was the casualty of his own civilian warfare. If he hadn't dreamt of an army uniform while he was at bat, he could have hit a hundred more homers.

"I'd like your autograph," Isaac said.

The old man covered his face with those big hands of his. "Go on. You're the Bomber now."

"Please," Isaac said.

And the Bomber signed the program notes the Christys had prepared on Isaac. *To the Commissioner. From Harry Lieberman, your biggest fan. November 29, 1982.*

Isaac wanted to cry, not out of that ordinary sadness of meeting the athlete as an old man with a grizzled neck. Isaac wasn't sentimental about anyone's mortality. But the Bomber had been the phantom player who'd entered Isaac's heart and then disappeared into some eternal children's league . . .

Isaac was led up to the podium by Schyler Knott.

People clapped.

Isaac's shoulders quaked. He could feel the worm writhe. But the PC hadn't brought his bottle of milk. He didn't care. Isaac wasn't going to be silenced by a stinking worm. He could have talked about the Black Sox scandal of 1919 and the ruin of Ed Cicotte, Swede Risberg, Chick Gandil, and Shoeless Joe, with his lifetime batting average of .356. But it would have been silly stuff, because Isaac knew about other gamblers, other fixed games that had never been publicized, never announced, and why should he tarnish the Christys' heroes? Don Isacco wasn't mean. But he wanted to rile the antiquarians a bit. He would have liked to mention Willie Mays, but he had to keep within the club's rules. And so he decided to talk about Josh Gibson, the great black catcher of the nigger leagues who was supposed to join the Washington Senators during World War II, but the Senators chickened out and Josh fell into a kind of madness, holding conversations with DiMaggio in his head, asking Joe why he wouldn't recognize Josh.

Josh Gibson and Joe DiMaggio.

That was the topic of Isaac's talk. But Schyler got in the way. He began a long, long introduction about the Christys and Isaac himself. ". . . a fellow antiquarian who saw Mel Ott play in the old green gardens of the Polo Grounds. Isaac Sidel is one of us. A brother to baseball. I don't need to list his credentials. He's the current Alexander Hamilton Fellow, traveling in behalf of the Justice Department. He captures psychopaths with his bare hands. It's Isaac who brought in that bank robber, Henry Armstrong Lee, the most dangerous man alive."

Isaac was embarrassed about Henry Lee. His best informant had told him where the bank robber was. And the media
had turned it into a scalp hunt. Now Isaac was growing
forgetful of Josh. He'd lost the music of his speech, and
Schyler hadn't finished introducing him yet. Don Isacco
gnashed his teeth.

"Brothers, sisters," Schyler said, "a big hand for the police
commissioner, Isaac Sidel."

It was too late. Gibson had gone out of Isaac's head. He
looked down upon a landmark of faces. He placed his elbows
on the podium. He stared like a rhinoceros, seeking the
riddle of his own words. He thought of Kingsley McCardle.
The boy would have loved the story of a black catcher who
hungered to play DiMaggio in the big leagues. The whole
goddamn country wouldn't let Gibson grow up. Josh, Isaac
muttered to himself.

Even with all his truculence he noticed a woman in the
audience. He smiled bitterly because he'd "captured" Henry
Armstrong Lee while the bank robber was sitting in a
woman's skirt. But this woman didn't look like Henry Lee.
She couldn't have been much younger than Isaac. But her
face wasn't ravaged at all. Time hadn't bitten into her yet. And
Isaac remembered her from forty years ago. The hair was still
pulled high. The lipstick was bloodred. The mouth was moist.
The cheekbones were fierce. Isaac started to cry.

"Anastasia," he said, before he tumbled into Schyler's arms.

4

There was a whole team of doctors around Isaac's bed. He was wearing some long hospital nappy, like an infant. There were flowers from Her Honor, Rebecca Karp. The bastards had drawn blood from Isaac. He could feel the pricks in his arm. The humidifier in the room purred like a little giant. The doctors all had white coats.

"Commissioner Sidel, have you ever swooned like that before?"

"Yes," Isaac said. "I'm a swooner. Go away."

"But you could have gone into shock . . . we would have had to—"

"Go away."

He started to rise up from his bed, and the doctors disappeared, except for Gordon Gould, the Department's chief pathologist, who served as Isaac's own physician from time to time.

"Gordon, where the hell am I?"

"Beth Israel. We brought you in an ambulance. Your blood

sugar was very low. You were hibernating . . . like a polar bear. All the essential functions had slowed."

"What time is it?"

"Time?" the chief pathologist said. "I'd say six in the afternoon. I'm not wearing my watch."

"And I've been lying like this for a day."

"Three days, Isaac."

"I don't believe it."

"But what happened?"

"Nothing, nothing. I saw a ghost."

"At the Christy Mathewson Club?"

"Why not?" Isaac said. "That club is full of ghosts."

"I'm considering a CAT scan."

"Gordon, what are you going to find? Bubbles in my brain? I have a worm. It fucks me whenever it feels like it."

"Yes," Gordon said. "It could have been the worm, eating up all your essential sugars. But I doubt it. Isaac, please . . . we'll have to take some tests."

"After Christmas," Isaac muttered. "I might be in a more festive mood. Where's Sweets?"

"Isaac, I'm not part of your cadre. I'm a pathologist."

"You still work for me. I want Sweets."

"All right. I'll send for Sweets."

And Isaac closed his eyes before his chief pathologist had left the room. He had terrible dreams. Lions were eating away at his body. He had no legs. He cried like he hadn't cried since he was a boy and his father had gone to Paris to become the new Cézanne.

He was still bawling like a baby when he woke up. There were no lions around. Only Frederic LeComte.

"Who let you in here?" Isaac asked without bothering to wipe his eyes. "I'm the Commish. I ought to have a guard outside my door."

"You do," LeComte said. His face was fuzzy. But Isaac recognized the blue color that LeComte had a fondness for. Powder-blue shirts ordered from Hong Kong. Blue silk ties.

Isaac dressed like a bum. He loved secondhand shoes, hats, and pants. His vision began to clear. He could see the cultural commissar's aristocratic nose. His lips were very, very thin. Isaac could imagine LeComte as the intellectual hatchetman for Cardinal Richelieu. There was something clerical about him, like a murderous priest.

"Isaac, we'll take care of all the bills. That's one of the advantages of being a Hamilton Fellow."

"LeComte, I have a hospital plan. I don't need Justice to watch out for me."

"We worked you too hard," LeComte said. "When you recover, you'll only have to do a couple of cities a week."

"I'm not going back to that gulag," Isaac said.

The aristocratic nose began to twitch. "Do you realize how many applicants I had, Isaac? One thousand three hundred and ten. And I picked you." LeComte walked from the window to the bed and back again. "And I picked you."

"LeComte, I never applied for your fellowship."

"That's the point. It was by invitation only. But people started applying . . . congressmen put on the pressure for their favorite candidate. But I got caught in a shitstorm and picked you. You didn't have one miserable supporter outside of me. And you call it the gulag. TV coverage in every city. Soon you'll have a fan club, like Jack Nicholson."

Isaac sat up in his hospital nappy. "LeComte, why'd you come here?"

"You're my protégé."

"Why'd you come?"

"To warn you, you motherfucker. I don't want your secret service looking for Maurie Goodstein."

"I don't have a secret service," Isaac said. "It's illegal."

"I know. I pay for it. I can have Burton Bortelsman deported, Isaac. I can send him to South Africa. If the blacks don't kill him, the Afrikaners will."

"It might get hairy," Isaac said, "if the *Washington Post* ever discovered that old Burt was a paid informant of the Justice

Department. You won't touch Burt. Now tell me what it is Maurie's done. Which don are you after?"

"Stick to your own cradle, Isaac. You'll live longer. Goodbye."

And Isaac settled into bed. The mayor called. Isaac was sleeping with Rebecca Karp twice a month. He would visit the little bunker under her office at City Hall or ride up to Gracie Mansion in the middle of the night. Their romance existed in some familiar territory between hatred and lust. She'd been a beauty queen, Miss Far Rockaway of 1947. Her popularity rose with Isaac's triumphs. Their lovemaking was born out of a loneliness of two people who couldn't make permanent attachments. Isaac had been married before he was twenty. His wife Kathleen fled to Florida. He was as intimate with her as he would have been with any stranger. She'd fallen out of Isaac's sphere of things. They'd had a daughter together, Marilyn the Wild. She kept getting married to spite her dad. She was living in Seattle. And when Isaac had visited that town as a Hamilton Fellow she wouldn't even take his phone calls. She'd loved his "angel," Manfred Coen, and Isaac had gotten him killed in one of his ploys against a tribe of Peruvian pimps. She'd never forgiven Isaac for that. The tapeworm had come from that tribe. The tapeworm was their gift.

And Becky Karp? She couldn't have found the time for marriage in her appointment book. Isaac suited her fine. He never made demands. Their minds were always elsewhere, but they had whatever tenderness their bodies could bring. She loved waiting up for Isaac and was just as happy when he left. That was the power of their alliance. Their forages in bed were almost like the City's own seal. Isaac was the gentlest lover she'd ever had.

"How are you, dear?" she said with her Rockaway accent. "Get well, will you, Isaac? I can't get any coverage since you're in the hospital. You've been monopolizing the six o'clock news."

"It's not my fault," he said. "I got dizzy and fell. But I'll be out of here in a day. I promise."

"I called six times," she said.

"I was probably asleep."

"Isaac, what's with Maurie Goodstein?"

Jesus, Isaac muttered. Even the mayor was into Maurie. The whole town had one preoccupation: little Maurie Goodstein.

"You think he ran off with one of his faigeles?" Becky asked.

"For a week, yes. But not a month. Maurie isn't that romantic."

"Then where is he?"

"I'd gamble that the Feds have him."

"But he couldn't survive in the witness protection program. He's too conspicuous."

"I agree."

"Then solve the riddle, Isaac. That's why you're my police chief. And get well."

Becky got off the line and Isaac grew more and more depressed. He waited and waited for Sweets, but his First Dep didn't come. And then Sweets materialized, out of the smoke and mist of Isaac's vaporizer. Isaac figured it was just another ghost who had come to haunt the PC. "Who are you?" he asked.

"Shit, you are a sight," Sweets said.

Isaac knew he was healthy again. "Goddamn, get me out of these baby clothes."

"Can't," Sweets said.

"I'm your boss, Mr. Sweets. I could laugh you right out of Headquarters. You'll love walking the South Bronx during the witches' hour."

"You can call me Captain Midnight. But you're staying in bed."

"There's a woman," Isaac muttered. "It's personal business, Sweets. I have to rely on you."

"Then tell me about it."

"There isn't that much to tell. I was speaking at the Christy Mathewson Club and there she was."

"Who?"

"Anastasia."

"Isaac, can you be a little more specific than that?"

"You know the history books. Anastasia was Czar Nicholas' youngest daughter. Most people think she was killed with the rest of the czar's family after the revolution. But every five or ten years a woman would show up, swearing she was Anastasia."

"And you met her at the Christys."

"No," Isaac said. "I knew another Anastasia, when I was a kid on the Lower East Side. She came to our school one winter, out of nowhere. It was during the war. She was a refugee. From Russia, I think. I don't know how the hell she escaped. But she was living with some uncle or an aunt. And she had all this European culture. She'd studied ballet in Moscow or Budapest. She could rattle off French until our teachers were dizzy. She'd read Turgenev and she was thirteen. We were all in love with her. And she played with us, said she was Her Imperial Highness, the Princess Anastasia . . . Anastasia with torn socks."

"And what happened?"

"I told you, Sweets. I was crazy about her. Once she took me home to tea. Her aunt was poor as a mouse, but she had a samovar, and we had this black, black tea with strawberry jam in glasses with a silver handle . . . it was high society."

"Did you kiss her?"

"I never had the chance. She only lasted one winter with those torn socks. And then she was gone . . . to a different uncle or an aunt. But Sweets, she had the whitest skin. You could almost feel the bones of her face, see them move."

"And you want me to find her?"

"Yes."

"What's her real name?"

Isaac held his cheek. "Anastasia. That's what we called her in class."

"Okay, you want me to find this anonymous article with a nickname who appeared and disappeared half a lifetime ago. How many men should I put on the case?"

"I told you. It's personal business. I want you to contact the Ivanhoes."

Sweets fished into his suit and slapped a gold badge into Isaac's hand. "I resign. I'm not working with those fuckers."

"Please," Isaac said.

"Isaac, Burton Bortelsman was with the security police in Johannesburg. Do you know how many black people he tortured and killed?"

"He was a homicide detective in Capetown."

"Yeah, that's his legend. But I know different. I'll kill him myself."

"I need you . . . and the Ivanhoes. Or I'll never find her."

"They're your jackals, Isaac. Use them all you want. But I'm not working with Bortelsman."

"All right," Isaac muttered, half his head inside the nappy. "But take back the shield. Don't resign on me."

Sweets clutched the badge in his paw. "Isaac, you'll find that princess. Didn't she come looking for you at the Christys? She'll look for you again."

"No, no. It was a fluke. I don't think she even recognized me. I was a little kid . . . and she was Anastasia. How would she know I'd become a cop?"

"She'll find you," Sweets said, tucking Isaac under his quilt, and the First Dep's voice seemed far away, like the mist out of some magic vaporizer. Isaac fell asleep in his nappy.

5

H̲e should have been sick
and pale, but he'd acquired a golden pallor in the hospital, as
if he'd swallowed some sun. He had documents to sign. The
mayor called. Isaac couldn't deal with the folders on his desk.
Anastasia. One of his sergeants caught him crying. The
sergeant's name was Malone. He was Don Isacco's bodyguard
and driver. Malone squinted at Isaac. Ah, the old boy's
bereaved. Must have been a death in the family. Isaac was
mourning himself. He missed the boy he had been, the boy
who would sneak into the Polo Grounds and watch the
Bomber play, sit with the high aristocracy in a Lower East
Side flat while he looked at Anastasia, longed for her into the
deepest night. Now Isaac understood the melody of his whole
romantic life. He'd married Anastasia, not Kathleen, but he
was a bridegroom without a bride. He'd missed her all these
years in some primitive spot beyond a police commissioner's
ordinary dreams. He hadn't thought of Anastasia; he'd lived
her absence in his bearish body. It was his daughter Marilyn

37

who had the same aristocratic mien. Marilyn had become his
memory of Russian tea.

Burt, the Afrikaner, brought him out of his gloom. He
arrived at One Police Plaza, which was forbidden ground to
the Ivanhoes. But Isaac was glad to see him. Burt would
understand all the enigmas of unrequited love. He wouldn't
plague the PC about Anastasia, like Sweets had done. He'd
come disguised as an Austrian police chief with a special
permit to see the Commish. His papers were impeccable.
Isaac had terrific forgers at that shirt factory where the
Ivanhoes lived. He was almost in the mood to kiss Burt. He
needed his Ivanhoes around him.

Burton whispered something.

"Can't hear you," Isaac said.

"Get that nigger off my back."

"Burt, what the hell—"

"I'm Herr Klein," Burt said, pointing to his Austrian police
chief's badge. Both of them knew the office was bugged.
LeComte had tapped into Isaac's side of the commissioners'
floor. His soundmen had also gone into Isaac's toilet. The PC
couldn't even crap alone.

They went down three flights to a neutral toilet.

"Your First Dep has been threatening me."

"Well, he's kind of ticklish about Afrikaners, Burt."

"I had nothing to do with security. I was with the criminal
brigade."

"I believe you. But I can't blame Sweets if he doesn't."

"Isaac, I will hurt him, hurt him bad, if he starts knocking
on my door . . . I traced the woman."

"What woman?"

"The princess Sweets told me about."

"Anastasia?" Isaac said. "Burton, how did you do it?"

"I stole the Christys' guest list. I talked to a couple of
people, including Schyler Knott. Told him I was with the
Treasury Department. He opened up."

"Well, who is she?"

"Her maiden name is Margaret Tolstoy."

"Maiden name?"

"She's married to a mob accountant."

"You're out of your fucking mind."

"Isaac, don't get cheeky. Her husband is a baseball nut. His name is Martin Crabbs. He works for DiAngelis. But he's not your usual lowlife. He was born Martin Krabnikov. His people are from the Ukraine. He graduated magna cum laude from Columbia College."

"That's my school," Isaac said between his teeth. He'd had one semester at the college before he dropped out to support his drowning family.

"Crabbs was on the fencing team . . . Isaac, are you listening? Or should I burn the file?"

"I'm listening," Isaac said. "When did he marry Anastasia?"

"Margaret, you mean."

"Yes, Margaret Tolstoy, with the hole in her socks."

A couple of deputy chief inspectors marched into the toilet, saw the PC with a stranger, and marched out again. Isaac was doing business, or he wouldn't have come down to *their* facility. He was the brain, the big mover, and they didn't question his motives.

The deputies distracted him, and Isaac had to repeat himself. "When did this Krabnikov marry Margaret Tolstoy?"

"I didn't say it was a legal marriage."

"Then she's his squaw. But how long have they been together?"

"A year or two at the most."

"And before that? Who was she with?"

"That's the puzzle, Isaac. There is no record of Margaret Tolstoy until she married the accountant. She suddenly surfaced. Out of some little black bottle."

"The mystery woman, Margaret Tolstoy. You're my catcher, Burt. I want a complete dossier."

"Isaac, I'm telling you, Margaret Tolstoy didn't exist."

"Don't die on me, Burt. If she had another identity, find it."

"There's nothing, nothing at all."

"Try Anastasia," Isaac said.

"I already did."

"Then go to Crabbs . . . or Krabnikov."

"That's difficult. He's in hiding. There's a rumor going around that LeComte's boys are getting ready to subpoena him. They want DiAngelis."

"So he's missing in action . . . like Maurice."

"Exactly," Burton said.

"Did you know that Schyler Knott went to school with little Maurie? And Maurie has a new boyfriend. Schyler says so. Some merry lad who's a male nurse. But Schyler can't remember the hospital."

"I could ease his memory a bit," Burton said.

"But be careful. I don't want Schyler bruised. And you'll have to zigzag a lot. LeComte is onto us."

"I told you, Isaac. He'll fuck me one of these days, LeComte will."

"Not without fucking himself. That's the main reason we take his money."

"Don't kid yourself," the Afrikaner said. "You're married to the man. You're his Hamilton Fellow."

"That's a thing of the past."

"Whose past? Yours or his?"

And Burton left him there, king of the john. Isaac hadn't even unbuttoned his fly. He stared into the mirror and could almost see the Bomber out in some center field behind the silvery dimensions of the glass. In a couple of seasons the Bomber had formed Isaac more completely than any other man or boy had done. Isaac still dreamt of himself as some ideal center fielder during the war. He couldn't imagine anything more heroic than hopping after baseballs in the middle of the afternoon. He was a Depression baby. He grew up with hunger all around him, when a free sandwich was the best sort of currency a boy could have. He was happiest during the war, when he stole ration booklets, defied the air-raid wardens, had Harry Lieberman . . . and Anastasia. He'd heard about the death camps, and he realized what would happen to him if the Nazis ever got to New York. But the Lower East Side had its own odd immunity. Not even the Nazis could have won the winter away from Orchard Street, where the clothing barrels would have served as a natural defense line. And he couldn't get the aroma of Russian tea out of his nostrils.

It wasn't so clever of him to walk down to Mulberry Street in the thick of a snowstorm and stand outside the Baron di Napoli rifle club, with its dark green windows, and pretend he was some scarecrow. The rifle club was under constant surveillance. A panel truck with the most sophisticated sound equipment the Bureau could buy was parked across the street. LeComte's soundmen could pick up Isaac's heartbeat. But Isaac preferred it this way, rather than a secret rendez-vous with Jerry DiAngelis, the youngest of the dons. DiAnge-lis hadn't been born into one of the Families. He hadn't married a Mafia princess. He'd made his bones in the street. His wife wasn't even a Siciliana. She was the daughter of a struggling Hebrew schoolteacher, a melamed who had nei-ther position nor wealth to aid a future don. Jerry DiAngelis was bitten in the ass by a witch, the Sicilians liked to say. He'd married crazily, for love. The melamed lived with DiAngelis and his wife, had retired from teaching and talked to the birds. But none of the dons dared joke about this *pazzo*, the dotty father-in-law. DiAngelis had survived bloody wars, he'd sat in jail. Other dons had tried to kill him. They'd blown up his car. They'd executed his chauffeurs. But DiAngelis walked out of the carnage. He killed when he had to kill, like some tycoon of the streets. LeComte had indicted him three times in the last two years. But he couldn't seem to put Jerry away.

Isaac stood in the fallen snow.

Nothing seemed to move behind the green windows.

And then DiAngelis came out with no bodyguard or winter coat. He was wearing a cardigan. He was five or six years younger than Don Isacco and he owned New York like no mayor or police chief ever could. Nothing got built, or moved, without DiAngelis. The mayor's *New York Times* was delivered in one of DiAngelis' trucks. The City would have come to a halt without Jerry DiAngelis. Isaac knew it, so did everybody but LeComte.

Jerry was an inch taller than Isaac. He was much better tailored. He had silver hair and no bald spots. But he curtsied to the police commissioner.

"It's an honor, Don Isacco. Are you bringing me a message from LeComte?"

"Come out, Jerry."

And Jerry DiAngelis waltzed onto the wet ground.

"Walk with me," Isaac said.

DiAngelis shut the door of the rifle club. He gave no other signal than that.

"How is your father-in-law?" Isaac asked.

"He worries about you. You're his favorite official. He'd heard on the news that you took a fall. He sent you flowers at the hospital, Isaac. Did you get them?"

"Probably. But you know. Every piece of merchandise is screened before it comes into my room. Thank him for me, Jerry. I'm fond of the old man. I hear he was one hell of a melamed."

"Isaac, what is it you want?"

"You have an accountant named Crabbs."

Jerry DiAngelis didn't pause in the snow. "Had an accountant. He ran away from home. LeComte would love to have him in court. But honestly, Isaac, Martin Crabbs has very little to offer LeComte. I do my bookkeeping in my head."

"It's not Crabbs I want. It's his wife."

Jerry stopped and did a tiny dance, soiling the rich leather of his shoes. "That bimbo, Margaret, Margaret Tolstoy?"

"She's a woman of culture," Isaac said.

"Of course she is. But why bother me about her?"

"I need her address."

DiAngelis started walking again. "Is that why you brought me out into the snow? You're as crippled in the head as my father-in-law."

"Jerry, her address . . ."

"Isaac, you have a hard-on for Margaret Tolstoy, that's your problem. I'm not her pimp."

"We went to school together. She was in my class."

"Margaret? She can't read English."

"She was in my class."

"When? In the dinosaur age? Isaac, I don't get it. She lives at Thirty-nine Grand Street. Apartment eleven. Satisfied?"

"Yes," Isaac said. "Thanks, Jerry, I'll return the favor."

And the PC started to walk. It was DiAngelis who had to call after him.

"Return the favor right now. Tell me where you're hiding Maurice."

Isaac pointed to LeComte's panel truck. And the two men shuffled around the corner.

"He's a wizard, LeComte . . . with microphones. The British secret service taught him everything he knows."

"Maurice," DiAngelis said.

"I don't have him, Jerry."

"Swear on your daughter's life," DiAngelis said.

"I don't want Marilyn brought into this. She's not a soldier."

"Swear."

"She's not a soldier, I said."

"It ain't good enough, *dottore*. Swear."

Isaac knew that Jerry could reach into Seattle whenever he wanted and it wouldn't have mattered what protection Marilyn had. But the prince of Mulberry Street didn't go after women. He was as ruthless and old-fashioned as Isaac himself. Almost another Ivanhoe. And the PC, who wouldn't have sworn on Marilyn's life to any other man, satisfied Jerry.

"I swear," he said.

"Then who the fuck has Maurice?"

"LeComte. That's my guess. He's squeezing your counselor."

"Maurie can't testify against me in court."

"He doesn't have to. Maurie can point LeComte in the right direction, like a Seeing Eye dog."

"And LeComte can have me sit in the can while his prosecutors work up one more phony case . . . but it's not like Maurie to sing, even if he is a faigele. I've been careful about the boyfriends, Isaac. I always check them out."

"Maurie doesn't have to sing," Isaac said. "All he has to do is disappear. LeComte figures you'll fold in court if Maurie isn't around."

"LeComte isn't alone in this. He likes to borrow your boys."

"I'm the police commissioner, Jerry. I don't buy and sell shirts."

"Does LeComte know I helped you capture Henry Armstrong Lee?"

"It wouldn't score points with him. He's pissed off that his own children didn't make the collar."

Justice had all the money in the world, but it couldn't understand the ways of New York. DiAngelis stole, cheated, killed, but he only killed *his* people. He was the best informant Isaac ever had. If a slasher was on the loose, or a black bank robber like Henry Lee, it was DiAngelis who pumped the streets, DiAngelis who found the leads, because the prince preferred a city without chaos. He was a crime boss, and Isaac's squads had him under surveillance, bugged his offices, his clubs, his mistress' rooms with sound buttons that LeComte supplied, microphones that could curl inside a pin. But Isaac left him alone. If Jerry was destroyed, Isaac would have to deal with another boss who might not be so reliable, and could start some senseless war where little old ladies would get killed.

Isaac said good-bye to the prince as the snow gathered between them. They didn't embrace, like comrades would.

They didn't touch, or even smile. DiAngelis returned to his rifle club. And Isaac tracked in the snow to Grand Street. He didn't care who was behind him, technicians who sat in trucks with cameras that could shoot right through a wall.

Thirty-nine Grand Street was attached to a shop that sold bridal gowns. The brides in the windows had burnt-red skin. The gowns were lavish, with long lace sleeves. Isaac had to stop and look, even though he had other business. The mannequins unsettled him. They were like no other dolls Isaac had ever seen. The dollmaker had endowed them with perfectly flowing arms under all that red skin. Isaac envied their lyrical lines. The dolls were as monstrous as any human.

He had no trouble breaking into Thirty-nine Grand Street. The front door had a pathetic lock. But Isaac began to shiver in the hall. He had a dizzy spell on the stairs. I'm not going to faint, I'm not going to faint, he muttered as he watched the filthy cracks in the walls. This wasn't a house where Anastasia ought to have lived. And then he laughed with all the bitterness of a lover with lesions in his heart. It's a perfect place for Margaret Tolstoy.

He stood outside the door, listening for noises that might tell him Margaret was inside. Then he removed the lockpicks that he carried in his coat, near the bottle of milk. He opened Margaret's door and stepped inside like any burglar. He wanted to breathe Margaret, unearth Anastasia in all he could smell. But Isaac sniffed dust and the odors of decay. This Crabbs couldn't have been much of an accountant. The furniture was older than Isaac's, with little lice marks in the wood. And there were no ornaments around, no pictures of Margaret, no paintings on the wall. And Isaac wondered if a genuine burglar had come before he did. The closets had been picked clean. There were none of Anastasia's underpants in the chiffonier. No lipsticks or perfumes. No checkbooks. No little signs of disorderly life that any couple would have had. The burglar, whoever it was, hadn't been a common thief. He or she worked for the government or Jerry DiAngelis.

Isaac's beeper began to whine. It was a Japanese gizmo with its own electronic message board. Isaac looked at the screen. PAY DAY. Her Honor wanted him at City Hall. He switched off the machine. His vertigo was gone. The world was pulling around him, and Isaac felt like a pygmy in the dark. He'd been on the road for two weeks and all the coordinates had changed. Some mother was sitting in the wings and running Isaac. And Isaac had to find who it was. And why.

6

Wrapped as he was, like a snowman in a tattered scarf and a coat that could have come from his dead mother's junk shop, Don Isacco arrived at City Hall. He didn't mingle with the newspaper folk or the mayor's entourage. He could have been a bum from the almshouse that had stood on this site. The old English masters had built a jail here, Brideswell, and had their own hanging tree. Isaac wondered when the tree had been felled. Before or after the Revolution? He went around to the side entrance of City Hall, descended a little flight of stairs, knocked on the door. One of his own policemen, assigned to Becky Karp, scrutinized Isaac and let him in. He didn't have to explain his whereabouts to a bodyguard. But it was close to Christmastime, and Isaac didn't want to be curt.

"Hullo, Tom. How's your wife? Give her my regards."

"I will, Chief. Would you care for some coffee now?"

"I'm too frozen to drink a cup," Isaac said. "I'd start to melt."

And the bodyguard laughed. He was from the old brigade,

47

when the Department was an Irish "castle," and the Shamrock Society ran half the show; the police commissioner himself was only an adjunct of whatever cardinal sat in the Powerhouse, St. Patrick's Cathedral. But now the Department had a Jewish PC and a black First Dep, and the Irishers had begun moving into the FBI, or were becoming sheriffs in Arizona or New Mexico, where they could hold on to their pensions and still carry a gun. And Isaac had to contend with the new Indian countries of Bushwick and the South Bronx. He couldn't reclaim them, because he couldn't reclaim the schools, which had become holding pens for moon children, kids who lived like marauders and maddened wolves. Nine-year-olds with knives.

He followed the bending lines of a water pipe into Rebecca's bunker. She was named after that Jewish witch from *Ivanhoe*. Rebecca. The monkish knight, Brian de Bois-Guilbert, dooms himself and dies out of his love for that storybook Rebecca. Isaac had never cared for Wilfred of Ivanhoe, the wonderboy of Sir Walter Scott's tale. But Brian de Bois-Guilbert had haunted him since he was nine, because he could never really pronounce that name, and Isaac was passionate about the notion of a monk with a battle-ax.

"Bois-Guilbert," Isaac muttered, while *his* Rebecca was waiting for him in the bunker's little bedroom. She was wearing a red robe. Isaac could see all the way down her throat. "You're late," she said, winding her wristwatch. She'd never borne a child, and she had the body of a twenty-five-year-old. She was still Rebecca of the Rockaways.

"Come to bed."

"Your Honor," he told her. "I'd like to resign."

"Cut the crap. This isn't the time for it. I have a three-o'clock at the Board of Ed."

"If you're looking for a chancellor, what about me?"

"Isaac, insanity isn't your best feature."

"But I'm serious," he said.

"We already have a chancellor."

"Alejo Tomás? He's an invisible man."

"And you never finished your freshman year at college. You're practically an illiterate from the City's point of view. And why would I want you down at Livingston Street? You'd ruin me with all your cockeyed schemes. We'd be fighting every minute."

"But it would help the kids, Rebecca. It would help the kids."

"What kids?" she asked. "Isaac, I know your worth. I couldn't get reelected without you at One Police Plaza. Come to bed."

And she pulled on Isaac's rags.

He sat down near Rebecca, as forlorn as Brian de Bois-Guilbert.

"Isaac, is it such a task to make love to me?"

"Becky," he said. "I'm no good as a police chief."

"Crazyhead, you're the number one cop in America. Didn't I lend you to Justice? The first fucking Alexander Hamilton Fellow."

"But it's the schools, Becky. That's where it starts." And Isaac made a hammer with his fists.

"You have a new cookie," she told him. "My deputies say, 'Get rid of that Pink Commish. He'll cripple you in the end. He's in love with Joe Stalin.' But do I ever listen? It's a cookie, isn't it?"

Her Honor leaped out of bed. She tossed off her robe, and Isaac could feel the music of her body, the deep chest, and the trim, athletic hips, calves that shone in the dark.

"Thank you, good-bye. I don't need you around while I get dressed."

He stood there, absorbing her punishment.

"Isaac, come with me to the Board of Ed. I'll tell them you want to be chancellor and I'll watch when they laugh in your face."

"They will laugh," he said. "And then they'll bow to a lackey like Alejo Tomás."

He marched out in his rags, while Rebecca cackled and started to cry. "I don't care if you have a cookie. I don't care. I don't care."

⚜

He went to the Christy Mathewson Club. There were new champions on the wall. Rabbit Maranville. Rogers Hornsby. Joe Judge. Where the hell were Babe Ruth, Tris Speaker, and Mathewson himself? Isaac smiled. What would his cryptographers at the Ivanhoe "division" have done about the new faces? Old men were drinking sherry in the main hall. But Isaac didn't see Schyler Knott. He climbed a flight of stairs to Schyler's office. He could come and go as he pleased. Who would have questioned the Commish? He stopped near the darkened glass of Schyler's door. He'd have to become his own cryptographer and look at the Christys' receipts. Perhaps there were notes Schyler had taken about Maurie Goodstein and Margaret Tolstoy.

Isaac grabbed for his picks. The door opened like a baby. But he'd have to rifle around in the dark. He couldn't risk putting on a light. He groped toward Schyler's desk, and that's when a pair of hands girdled his chest with the force of a python. Don Isacco couldn't breathe. Bubbles formed in his mouth.

"Keep still."

Don Isacco stopped fighting.

A light went on. And Isaac recognized one of the Bomber's mitts. Harry Lieberman, formerly of the New York Giants, stood behind Isaac.

"Can I turn around?" Isaac asked.

"Yes," Harry answered, breaking his grip.

Isaac coughed. The Bomber gave him a glass of water. "Drink slow," he said.

To be squeezed to death by his very own hero. It seemed proper to Isaac. But there was nothing cruel in the Bomber's face. He was an aging boy from the Polo Grounds, carrying out some mission for Schyler Knott.

"Sorry, Commissioner," the Bomber said as Isaac sipped from the glass.

"Where's Schyler?"

"I'm not allowed to tell."

If only Isaac could have had his own team, with the Bomber in center field, he wouldn't have needed the Ivanhoes. "Harry, I'm your friend."

"Schyler doesn't think so."

"What happened?"

"This guy came around and started to threaten."

The Afrikaner, Isaac muttered. Burt. "Was he a stocky fellow with a bald head?"

"Something like that. He came again and I had to throw him down the stairs."

"I apologize," Isaac said. "He's one of my investigators. I should have kept him on a leash. But I was desperate. I'm looking for someone named Margaret Tolstoy."

"Never heard of the babe."

"She has a husband. He's a member of the Christys. Martin Crabbs."

"The accountant. Why didn't you say so? I didn't know he was married."

"But she was here . . . the night I gave my speech."

"You didn't give your speech, Commissioner. You disappointed us. I was waiting for a month."

"But it was because of Anastasia. Margaret, I mean. She was a childhood sweetheart. Not a sweetheart exactly. I was in love with her and—"

"I remember the babe. She had blond hair. A peach. She'd never been to the club before . . . Schyler had two other guests."

"I don't understand."

"Two other guests. They scratched his cheek with a knife.

They started to strangle him with his tie . . . here at the club."

"What did they want?"

"Maurice's address. But they couldn't get it. Schyler wouldn't betray a Christy."

"But why didn't he go to the cops? He could have called me."

"They were cops," the Bomber said.

"Are you sure of that?"

"Schyler didn't tell no one but you that Maurice was a member of the club. They were your people, Mr. Isaac."

"They were not," Isaac said. None of his Ivanhoes would have touched Schyler's face. "Listen, Bomber."

"I'm Harry," the Bomber said. "Don't take privileges."

"It's a mess. Schyler's in danger. He has to come to me. If he does know where Maurie is, there will be more trouble."

"We take care of our own, Mr. Isaac. We don't strangle. We don't use knives. But we were scrappers once, and we haven't forgotten how to fight."

"Dammit, Harry, there are enough detectives in town. Warn Schyler, will you? He has to get in touch."

"I'll see," the Bomber said.

"Why did you change the pictures on the wall? You had Babe Ruth . . . and now there's Joe Judge."

"We have our own message system, Mr. Isaac. It's internal to us. And you're not a Christy. Don't get smart. You can't break our codebook, even if you are the biggest cop."

"Harry . . ."

"If you come again, wear a tie. That's house rules. And don't bring your fancy needles. We're gentlemen. We don't pick locks."

And Isaac skulked away like a dog. The Bomber had unmasked him as a thief. And crazily, as the snow flew around him, Isaac started to cry. The worm hadn't bothered him once in the Christys' bluestone building. But he sucked on his bottle of milk.

He trudged to the Lower East Side, and even in his ragged coat, people recognized him. They kissed his hand. Old Jewish men, Chinese seamstresses, Irish widows, and Latino dowagers of Loisaida. He couldn't escape his bearish self. "Don Isacco, Don Isacco." The drug dealers had fled with a police chief in the neighborhood. The holdupniks had to think twice. Isaac kept a flat on Rivington Street. It was his official address, a rent-controlled apartment that cost him under two thousand a year. There were no burglaries with Isaac in the building. There was enough hot water for a king. And even if Isaac's tub was in the kitchen, what did it matter?

He could walk into any health club, or shower at the Pierre.

Women wrote him love letters, sent him pictures in the mail, with marriage proposals and lists of all their assets. But Isaac wasn't looking for a millionairess. Columnists quoted him in the papers about crime. His figure could be seen on the six o'clock news, the great detective in the clothes of some cadaver. He was much more popular than Rebecca Karp. He'd been offered movie contracts. All Isaac had to do was play himself. Suddenly his very ruggedness had become chic. But all he could think about was Anastasia.

He'd never find her again.

He had a terrific appetite to bargain with the merchants of Orchard Street, as he'd done before he'd been a famous cop. It was in Isaac's blood. His mom and dad had been traders once upon a time. And Isaac loved to shave off a dollar or two from a merchant's price. But it was difficult for him now. The merchants wouldn't take a penny from Don Isacco. He had to reach into his pocket for a false nose. He warmed up the putty and fit the nose to his face.

He went into Abraham's, where he'd bargained as a boy. The old man was over eighty now, and he had a young black assistant who babbled a stronger Yiddish than Isaac ever could. *"Traif,"* the assistant said when he had a look at Isaac, meaning that this bum was unkosher and wasn't worth a minute of the old man's time.

"Pajamas," Isaac said with his false nose. He saw himself in the old man's mirror: half Fagin, half Frankenstein.

"Wash-and-wear, or what?" the old man asked.

"Flannel," Isaac said, as if there could be no other pajamas in the world.

"For flannel you gotta pay," the old man said.

"*Nisht*, Abraham, *nisht*," the assistant said, trying to discourage the bartering that was about to begin.

"Show this gentleman our merchandise, will you, Al?"

"He's a schnorrer."

"Show!"

"I'm big around the chest," Isaac said. "I need extra large."

"What about the bottoms?" Abraham asked.

"I like to roll them up around my knees."

And the assistant carted out great brown boxes of Abraham's flannel pajamas. Isaac sifted through the boxes, happier than he'd been in a long, long while. He found a pair with white stripes in a blue field. They looked like prison pajamas. "How much?"

"Fifteen dollars. They cost me sixteen. But they're on sale."

Isaac had to be cautious. Abraham was temperamental about his prices.

"Thirteen," Isaac said.

"Mister, go home."

But Isaac could read the signs. Abraham hadn't closed the boxes.

"You are a schnorrer," Abraham said. "I give you from Hong Kong. Merchandise. The best."

"Thirteen."

Abraham took the thirteen dollars and thrust the pajamas into a paper bag, while Isaac's heart swam with all the delirium of a curious kind of kill. "Now take off that miserable mask," Abraham said. And Isaac was gloomy again.

He pulled off the nose and picked at the putty.

"How long I know you?" Abraham asked.

"Forty years."

"Longer," the old man said. "And you still take advantage. Next time you come to bargain, come without the nose."

And Isaac waltzed out into the snow with his striped pajamas. Perhaps he should consider a movie contract. No one could really police New York. And as he crept toward his apartment, he could feel a shadow behind him. He wasn't carrying the gold-plated gun LeComte had given him to start his career as a Hamilton Fellow, an expensive toy from the gunsmiths at the Justice Department, with the attorney general's signature engraved on the grip. Isaac didn't require such an immaculate piece. He had his own hands to play with. He glimpsed into the shop windows. The shadow was wearing a homburg, with rubber boots and a long coat. Isaac began to muse. They send infants in galoshes after me.

He would lead this shadow on a merry chase. It had to be a package from LeComte or Jerry DiAngelis. Isaac decided to take the package home. He trudged toward Rivington Street, turned the corner, ducked into a doorway, and when the package appeared, breathing hard and clomping along in his rubber boots, Isaac leaped at him like a werewolf, spun the package around. The homburg fell off. He was looking into Anastasia's almond eyes.

Part Two

7

He couldn't have told you if it was a dream or not. But Isaac had grown philosophical since his fiftieth birthday. And he'd have argued that it wouldn't have mattered much. What was fixed in his memory had its own tactile life, could be touched like the teeth in his head. Had he dreamt Kingsley McCardle? Was the Justice Department or LeComte himself one more ghost? LeComte couldn't bother him now. And McCardle had entered so deep into his psyche, the kid belonged to Isaac's tribe. But he was thinking of an icon, the figure of Jesus painted on a wooden panel, Jesus wearing thorns of gold. Isaac had seen the icon in Anastasia's household and had to ask what the hell it was. He knew all about the Son of God. There were even churches on the Lower East Side with onion domes, where all the Ukrainians went. The priests wore big hats. And they carried pendulums of incense. They had beards like the zaddiks of Brooklyn, but they were taller, brutish men, and their eyes burnt in the middle of the afternoon with a samovar's yellow flame.

But it was the icon in Anastasia's house, that Jesus with the golden thorns. His face had all the sadness of a man who must have sinned. It was only logical. *Their* Jesus was a Jew, like any haunted ragman of Hester Street, with a bundle of clothes on his back. But Isaac would sit and drink Russian Orthodox tea, black as blood, while Anastasia's aunts crossed themselves and asked mercy from the icon for having a little Jew in the house. They loved talking to a piece of painted wood. And that wood had become a deity for Isaac, like the images of Moses on the mountain, Moses with a blackened face. Anastasia had wakened him when he was fourteen. He could still feel the thickness of her stockings, see the little hairs on her aunties' chins, and that Son of God on the wall.

She was so weak, this Margaret Tolstoy, Isaac had to carry her up the stairs. He didn't have black tea to offer her. He wasn't a collector of samovars. He prepared a broth with noodles. She wolfed it down, her hands trembling as she held the bowl. Not a word passed between them, not a smile, not a single grunt of hello.

"Margaret," he said.

"You've been hearing rumors."

"Aren't you Margaret Tolstoy?"

"I'm Anastasia."

"But you're living with the accountant. Crabbs."

"I'm still Anastasia."

"Please," Isaac said. "I'm a cop. I had you traced. You call yourself Margaret Tolstoy."

"Mostly to strangers. It means nothing. It's a professional name."

"What profession?" Isaac asked.

She put down the bowl and pulled his ears. "Oh, Isaac. I'm Crabbs' whore." He wouldn't listen, but the sound of her voice brought him back to the country of samovars and baked apples. He was that boy again, Anastasia's slave.

She was shivering. "Your clothes are wet. . . . I'll give you something to put on."

The big bear searched his closets. Imbecile, he muttered. He let her have the pajamas he'd bought at Abraham's. He surrounded her with slippers, socks, and a cashmere robe his wife Kathleen had given him when he graduated from the Police Academy. Anastasia undressed in front of Isaac. He closed his eyes. She laughed from deep inside her throat, like a growl that was half-liquid. "Still my beau, aren't you, Isaac? My Jewish knight."

He opened his eyes. She stood in his pajamas and her rubber boots. "Then you do remember me," he said.

"How could I forget? You followed me home from school. Isaac, you were like glue."

"But we never kissed."

"We didn't have to," she said with a smile that broke onto her face. There was webbing under her eyes, pockets in her cheeks, but she hadn't misappraised Isaac. He was her knight, and she was his mam'selle without mercy. All his accomplishments fell away. His commissioner's status. His gold shield. He'd have killed for her and wouldn't even have asked for a kiss.

"You remembered me . . . all these years?"

"I'm not a saint, Isaac. I remembered. I forgot. But you're a famous man."

"And my lecture at the Christy Mathewson Club. Why did you come?"

"Ah, I love Babe Ruth . . ."

"But you're Russian," he said.

"Roumanian."

"That icon," Isaac said. "And your aunts."

"They weren't my aunts. I was their little housekeeper."

"And then you disappeared."

"It happens when you're an orphan. I moved around a lot."

"But you didn't even say good-bye."

"Oh, the agency writes love poems every time they send you to one more aunt. Isaac, I didn't even have the time to pee. I was a transient. What was the point of good-byes?"

"But I would have known. It wouldn't have been such a mystery."

"Isaac," she said, pulling his ears again. "You thrive on mysteries." She understood his nature. That's why he'd loved her. She'd sensed the police chief in him when he was fourteen.

"Your husband's a Christy. Did he turn you on to the club?"

"I told you," she said. "I'm his whore. Or at least I was."

"I don't get it."

"Now I have some kind of widow's status. DiAngelis' people took care of him. And they'd love to take care of me. That's why I was at your lecture. I needed help, Isaac. I'm sorry if I'm not sentimental about our past. I had lots and lots of beaux. Some of them I kissed. Some of them I didn't."

"But I saw Jerry DiAngelis. He promised me that he didn't whack out your husband."

"It was one of his crews. Let him say what he wants. He can't control them all."

"But he's the Man, Anastasia."

"When he goes to the toilet. When he shakes hands. But not out in the street."

"Then what crew was it?" Don Isacco asked.

"His brother's."

"Teddy Boy? The Nose? He's Jerry's legman."

"Then he has some pair of legs. He's been trying to put out my lights for a week."

It makes no sense, Isaac muttered. The Nose was Le-Comte's spy. LeComte had caught him dealing drugs and had turned the Nose around. Ted had compromised his brother's gang. He was the rat Jerry DiAngelis was looking for. But Isaac wasn't allowed to tell. Isaac was the PC. He couldn't snitch on LeComte and the Bureau. Nose was registered with the FBI. LeComte let him pull stickups and slap people around. Nose did his brother's dirty deeds and was also bleeding him dry. He could afford to be a maverick and have mad fits. But who would have licensed him to kill Martin

Crabbs? Not LeComte. It had to be Jerry. The Nose didn't have to worry about any indictments. He was the rat prince.

"Anastasia," Isaac said, looking at the pajama lady. She was spectacular in prison stripes. His heart beat with such hunger, the Commish was beside himself. Would he ever kiss Anastasia? But he was still Sherlock Holmes, the subconscious detective. "It has to be more complicated than that. Did Teddy turn on to you?"

"Isaac, I said I was Crabbs' whore. I wouldn't go near the Nose."

"I didn't ask you if you liked him. Did the Nose like you?"

"He wouldn't have minded getting into my pants. But that didn't stop him from sending his shooters after me."

"Are you sure it was the Nose? I mean, what if it was a mix-up, and another crew was trying to put the blame on Teddy Boy?"

"It was the Nose. He was wearing Crabbs' tie. He wanted to strangle me with it. But some neighbors happened to knock on the door. And Nose waltzed out the window. That's when he started sending his shooters around."

"Did he give you a reason?"

"Not really."

"And why are you convinced your husband is dead?"

"Didn't the Nose have his necktie? And he told me, 'That bastard is sleeping for good. You're next.' . . . Hey, I'm cold in these pajamas. Can't you offer a girl a simple glass of tea?"

"Sorry," Isaac said. "I don't have a samovar."

"Who the hell does?" Anastasia asked him, and Isaac was perplexed. She didn't talk like the old Anastasia. All that refinement was gone. And where was her French vocabulary? Crabbs' whore. He had a touch of sympathy for the Nose. He would have finished Crabbs himself.

He boiled the hot water, prepared little biscuits from the appetizing store, presented her with an apple he'd baked in his oven. He couldn't eat in restaurants anymore. People would arrive from every corner, bend on their knees, and beg favors from the Pink Commish. It was embarrassing for Isaac, and he couldn't digest his meal. So he gave Herbert, the appetizing man, an extra key. Herbert would stock Isaac's refrigerator with whatever delicacies he'd prepared for that day. And Isaac would walk around with sturgeon in his coat and a bottle of milk. The worm had gotten used to Isaac's diet and didn't writhe so much.

Isaac discovered blinis in the fridge, prepared by Herbert's own hands. He broiled them and served the blinis with sour cream and a split of champagne. He had dark, crusty bread and pumpkin pie, even though Thanksgiving had come and gone without much notice. He still couldn't believe Anastasia was in his own kitchen wearing Isaac's pajamas, pajamas he'd never worn. He had no appetite. But Anastasia tore at the blinis like a Roumanian princess. She belched once and excused herself. She drank the champagne, her mouth moist with some secret pleasure. She rocked in her chair and sang a song in a language Isaac had never heard before. She didn't seem scared. And it puzzled him. Her breasts heaved under the pajamas. He drank in her perfume.

That's when he noticed a shadow creeping up the kitchen wall. Isaac turned. A man stood on the fire escape with a scattergun. He wore a hood with eyeholes. Isaac recognized the gun. It was a 12-gauge Mossberg Persuader with enough smack to tear off Isaac's head. But the Mossberg wasn't aimed at him. The man had come for Margaret Tolstoy. Isaac threw her under his table with as much force as he could. Her almond eyes clicked once at the Pink Commish. The gun went off. The table splintered like a huge wooden pie.

Isaac leapt at the window, but the man in the hood had climbed down the ladder. Isaac returned to Margaret Tolstoy. She was lying on the floor in a great sea of wood and sour cream. He held her in his arms. Now it was Isaac who sang. It was a nonsense song his mother had taught him about a band of runaway dogs. A lullaby. He sang Crabbs' widow to sleep.

He was Don Isacco, and he could have caused a big stink. But he didn't want his own Department tracking in the ruins of his kitchen, labmen with their latex gloves and little pincers, detectives in their rubber soles. He hired a carpenter and a glazier and had the kitchen redone. But the neighbors seemed less sure of his residency now. The godfather of One Police Plaza was as vulnerable as they were. No reporters came around. There was nothing on the six o'clock news. And meanwhile, Isaac's brains were boiling. The Nose or one of his shooters had entered Isaac's territories. And someone would have to pay. But first Isaac would have to find shelter for his old sweetheart.

He brought her to the Ivanhoes. Burt was out on a mission. And Isaac entrusted her to Allan Locksley, his chief cryptologist. Locksley had been a professor of Greek and Latin at one of the inner-city colleges. But when Latin and Greek were dropped from the curriculum, Locksley resigned, gave up his tenure, and joined the Ivanhoes. He loved secret languages and had a passion for breaking codes. He brewed that dark tea Anastasia adored.

"Allan," Isaac said, "when Burt comes back, I want you to go uptown to the Christy Mathewson Club. They have some kind of fucking code on the walls. They use portraits of baseball players as flags. That's how they signal to themselves. I want you to break that code. I think they're hiding Maurie Goodstein. . . . Anastasia, did you ever meet Maurie?"

"Nose's lawyer? Of course. He's a little guy."

"Did he tell you anything?"

"That faigele? He didn't even flirt."

"What about Crabbs? Did they ever huddle?"

"Crabbs and Maurice? Was there anything between them? I doubt it. I never saw them kiss."

"Business, I mean. Did they do business together?"

"Yes. They had to. Crabbs was the Family accountant."

"And did your husband ever mention Maurie?"

"Once or twice."

"Did he give you any of Maurie's papers to hide? Think, Anastasia. It's important."

"No. I didn't like to mingle in his affairs. . . . Isaac, when are you coming back?"

"Soon."

"It's dark here. Like a factory."

"It is a factory. That's why it's safe."

And Anastasia pulled Isaac's ears in front of Allan Locksley. She kissed Isaac on the mouth. Forty years. That's all Isaac could think about. Took him forty years to accomplish that kiss. He might have sucked harder on her lips if Locksley hadn't been around. He couldn't let his feelings "surface" among the Ivanhoes.

He walked down to Cleveland Place, next to the old Police Headquarters, where Jerry DiAngelis lived in a modest house with a brittle front porch. DiAngelis had been poor most of his life. He had a wife, a melamed, and an older brother to support. He'd sat in jail six or seven years. His rise to power had been mercilessly slow and then very, very swift. He'd been the captain of his own crew. Other dons had tried to kill him. But he'd stepped over their bodies. And now the Family was his. He was forty-seven years old. He didn't have tiny button eyes like his brother, Teddy Boy, who'd never married and lived under the same roof, a bachelor who was Isaac's age.

Bodyguards lingered near the porch and Isaac had to announce himself, step in front of DiAngelis' closed circuit TV, the same high-tech model the Israelis used at their consulate. "Jerry," Isaac said, standing there like a fool. "It's me."

"I know it's you," a voice crackled from inside the circuitry. "I'm not fucking blind."

"Can I come in?"

"Don Isacco, I think I've had enough of you for one week. . . . I'm with my wife, you motherfucker. We're celebrating Christmas."

"Shouldn't curse," Isaac said.

"Don't lecture me."

"My mother was trampled to death by a bunch of wild kids."

"That breaks my heart."

"It should, Jerry. It really should. And nobody celebrates Christmas on December ninth."

"Jewish Christmas," the same voice croaked. "My father-in-law was a Hebrew teacher. And my wife's a Yid. What's the matter, Isaac? Did you lose your religion?"

"Ah, bless all the saints, it's Hanukkah time. Thanks for reminding me. But I need to come upstairs."

Isaac heard the tiniest of clicks. The front door opened. It was plated with steel and had once belonged to an icebox. No sledgehammer could have solved that door. It would take a cannon to get in. Isaac climbed the stairs. The melamed was waiting for him on the landing. Isadore Wasser. There was nothing religious about the old man. He wore one of Jerry's old jackets and a pair of slippers that resembled snowshoes. His hair was marvelously white. He'd aged like some golden child.

"Shalom, Iz," Isaac said.

The melamed hugged him. "How is my favorite Stalinist?"

"Not so good, Izzy. Not so good."

DiAngelis appeared. "You don't have to kiss him, Dad, for God's sake. He's the fucking police commissioner."

The melamed was furious. He shook his entire head of silver hair. "Sonny boy, he's also our guest." And he invited Don Isacco into the living room. And Isaac understood Jerry's reluctance to have him in the house. A pair of soundmen were sweeping the room for bugging devices. One of them had a long electronic sleeve that he used to suck at the ceiling. The other carried a little pipe in his ear and listened to the walls, as if he were looking for some lost fragile heartbeat. And Isaac felt a little guilty. LeComte had "needle" mikes planted in the walls of the buildings on both sides of Jerry, who was caught between a kind of powerful parabolic sandwich. Isaac knew which of Jerry's rooms were "live," and which were "dead." He'd come like a robber with nothing to steal.

Jerry started to rant. "LeComte, you cocksucker, you hear me, LeComte? I hope you die of measles on your ass."

"Sonny," the old man said, "it's not so smart, talking to a wall."

"He's crucifying me, Dad. And Isaac works for him, that piece of dreck."

"LeComte isn't my boss," Isaac muttered.

"Sure," Jerry said. "He sends you out on the road, like a fucking comedian . . . you hear me, LeComte?"

The melamed ushered Isaac and Jerry into the kitchen, while the soundmen probed for mikes they'd never catch.

The kitchen was larger than Isaac's whole apartment. Eileen DiAngelis stood around the stove with Teddy, the bachelor boy who was being run by LeComte. The Nose was a great big giant. He couldn't meet Isaac's eye. He was homicidal, but he lived like a baby in his brother's house. He never missed a meal. He'd earned his nickname because he'd had a constant erection while he was a boy, and kids would laugh at the "schnozzola" inside Teddy's pants. He'd bullied his younger brother until Jerry grew bulky enough to absorb all his brother's blows, and then he went after him with a hammer. Ted was underboss of the Family. He ruled whenever Jerry sat in Green Haven or the Metropolitan Correctional Center during one of LeComte's searches and seizures. It made terrific sense that LeComte didn't want Jerry around. He could have a crime family of his own to play with.

"How are you, Nose?" Isaac asked.

"Shut up and sit down," Eileen said. "And don't pick on the kid."

They sat at the table and ate spaghettini puttanesca, stabbing black olives with their forks. They ate in silence except for the old man. "Tell me again, Isaac, how Stalin was such a genius he had to murder twenty million of his own people."

"He was no worse than any of the czars," Isaac said. "The ultimate paranoiac in a paranoid world."

"Poisoned his own wife," the melamed said. "Lovely man."

"But he survived, Izzy, that's the point. I'm not congratulating him."

"Got rid of all his generals and the best poets the world had ever seen. He was a ratty-eyed seminarian, a police informer."

"But Trotsky had the whole Red Army and it couldn't help him."

"Jesus Christ, you're giving me a headache," Jerry said.

"Sonny," the melamed said, "it's our conversation. Keep out." Isaac adored the old man. Izzy Wasser had had a career long before he was a melamed. Isaac had read his rap sheet. Izzy graduated from burglary to Hebrew schools. His son-in-law would never have become a don without him. The melamed was Jerry's private *consiglieri* and tactician, a teacher of crime.

"Trotsky wouldn't have touched the poets," Izzy said. "There was your genius. He liked the company of educated men. You wouldn't have had the show trials and the pogroms."

"You would have had worse," Isaac said. "Philosophers tearing at each other's throat while the country starved. Your poets would have had to scribble with their own blood. And Hitler would have sat in the Kremlin if it hadn't been for Uncle Joe."

"The Little Father of his people," the old man said. "The perfect policeman. Like yourself."

"I'm going crazy," Jerry said. "Dad, Dad."

"I'm finished," the old man announced. And Eileen laughed. She'd been Jerry's sweetheart since junior high. The melamed had encouraged their romance. He admired Jerry's persistence, his ardor over Eileen. He was an anarchist, and he didn't care about kosher things. He was moved by strong-willed men. It didn't matter that he lost several pupils, their parents angry at the melamed for bringing Jerry DiAngelis into a Jewish house. He spat at the money that flew out of his fingers. He was Isadore Wasser, the best melamed in town.

"Apologize," he said, glaring at his son-in-law, the don of all the dons, even if the mortality rate was high for a Mafia king like Jerry.

"Apologize for what?" Jerry said, his teeth glinting like a wolf.

"I heard you on the intercom. You insulted the memory of Sophie Sidel."

"Who the fuck is Sophie Sidel?"

"Isaac's mother, may she rest in peace."

"How did I insult? Who remembers?"

"You called the Commish a motherfucker. She had a violent death, Sophie Sidel. And you told him, 'That breaks my heart.'"

"Dad, it was just an expression . . . Jesus Christ."

"There was malice behind it."

Jerry stood up at the table, bowed, and kissed Isaac's hand. "I apologize, Don Isacco."

"Without sarcasm, please," the old man said.

"Isaac, I've been under a strain," Jerry said. "LeComte has been grabbing at my balls. Forgive me . . . now can I finish my meal?"

Jerry adored the old man as much as Isaac did.

Eileen ladled out chunks of an enormous pie that was filled with berries and walnuts and pears. Jerry had his *comare*, whom he visited twice a week, but the *comare*, who was blond and beautiful, and Argentinian by birth, couldn't have prepared a pie like that. Isaac himself was a little in love with Eileen, who knew about the *comare* and never mentioned her. She was as fierce and proud as the melamed. And she'd fashioned a family in this landscape of thieves. She couldn't have children. Isaac didn't know the reason why. He wouldn't have asked. Jerry had had a child with the *comare*, a ten-year-old boy. And it was this that ate at Eileen. She would have liked to add the boy to her household of waifs, the

melamed who began as a burglar, the husband who would rot
in jail or die in some meaningless Mafia war, and Teddy Boy,
who depended on her when he wasn't out strangling people
with a necktie. She was fond of Isaac also. She recognized the
wayfarer in him, with all his captures and glory hours on TV.

"Isaac," she said, "another piece?" cramming the commissioner's plate with a mountain of berries. And then she
prepared black coffee with a lemon peel and hot milk for
Isaac's worm. She was familiar with all his maladies.

When the meal was over, Isaac and Jerry wandered out of
the kitchen and into a closet that Isaac chose, because it
wasn't within reach of LeComte's parabolic mikes.

"I'll figure out his fucking equipment, Isaac. Don't you
worry. I have the best sweepers in the business."

"You're wasting your time. LeComte is always a year ahead
of the competition. No one's immune. He's bugged my office
too."

"That's indecent," Jerry said. "You're our highest cop."

"Means nothing to him. But I have a problem, Jerry. You
lied to me."

"About what?"

"Margaret Tolstoy."

"Isaac, are you sick? She's not even Crabbs' *comare*. She's
a bim."

"Well, your brother tried to strangle her and almost
succeeded."

"What the hell for?"

"That's what I would like to know. He doesn't have too
many ideas in his head."

"And you're saying I arranged it, huh? I have no interest in
the merchandise, no interest at all."

"And she swears that Teddy Boy iced Mr. Crabbs."

"Crabbs is as alive as you . . . or LeComte."

"That's hard to believe. Someone was outside my window,
Jerry, with a shotgun."

"Some local kid with a gripe . . . or a fucking addict."

"Addicts couldn't afford a Mossberg Persuader. Your Family is fond of that particular gun."

"Did you have a peek at the cocksucker?"

"He was wearing a mask. And he dropped both barrels into my kitchen, Jerry. Shot the place to shit. He was after Margaret Tolstoy."

"It's insane, Isaac. Come on."

They stepped out of the closet and returned to the kitchen, where Teddy Boy was devouring the remains of the pie. His hands were thick with blood from all the berries. His brother caught him while he was trying to cram another piece of pie into his mouth. Jerry threw him off his chair, grabbed his grizzly head, and banged it against the floor. "Nose, are you free-lancing again?"

"I wouldn't do that."

"You went after that *puttana* Margaret with a necktie . . . and you had a shooter waiting outside Isaac's window, the fucking chief of police."

Jerry got up, stood over his brother, and started to drag him around like a sack.

Nose started to cry.

The melamed entered the room. "He's your own blood, Jerry. You'll kill him."

"I'll do worse than that," Jerry said. "I'll make him wish that being born is something he'd like to forget."

But when Eileen appeared, her black eyes boring into Jerry, he stopped dragging his brother. "How the fuck can I operate? I have retards who want to blow the commissioner away."

The melamed clutched his silver hair. "The walls, Jerry, the walls."

"I know about the walls, Dad. Teddy, I want that shooter of yours whacked out. . . . Are you hiding Crabbs?"

Nose shook his enormous head.

"Then take Isaac to him."

Nose started to rise like a whale. He whispered in his brother's ear.

"I don't give a flying fuck," Jerry said. "The man has to explain himself to Isaac. Get your car keys, little brother." Then he turned to the Commish. "Isaac, do me a favor. Hold his hand. And make sure his jalopy isn't wired for a bomb. My crews have gone crazy. And there's a rat running around. LeComte might have paid him to finish off my little brother. I wouldn't mind. He's a nuisance. But the wife would miss her teddy bear."

And so Isaac started down the stairs with Ted. The melamed called to him. "Remember, Isaac. Stalin also got it in the end. I don't care what the Soviets say. Beria poisoned him."

"Maybe he did. But Beria died the same year. That doesn't make him another Stalin. See you, Iz."

8

Isaac's teeth rattled in his head. He waited for a violent pull of the worm that always signaled an attack of vertigo. But it didn't happen. He'd been dying to tell Jerry and Eileen and Iz who the rat really was. He wished Jerry had dragged the life out of his little brother. But Isaac would have to resign if he revealed who Informant M (for Manhattan) 76666 OC/TE was. Teddy's FBI code name was the Four Sixes because of his uncommon serial number. Four Sixes was LeComte's star in the case that was building against Jerry DiAngelis and the crime family he'd inherited from the Rubino brothers, Vincent and Paul, who'd opened their "book" to Jerry, initiated him into the clan, and then tried to kill him when his own Manhattan crew seemed almost as powerful as the Rubinos themselves and their nephew Sal. But the Rubinos had died in that war. And now Jerry was prince of the Family, with a couple of rebellious crews that were still loyal to Sal and were ambiguous about Jerry and his brother. And so the prince had to walk out of bombed cars and pacify the crews that were against him. He didn't favor

74

shotgun parties. He wanted to heal old wounds. But he'd had to kill a captain or two. And while he danced and did all his politics, Source 76666 met with LeComte and sang his brother's life away.

They walked to Ted's cream-colored Coupe de Ville. Isaac slid down under the sedan to see if the car was wired. But it was an idle move. The bomb could have been triggered by remote control, and it would have taken Isaac half an hour to unearth the "clock." Fuck it, he said. The FBI was shielding Ted. LeComte's own experts had probably vacuumed the car for plastique.

They climbed in, and Isaac sat with Ted. The Nose wasn't as dumb as he seemed. It was easy to play the imbecile. But he was LeComte's kingfish, the Four Sixes.

Ted drove out of Manhattan, crossed the Washington Bridge. And Isaac had to smile when Ted stopped at the Red Apple restaurant, gateway to the Catskills and the Borscht Belt. The Red Apple had been a Jewish colony during Isaac's boyhood. Now it was a glorified hot-dog stand. The Nose gobbled half a dozen dogs. It was only an hour since he'd attacked Eileen's pie. Isaac recalled the political discussions he'd had on a Red Apple bench with fellow waiters who were working the Borscht Belt to find a rich man's daughter to marry . . . or lacking that, get laid.

"*Das Kapital*," Isaac muttered.

"What?" Four Sixes said. "You ain't gonna snitch, are you, Isaac? I mean, what I did, I had to do. The Big Man, he had me in a bind. I couldn't last it out in a prison cell. The grub's no good. And I can't take a crap with the screws watching all the time. I need Eileen's cooking."

"Shut the fuck up," Isaac said, "or I'll finish what Jerry started."

"He's my big brother," Four Sixes said with a lunatic smile. "He can touch me all he wants."

"You're five years older than Jerry."

"He's my big brother. He looks after me."

"And you betray him to a shitband of FBI men."

Ted started to bawl. "I can't do time. My brother can. But I can't."

They drove to Swan Lake, and Isaac fell into a poisonous mood, because he didn't want to consider his days and nights in a Borscht Belt kitchen at seventeen, when he'd had to fight whole crews of busboys to find a place for himself. Teddy Boy stopped a hundred yards from the lake, and the borders of a deserted hotel. The lake was frozen through. It was winter in the Catskills. The ice made little crackling sounds, like breathing skin. Isaac recognized the hotel. Its signboard had been torn down. But it was a big white house over the water, with porches that went as high as the roof. The Hotel Gardenia, where Isaac discovered Lenny Bruce in the main casino. It was just after the war, and Bruce was a struggling comic, a famished Jewish kid. They'd come out of the same whirlwind, like inmates of an orphan asylum where money and social standing were as meaningless as the moon. Isaac still lived in that orphanage. He didn't even have a thousand dollars in the bank. He was a pauper with a big salary. And he'd worked this hotel, slaved in its kitchen, danced with doctors' wives, made brutal love to them while their hubbies were in Manhattan.

"What the hell is Crabbs doing here?" Isaac asked as they climbed the hill over the lake and listened to the ice. Had the Mafia seized the Borscht Belt after it had become a graveyard?

"It's a beauty, ain't it, Isaac? Like a fucking castle. And you can't approach it from the back. The hill's too steep."

"Who found this place?"

"I did."

"It's not one of LeComte's warehouses?"

"LeComte never heard of this hotel."

"So you were taking a Sunday drive, and bingo, you saw the white hotel and you said to yourself, 'This is for Teddy Boy.'"

"Something like that. But I had an edge. Crabbsy's been to the lake before. He's familiar with the terrain."

"Familiar with the terrain? That's LeComte talking now. Did he take you through the FBI course at Quantico? Did he send you to school with all the G-men so you could be an educated rat? Mr. Four Sixes. Is this where you'll retire, Nose, when they put you in the witness protection program?"

"I ain't going into the program. I wouldn't hurt my brother."

"You'll just nibble at his fingers until he's all gone. I asked you, Nose, why the fuck is Crabbs here?"

"He's hiding."

"From whom?"

"The government."

"So now you're his guardian, huh?"

"I'm his friend. He does my taxes. He gives me an allowance. He invests my cash. But I can't tell."

A man stepped out onto the bottommost porch. He was carrying a 12-gauge Mossberg, like that guy with the mask. He didn't look like any accountant Isaac could imagine. He didn't have spectacles or a splayed ass. Isaac was instantly jealous. "Margaret's husband," he muttered, because he had the feeling this wasn't some Buffalo Bill of the Catskills. It was Crabbs. He had dark eyes and a thick crop of hair, and that peculiar stink of intelligence.

"Nose, are you nuts?" he said.

"Crabbs, I want ya to meet—"

"I know who it is. The singing policeman, Isaac Sidel. I've sat next to him at banquets. I've seen him on the news. Nose, you shouldn't have brought him out to the lake."

"I didn't have no choice, Crabbs. He visited my brother. He told him about Margaret and—"

"Will you come inside," Crabbs said. "You're turning us all into targets. There's a terrible glare off the lake."

They went into the Hotel Gardenia. The lobby had been gutted. The chandeliers were gone; the front desk had been ripped right out of the wall. There weren't any portraits of the Gardenia's Jewish greats: Hank Greenberg, Al Jolson, Eddie Cantor . . . cardboard cutouts that had stood in the lobby and had seemed so lifelike to a boy of seventeen that Isaac could remember mumbling to Al Jolson and asking Hank how come he'd retired in 1947 after hitting twenty-five homers for the Pirates.

"Mr. Crabbs, are you an old Borscht Belter?"

"Away from the windows, will you? There's still a glare." Crabbs put a blanket around his shoulders. "Yes, I'm a veteran of Swan Lake. I did some time at the resorts. But not at this particular cheesebox . . . I always loved it up at the lake. You could hear your echo for miles. It was beautiful then. Lanterns over the water. Midnight boating parties."

"Who are you hiding from? LeComte?"

"Commissioner, this is my vacation."

"The Mossberg isn't a birdgun. It's for maiming people and bears. What are you afraid of?"

"Cops like you . . . don't you get it? Jerry's going down. And I do his arithmetic for him. The Feds have me marked. I'm the monkey in the middle. When they serve their papers, I don't intend to be around."

"So you've become the hermit of Swan Lake."

"It's better than a coffin."

"But who exactly wants you dead?"

"Right this minute? I wouldn't know. But I can see the handwriting. Mob accountant indicted. His throat gets cut at the Metropolitan CC."

"Has LeComte made any overtures?"

"He doesn't have to. Commissioner, don't be dense. I'm trapped. LeComte's got most of the firepower. Jerry has his good looks and a sensational father-in-law. But he can't control his crews. One day they'll whack him out. And I don't want to be there. I'm closing all the books."

"Does that include Margaret Tolstoy?"

Crabbs hunched under his blanket. He held the Mossberg

to his chest. His eyes seemed to lose their liquid in that enormous lobby of the Gardenia. "That woman is my business."

"Not when you send Nose out to strangle her."

"It's a family matter."

"Attempted homicide? I could bring you to Headquarters right now."

"But I'm holding the Persuader," he said.

"Then use it, Mr. Crabbs. Because I'm not leaving without an answer."

"Is Madame Tolstoya a friend of yours?"

"I met Margaret when I was fourteen. She called herself Anastasia then."

"Yeah, the last of the Romanovs. She's a dime-store slut. I married her. But the trouble is I already had a wife."

"So Margaret was your *comare*."

"'Bloodsucker' is a better word for that little bitch."

Isaac slapped the accountant. The Mossberg dropped to his feet. Neither Crabbs nor Teddy Boy reached for the gun. Crabbs drew further into his blanket. Teddy rocked on his heels. And Isaac thought he'd come to a home for catatonics on the south shore of Swan Lake.

"What did she have that could hurt you so much?"

"Details," Crabbs said. "Angles she could have given to the FBI. Little notes I'd left with her in case I had to run. She was dreaming of blackmail, Margaret was."

"Did she name a price?"

"No, but I could see it in her eyes. I wasn't safe, Mr. Sidel, long as Margaret's alive."

Isaac slapped him again. "You prick. You were scared shitless so you settled on Margaret as your scapegoat."

Crabbs wiped a fleck of blood from his mouth.

"Please don't hit him," said the Nose, whose mitts were almost as large as old Harry Lieberman's of the New York Giants.

"Goat?" Crabbs said, his crazy laughter rising to the roofs.

"She had Jerry on a string. She was his woman. But he had a wife and a *comare*, and he couldn't handle Margaret. So he passed her on to me. I was Jerry's garbage pail."

"How did Jerry meet her?"

"She appeared," Crabbs said. "Out of the blue. And she fell in with the gang. Or maybe Jerry inherited her from one of the Rubinos. I can't remember."

"First she wasn't there," Nose said. "And then she was."

"Just like that," Isaac said. "She flew out of a magician's glove."

Nose pondered what Isaac said. "It's possible."

"And she never talked to you, Mr. Crabbs, about where she was or who she was with until she became your *comare*."

"I told you. She had a tight lip."

"Even about baseball?" Isaac said.

"She's Roumanian, for Christ's sake. Bucharest was her territory. Not baseball."

"But you're a Christy, aren't you?"

"So what? I happen to love the game. It's not relevant to Margaret."

"And did you know that Schyler Knott has disappeared from the club? Someone tried to strangle him . . . with a necktie. Doesn't that sound familiar?"

"Nose was never near the Christy Mathewson Club, were you, Nose?"

"Who's Christy Mathewson?" the Nose asked.

"A pitcher with the New York Giants," Crabbs said. "Won thirty-seven games in Nineteen hundred and eight."

"I wasn't around in Nineteen hundred and eight," Nose said. "And baseball isn't my business."

"You see," Crabbs said. "He's clear on that subject."

"And what about you?"

The accountant emerged from beneath the blanket. "Me?"

"Yes. Maybe you and Schyler disappeared for the same reason."

"And what's that?"

"Maurice Goodstein . . . of the Christy Mathewson Club."

"I wasn't close with Maurice."

"You were close enough. Tell me, who got you the job as Jerry's accountant? You're a lone wolf. You don't have the backing of a big firm. You're not associated with companies that could hide Jerry's assets . . . who got you the job?"

"Maurice. We knew each other from the club. He recommended me . . . and set up the meet with Jerry."

"And that's how you found Margaret Tolstoy."

"I already told you. Jerry introduced us."

"Gave her to you. Like some exotic bird . . . a Roumanian princess."

"A princess who was born in the street."

Isaac's eyes turned to beads in the dark well under the Gardenia's roof. He could have been some grand inquisitor from another time, long before white hotels arrived on Swan Lake. "Where's Maurice?"

The accountant tried to duck under the blanket, but Isaac wouldn't let him. "Where's Maurice? Are the Christys holding him?"

"I think so. Look, I'm not part of the inner circle. Schyler would never trust me."

"You're not even the club's accountant. Yet Maurice recommends you to Jerry. And you both disappear at the same time. Do the Christys have their own haunted hotel?"

"They might. How should I know what's in Schyler's head?"

"But Maurice isn't like you. It would take an awful lot to get him to run. Maurice rolls over everybody, like a fucking tank."

"But LeComte changed the complexion. It's spooky out there. Jerry's gang is split. LeComte creates his own battle circus. He's FBI, CIA, Treasury, you name it. He has secret services coming out of his ass. Nobody can win. It's not one agency, Commissioner. It's the whole United States. Le-Comte proves the existence of a crime family in court, and Maurice can't separate himself. He's part of that family. The money he collects from Jerry is tainted, like Jerry himself. He had no options, Commissioner. He had to run . . . or join LeComte. Maurice is no joiner. And neither am I."

"So you'll sit here in your white hotel and wait for what?"

"Until LeComte finds another hobby. Or gets sick of chasing Jerry DiAngelis and decides to run for secretary of state."

"That's not an elective office," Isaac said.

"With LeComte it is."

Isaac couldn't argue with the accountant. He left Crabbs in his tiny kingdom on Swan lake. The worm in Isaac's gut told him Crabbs didn't have much longer to live. One gang would get him, and it didn't matter which. The wind blew off the ice. And the lake howled at Isaac as he climbed down the hill with Teddy Boy. Isaac couldn't see a star in that Catskill sky. Just a piece of the moon like some crescent in an endless flag. Nose tried to lure him into a conversation, but Isaac walked ahead. The stars had abandoned the Borscht Belt. And nothing in the world could bring back Brazilian Night in the big casino, when Isaac had danced the samba, wearing a white tux, with the sweat of the kitchen behind his ears, and the dream of connecting with some doctor's daughter, preferably a Stalinist like himself.

9

Isaac returned to his Ivan-
hoes. It was three in the morning, and fresh snow had begun
to fall. He loved the winters, even though his flat on
Rivington Street was like Little Siberia. The wind would howl
across the rooms and leave Isaac in a deep shiver. But he was
at the shirt factory now. Locksley, the Greek and Latin prof,
was acting as some kind of duty officer, and Isaac didn't have
to wake him. The other Ivanhoes slept in their cots.

"Allan," Isaac said, "how did it go at the Christys? Did you
make any sense out of the portraits on the wall? . . . Well,
did you decode them or not? You're dealing with amateurs,
for Christ's sake."

"That's what makes it doubly difficult," Locksley said.

"So you couldn't read their traffic."

"Didn't say that. But it took a little doing." And Locksley
held out a tiny memo pad with a green cover. "We broke into
the place and found this in one of Schyler Knott's back
drawers. It was sloppy of him, if you ask me."

"What is it?"

"Schyler's codebook."

"All right, Allan, tell me the grift."

"It's an x plus y plus one affair. Like a recurring melody. A constellation almost. Schyler invents his own alphabet. Nothing to do with the names themselves. That would be too modest. Schyler's in love with birthdays. Look at Babe Ruth. Born February sixth, Eighteen hundred and—"

"I don't want the whole megillah. The message, Allan, what's the message you caught last night?"

"From the birthdays of the men on the wall?"

"Yes, Allan. Do I have to rock you like a child? Give me the fucking message, will you, please?"

"Well, each birthday has its own shorthand."

"I trust you, Allan. You're a Houdini with a codebook."

"Crash Landing."

"What the hell does it mean?"

"I'd say they're moving Maurice. And they're in an awful rush."

"But it's speculation. It could mean almost anything. And suppose Schyler planted the notebook for us to find."

"I doubt that, Isaac. It's too detailed."

"But he could still be having fun at our expense. Where's Margaret Tolstoy?"

"She fled the coop while I was with the Christys."

"You left her all alone?"

"Isaac, she had six Ivanhoes as her baby-sitters."

"But I told you not to leave her until Burt got back."

"He did get back, but he had to go out again. . . . Isaac, there was nothing we could do. We're not her jailors. The princess said she had to go to the toilet."

"Princess?" Isaac muttered, his eyes like bones in his head.

"Isaac, you called her Anastasia. And I'm a cryptologist. I'm always searching for names in the dark."

"So she waltzed into the toilet and disappeared on you. My champions. My best fucking men."

"Oh, we could have shackled her, but that's not the

message we got. A friend of yours from way, way back. Looking for a bit of sanctuary, which we supplied."

The phone rang, and Isaac's deepest wish was that Anastasia was on the line, ready to purr for Isaac and say she was a naughty girl who'd gone out for a ham sandwich in the middle of the night. But the factory was stocked with ham and all the bread Anastasia could eat. It was Burt, calling from a public phone.

"We found the faigele," he said. Burt had to repeat himself because Isaac was still dreaming of his Roumanian princess. "Isaac, the male nurse. Maurice's boyfriend. We're holding him for you. At the candy store."

It was one of Isaac's safe houses, like the shirt factory. Isaac had them all over town. The candy store was a cellar in the East Village, across from a Ukrainian cathedral. He took a cab to the church, waited, waited, then ducked into the cellar like the police chief he was, his nostrils flaring. He knocked once on the cellar door and listened for Burt's growl. "Who is it?"

"Brian de Bois-Guilbert."

The door opened, and Burt stood in a doctor's gown.

"Jesus," Isaac said, "did you kidnap the poor bastard?"

"We bloody well did."

"Played the doctor and stole him from where?"

"St. Jude. It's a nursing home at the upper end of the island. Run by the Catholic Charities, I think. Anyway, we had to swindle him past a couple of priests."

"Does he know who we are?"

"Not yet, Isaac. I didn't know how you wanted to play it. But the lad is scared. I planted a little light bulb in his head, told him he might not survive the night."

Isaac reached for his putty nose and then returned it to his pocket. "What's his name?"

"Jaime Cortez. A real Latin beauty, with eyelashes like a little girl."

Isaac followed Burt into the depths of the candy store. Jaime Cortez sat in a simple chair. He did have a gorgeous face, like a slightly brutal choirboy who'd grown too big for his pants.

"Jaime," Isaac said, "do you know who I am?"

"Yes," the boy said. He couldn't have been more than nineteen or twenty. "The big policeman."

"Then you'll understand that we don't wish Maurice any harm. We just want to communicate with him. Do you believe me?"

"No. You have too many ballbusters, like this one. He shouldn't have been so rough with me."

"Ah, but you wouldn't have come along, Jaime, if he asked you in a quiet way."

"It doesn't matter. The big policeman is supposed to be on our side."

"I am, Jaime."

"Then why you let him steal me, huh? You come to St. Jude's. I talk. I fix some cocoa. I make it with hot milk."

"But the news might have leaked. It wouldn't have been kosher for Maurice. Other people might have come, bad people."

"He's bad," Jaime said, pointing to Burt.

Burton sighed. "Isaac, are you going to let him pussy around?"

"Shhh," Isaac said, kneeling in front of the nurse. "Jaime, we want to help. But we can't without you. Has Maurice been in touch?"

"Yes."

"Why did he vanish?"

Jaime smiled. "He don't vanish from me, Mr. Isaac. He calls. We meet. We make love. He bought me a wedding ring, but I don't wear it at Jude's. The fathers wouldn't like it. I'm a good nurse."

"And where do you meet?"

"In safe houses," Jaime said with a luster in his eyes that diminished Isaac and all his Ivanhoes. "Once he took me to the club."

"What kind of club?"

Jaime clamped one fist over the other, as if he were clutching a baseball bat.

"He brought you to the Christys?"

"We went upstairs," Jaime said. "We danced. We had chicken and cherry pie. We took a shower."

"Lord," Burt said with a bitter face. "Do we have to listen to the details? Isaac, are you going to crack his skull or do I have to? . . . Bloody fuckin' faigel. Dancing with Maurice like a regular bride. It's enough to make me puke."

"Shut up, Burt."

"I will not. Sack me, Isaac. But I found the faigel. And you bloody well bleed what you can out of him. Because he's talking rot."

"Wait for me outside, Burt. Thank you."

"I do the dirty work. I steal the sod. And then I'm punished for it."

"Burt."

"All right. But if he's not a good canary, boss, beat him around the ears. Then he'll talk. Wouldn't want a child of mine around a yob like that."

"You don't have a child," Isaac said.

"That's immaterial. It's the principle of the thing."

And Burt walked out of the candy store.

"Dance with me," Jaime said.

"But there's no music . . ."

"Dance with me."

"I wouldn't know how," Isaac said. Jaime stood up and Isaac danced him around the store. It was an odd sensation, because in Isaac's arms Jaime could have been a girl. The PC had Margaret on his mind.

Jaime sat down again.

"He says no one can help him. Not you, Mr. Isaac. Not Jerry DiAngelis. He's running from the Devil."

"Is the Devil's name LeComte?"

"Maurie didn't say. The Devil, that's all."

❦

Isaac let Jaime go back to St. Jude's. But he couldn't find Burt outside the candy store. He looked across the street. The commandant of the Ivanhoes was sitting on the steps of the Ukrainian cathedral, sitting in the snow, as forlorn as some forgotten gargoyle out of Isaac's past.

"You jeopardize us, Isaac, give our positions away, and we don't even nab Maurice."

"Did you see Margaret Tolstoy at the factory?"

"I did not. I was having a busy night . . . acquiring the nurse."

"I'd like you to go to Swan Lake. Margaret's husband is hiding out in a white hotel that looks like a Southern mansion. You can't miss it."

"Where the hell is Swan Lake?"

"In the Catskills, Burt. I guess they didn't have a Borscht Belt in Capetown."

"You're bloody right. And what am I supposed to do with the man? Be his baby-sitter?"

"Yes. He doesn't have much of a future. I'd like to keep him alive if we can. Take two of our boys, Burt. Just in case."

"Who's after the bugger?"

"I'd say Jerry's rivals, but I'm not sure."

"The old Rubino bunch?"

"It's my guess they're being financed by the other Families . . . or else they're free-lancing and they'd like to capture Jerry's bookkeeper, squeeze him as hard as they can, and kill him."

"Rubino's captains? They're ragtailers. Jerry could squash them like a bug."

"Not if they've been given a boost."

"Angel on my shoulder, is that it? The great white father LeComte? Meddling as always. Playing half the gang against the other, so he can put brother Jerry into the pen. Plucky bastard, ain't he? Our nominal leader, crown prince of the Ivanhoes. Wish we could survive without his cash."

"That's easy enough," Isaac said. "Mount a commando operation and rob a couple of banks."

"We'd be better off in the long run," Burt said.

"I agree. But it's the short run I worry about. Ride up to Swan Lake, will you? And hold that accountant's hand."

Burt got up from the steps of the cathedral and shoved off into the snow. Isaac kept looking for him, but the Afrikaner was invisible after thirty yards. *Mandrake the Magician.* The PC had idolized him as a boy. Mandrake could conjure up warm-bodied ghosts and have them melt into snow. He was in love with Princess Narda. He wore a top hat and a cape, even when he was stuck in some bayou. And he had Lothar, the big black giant in a fez. Mandrake and Isaac had their princesses, but Narda was a little more reliable.

The PC got to Rivington Street, hoping Anastasia would be outside his door. But he had nothing but the worm and the thick beat of his own black heart. He wasn't Mandrake. He fell asleep in all his sloppy clothes.

10

Isaac had to rise at six. He was touring the City's schools. He didn't have a proper invitation from the Board of Ed. The PC had invited himself. He was feuding with the chancellor, Alejo Tomás, an hombre who was tied to the Democratic machine. Tomás had prettied up all the dropout reports. He prattled about innovations. He juggled the schools' reading scores so that illiteracy was one more pink elephant. He talked of computers in kindergarten classes and of preschool programs that existed only on paper. Tomás couldn't control the unions, the teachers, or the schools. Prostitution flourished among twelve-year-old girls. Fourteen-year-old kids ran dope rings. There were thirteen-year-old expectant mothers in Alejo's school system. Janitors were sleeping with boys and girls. One brand-new high school was sinking into the ground. Another was infested with rats. But Alejo still had his chancellor's chair. And Isaac was determined to push him out.

His chauffeur, Sergeant Malone, arrived at seven. They had coffee together in Isaac's tiny kitchen. Isaac boiled him an egg. And Malone felt sorry for the PC, who lived worse than any rookie cop, with a tub in his kitchen and a dining room without windows. Where does his pay go? the sergeant wondered. Does he squander it on society gals or medicines that put his worm to sleep? He'd gotten his own "angel" killed, Manfred Coen, who had the misfortune of attracting Isaac's daughter to himself. But you couldn't talk about Coen to the Commish. Isaac's worm was attached to Coen's death in ways the sergeant couldn't quite comprehend. Isaac had been dueling with a family of pimps. He went underground, lived with the pimps in their candy store. And the pimps, who'd grown up with Manfred in some miserable sector of the Bronx, had given Isaac the worm. But it wasn't a tale that one even whispered about, because that worm had a secret sense. The worm was like fucking radar on anything to do with Coen. Let the spirits lie low, the sergeant liked to say. Best not to get too close to this Commish, or the daughter might arrive, and then where would you be?

"Did you bring your tux?" Isaac asked.

"That I did."

And it was another wondrous thing to Sergeant Malone. The police commissioner of the City of New York borrowing a tuxedo from his chauffeur for the Governor's Manhattan Ball. Their build was the same, that was true. The tux had belonged to Malone's dad, and his dad before him, in County Clare. And Malone himself had worn that tux to a hundred weddings and wakes and meetings of the Shamrock Society. The crotch had tightened after all those years. The cummerbund was a bit too shiny. A shoulder sagged. But Isaac, who'd seen Malone in the monkey suit, had insisted on wearing it to the Ball. "Should I bring it up right now, Chief? Will only take a minute. You can try it on. And if there's a problem, well, the missus can always mend it. She's a bit of a tailor, you know. Always was."

Isaac shrugged. "There's plenty of time."

And there was no way to hazard a guess what the PC was

thinking about. Sly lad he was. Sherlock Holmes without the violin. And suppose he was a sheeny. He'd stood for the Irish at One Police Plaza, addressed the Shamrock Society, done honor to the lads, even though he had a nigger First Dep. The Irish had owned the Department under the former PC, Tiger John Rathgar, but Tiger John was sitting in a cell at Green Haven, a bloody thief, and a shame to all his countrymen. It was Isaac who'd been his First Dep, tutored and suckled by the lads themselves, accepted into the fold, sheeny as he was, because he had a drop of the old blarney in him and had taught himself to speak with a bit of a brogue. Now another sheeny sat in City Hall, Rebecca Karp, and the Irish were being pushed out of office. No matter. Malone was secure around Isaac the Brave. Isaac wouldn't desert the brethren. But he was the Last of the Mohicans because as sure as piss, Mr. Sweets would be the next PC.

They had their second coffee with steamed milk. And then Malone and Isaac descended into the street. Isaac wouldn't ride in a limo. He preferred an old Dodge that had been slapped together at the Department's body shop and garage. A man of the people Isaac was. The Pink Commish. But he wasn't a bolshie, no matter what the politicians said. He had an Irish heart, Isaac did. Blunt and black with tears. Hadn't he picked a colleen to marry? The good Kathleen, who accompanied him to the Shamrock Society dinners in the old days, her with the red, red hair. The colleen had gone out of his life. But he was still bound to the sons of Shannon.

"Where to?" Malone asked after he got behind the wheel.

"Sweets' place," the commissioner said, and Malone turned gloomy, because he hadn't expected to chauffeur the black giant. Isaac and Sweets had separate offices and separate lives. Malone picked up Sweets at his house in Greenwich Village. Six foot six he was. And he had to duck for all he was worth to get into the Dodge.

"How's the shop?" Isaac asked.

"I'm still trying to make peace with the Hasidim, Isaac. They consider me a dybbuk."

"But you have Crown Heights under control."

"For the moment." And then, with his legs almost as high as his chest, he asked, "How are you, Mr. Malone?"

"Grand, Commissioner, grand."

There was a new subway bandit on the prowl, a Latino who exposed himself in subway cars and grabbed women's purses, and it was Sweets who went before the television cameras, Sweets who took the interviews instead of Isaac. "I don't think I ought to appear alone, Isaac. I shouldn't set policy. It doesn't feel right. The press is starting to call you the invisible man."

"I'm flattered," Isaac said. "Sergeant, tell him. Didn't he look like he could break a couple of heads while he was on the tube? How was he?"

"Grand."

"Now no more words about protocol," Isaac said.

"But why am I on this tour?"

"Because I want you to see the schools firsthand."

"I've visited them with the chancellor, Isaac. I've spoken to high school seniors about the Department."

"That's not a visit," Isaac said. "Tomás prepares himself, dummies things up, hires extra guards, and targets one school, straitjackets it, hides the bad kids in the basement, and you don't get to see shit."

"Isaac, I don't want to be involved in your feud with Chancellor Tomás. Conduct your own guerrilla war with the Board of Ed. I have enough problems."

"Will you just sit," Isaac said, "and decide for yourself?"

"And you think the chancellor will be quiet while you enter his domain?"

"Let him howl his head off."

"But we have no jurisdiction, Isaac. The schools are his."

"I'm the police commissioner," Isaac said. "The whole fucking city is mine."

"If Tomás wanted to be strict about it, he could force us to get a warrant. And you might not find a friendly judge. Tomás is the Party man, not you."

"Warrant?" Isaac said. "I haven't come around to make arrests. We're on a fucking survey."

"What survey?"

"Tell him, Sergeant."

And Malone had to provide a bit of Isaac's own blarney. "To see if the janitors aren't divertin' the electrical current for their own private use . . . and if the boys and girls are getting fresh milk in the free lunch program."

"That's not police business," Sweets said.

"Haven't finished yet, sir . . . to see if sexual molestations aren't abounding on school property, if hoodlums and addicts aren't taking advantage of the facilities, if the clerical staff is not derelict in—"

"Enough," Sweets said. "I'm convinced. It's a survey." The First Dep was riding with lunatics, and he'd join their company if that's what Isaac wanted of him. He knew the chancellor would scold Sweets one of these days, because Alejo Tomás wouldn't speak to Isaac any longer, and Sweets would have to bear the burden, as he always did, covering for this crazy Commish. The PC would twist the law around to his advantage, but he didn't have bankbooks stashed away, like Tiger John Rathgar, the old, disgraced Commish who sat in Green Haven. Isaac would visit him from time to time.

The PC had no prescribed route. He was Mandrake the Magician, without a cape. He went with his chauffeur and Sweets into the hinterland of Manhattan. The first stop was a junior high on Avenue A. The school's fence had been ripped apart. Kids lounged in the schoolyard, wearing Halloween masks in the heart of winter.

"Hello, papa," they said to Isaac, but they kept away from the black giant.

"Isaac, should I give them a toss?" Sweets asked. "They could be carrying some kind of shit."

"We're guests," Isaac said. "Wouldn't want an illegal search

and seizure on our conscience, would we? Besides, Tomás'
lawyers might climb on our backs. I haven't come to provoke,
Sweets. We're tourists in the neighborhood, that's all."

They entered the school, the three of them, Isaac, Sweets,
and Sergeant Malone. The school guard was mortified. He
recognized Isaac and figured it was a bust. He had a roach in
his back pocket and a dime bag of cocaine. But Isaac didn't
hassle him. "Are you working hard, son? Keeping out the
stragglers?"

"Yes I am, Commissioner Sidel."

"You can call me Isaac."

And the PC headed for the principal's office to announce
himself. But the principal had suffered a nervous breakdown
and was on a very long leave, living in Miami. No one could
say where the assistant principal was. It was an ordinary clerk
who took Isaac around.

The school psychologist poked her head out of an open
door. "Is that Norman Mailer?" she asked, seeing Isaac's
bushy white hair. "You're not Mailer. You're our fascist chief
of police . . . you hurt black people."

"I wouldn't let him, ma'am," Sweets said.

"You, you're his Uncle Tom. You helped him capture
Henry Armstrong Lee."

"Henry Lee was a bank robber, ma'am. He was at the top
of the FBI's Ten Most Wanted list."

"That's just hype," she said. "He was our Robin Hood. He
took from the rich and gave to the poor."

"But most of the banks he robbed were in Harlem, ma'am,
where poor people kept their money."

"What would you know about poor people?" she muttered.

Isaac had to edge Sweets away from the woman with his
elbow. "You'll never win, Sweets. Henry Lee did light up a lot
of Christmas trees. He was poor as a church mouse when we
took him. I was fond of Henry Lee."

And they marched unmolested from class to class. Isaac saw
the same dead eyes he'd discovered at the children's shelter

in St. Louis. He missed Kingsley McCardle. The classrooms
had a quietness that always scared Isaac. There were no
barterings, no exchanges between the children and their
teachers, who seemed caught in some eclipse. It was blue
midnight at nine in the morning. Half the students had no
books. They sucked on their own spittle.

"It's one school," Sweets said. "The principal's gone. There's
no one to run the shop. Isaac, could you have taught those
kids?"

"Open your eyes. It's too fucking late. Half those little girls
will be pregnant by next year."

"You don't know that," Sweets said. "You're just pulling
statistics out of a paper hat."

"And even if I am," Isaac said. "Even if I am, I'm only a
little off."

It was the third school. And Isaac had gone up to the
lunchroom. He'd seen those thin miserable sandwiches,
the country apples, the glasses of milk. And he started to cry.

"Is it the worm, Chief?" Malone asked. "I could borrow a
glass of milk."

But Sweets understood what the crying was all about. It
wasn't an ordinary attack of melancholia. There was a hope-
lessness in the schools that Sweets could never have imagined. He'd played ice hockey at Horace Mann. He'd been on
the debating club. He'd had pocket money, and roast beef for
lunch. He'd written papers about Malcolm and Martin Luther
King. And now, as the first deputy police commissioner, he'd
spoken to the very best seniors at the Bronx High School of
Science. He'd met with Parents-Teachers Associations. He'd
visited model junior high schools with Alejo Tomás. But he
hadn't been to schools like this. Sweets blamed himself. It was
his very own borough, not some dune out in the Bronx. It
was worse than Riker's, where prisoners could scream or crap
on the floor in protest. These kids looked like some vampire

had bitten them on the neck. Sweets didn't have Isaac's ability to cry. He sat down and ate an orange with one of the kids. Then he got the hell out of there with Isaac and Malone.

"Fuck Alejo Tomás," he said in the backseat of Isaac's Dodge.

"He'll run to Becky Karp and make a stink. She'll demand apologies."

"Fuck Becky Karp."

"Ah, that's the ticket," said Malone, who was beginning to like the big black giant. His stomach felt tight and for a moment the sergeant believed that he'd inherited Isaac's worm. He didn't notice any Irish children in these schools, but that didn't matter. Black they were and a little brown. But Jesus, they could have been on a starvation diet. He saw one lad vomit a thin, colorless bile into a wastepaper basket. The security guards looked like dunces who belonged in the asylum at County Cork. The professors here could have been tired animal trainers. It wasn't a house of education, not even an efficient zoo, but a morgue where the cadavers had their own little chairs. This was no place for children.

He deposited Sweets at One Police Plaza. And then he took his granddad's tuxedo out of the trunk. Isaac didn't smile.

"Where's the cape?"

"The cape?" Malone said. "The cape? It went out of style a hundred years ago."

"But I saw you wearing the cape," Isaac said.

The sergeant had to think. "Ah, at the Halloween party. It was for a gaff, a bloody piece of humor, Isaac."

"I can't go to the Ball without a cape."

"Then I'll take you home to the missus," the sergeant said, "and she'll iron the cape for you."

"Grand."

11

He didn't have Mandrake's perfect profile, or the penciled mustache and slick black hair that reminded him of Warren William, a long-forgotten movie actor who played the Lone Wolf during Isaac's boyhood. The Wolf was a reformed jewel thief who had his own valet. He liked to wear opera clothes and was constantly getting women out of trouble. Isaac always linked him in his own mind with Mandrake the Magician.

He was looking in the mirror, attempting to clasp his bow tie, when he heard a knock on the door. "Come in," he said without even considering the holster in his drawer. He wasn't Pancho Villa.

It was Burt, back from Swan Lake, and he laughed at Isaac's costume. The top hat, the cape, the bow tie that rested at an angle. "Be useful, will you?" Isaac said. "And fix this bloody thing."

The Afrikaner reached around Isaac and clasped the bow tie.

"How's the bookkeeper?"

"Dead."

"It figures. But how did he catch it?" Isaac asked.

"That's the interesting part. There was no sign of struggle. Even if someone tried to clean up after the kill, I would have felt it. I'm psychic about things like that."

"No you're not. You're just a good policeman."

"He caught a bullet in the ear from up close."

"Find the gun?"

"No. But from the look of the hole, I'd say it was a very small piece. Like a derringer you could hide in your purse."

"A ladies' gun, you mean. A single-shot."

"Isaac, I didn't bother with our ballistics people. I left him alone. One of the local sheriffs will find the body."

"But you're hinting it was Margaret Tolstoy who knocked on her husband's door, romanced him a little, and shot the poor fool in the ear."

"Yes, it might have been a woman, or someone who fancied derringers and wanted to make us think it was Margaret."

"And what's your opinion, Burt?"

"It points to Margaret."

"And the motive, Burt?"

"Isaac, I'm not a magician. But the woman arrives out of nowhere, calls herself Margaret Tolstoy, crawls in with Jerry's people. It's not kosher. She comes to you, the great love of your life."

"I never even kissed her."

"Makes it all the more romantic. Swears the Nose is trying to whack her out. You leave her with us. She runs away. She could have followed you up to Swan Lake. She might have been looking for money. Or following orders from somebody else."

"The Rubinos."

"Why not?"

"And you're saying she's a professional."

"What do you know about the woman from the time you first met her until now? There's a big bloody gap."

"Then find her for me, Burt."

"But what if she's not the friendly type and I have to break her neck. Will you blame me, Isaac?"

"Yes, I will."

"Then send another Ivanhoe to pick up the package. I'm not feeling suicidal this week."

"I didn't say bring her back. Just locate her."

"You mean, give you the grids on Margaret's map."

"Yes, if you have to."

"I should have stayed with the Boers. I'd have had a better chance to survive."

"You killed a man, Burt. You were a tainted cop."

"Like yourself, Isaac . . . but I will say, I love your suit. You'll be the life of the party. Can't miss. Give my regards to the Gov."

It was five hundred dollars a seat, a charity banquet and ball. The governor didn't take a nickel for his own pocket. The whole boodle went to the City's hospitals and schools. But the Manhattan Ball wasn't really about the gathering of gold. It was a show of faces. The cardinal was there. The mayor. The giant realtors. The Ball had grown into a politician's paradise. Deals were made behind the bones of a turkey breast. But it was a curious sort of higgledy-piggledy. Because the governor, whose Ball it was, had little power here. He was exiled to the intrigues of Albany, even though he spent half his time in Manhattan. He oversaw the City's budget, could unseat mayors and chancellors and police chiefs, but he wasn't much of a player in Manhattan's woolly life. He was an elder statesman who was younger than Isaac or Becky Karp and Alejo Tomás . . . and James Cardinal O'Bannon, aka Cardinal Jim, defender of the Archdiocese of New York, which meant Staten Island, Manhattan, the Bronx, and seven other counties. But his influence fell everywhere. Realtors kissed the ring that the pope himself had presented to Cardinal Jim. He was sixty-six years old and he had a longshoreman's grip. He liked to flirt with the ladies and have a thimbleful of whiskey, drinking to the health of Catholics, Protestants, and Jews. He'd become cardinal to the entire village, and most of the village had to pay its respects.

But Isaac wouldn't line up to kiss the cardinal's ring. He had no favors to ask. He could catch Cardinal Jim at a more practical moment, far from the politicians, where they could discuss the New York Giants, Joe DiMaggio's swing, or the Dublin that Isaac had visited, and the endangered species of Irish cops in New York City. The cardinal loved to smoke in private and tell bawdy jokes.

And so Isaac mingled among the pols at the penthouse ballroom of the St. Moritz. He wasn't so eager to talk. He stepped out onto the terrace and stared at that long, deep hallucination called Central Park, with ice over the Reservoir and the lakes. The Commish was almost happy, considering who he was, a melancholic detective who had his own little diocese. He was wearing Malone's monkey suit, with the cape that fell over his shoulders like a Confederate general. He sucked on his bottle of milk. Councilmen couldn't get him into a conversation. But Cardinal Jim got rid of all the handshakers and strolled out onto the terrace to breathe the air with Isaac. The cardinal wore the red-lined cape of his office, and Isaac realized how foolish he was in Malone's monkey suit. He wasn't Mandrake the Magician. He was a relic from the Civil War via Malone and County Cork.

Isaac curtsied a bit to recognize the cardinal's station. "It's a grand view, isn't it, Your Eminence?"

"Beg off the titles, will you now? I've had enough curtsying for one day, thank you. . . . Isaac, they're like maggots. They never leave you alone."

"Then why do you come to these affairs?"

"I can't desert my flock. Congratulations, by the by. For cuffing Henry Armstrong Lee. It took courage, Isaac. Admit. Going into a deserted building to claim the FBI's Most Wanted Man. And there it was, on the TV. I prayed for you,

Isaac. My heart was beating so. I couldn't contain myself. I was blubbering in front of all my priests."

"But he wasn't even armed."

"All the worse for you. Made him twice as dangerous, in my opinion."

"He was wearing women's clothes."

"To disguise himself and his foul temper. Don't get modest on me. Accept an old vicar's congratulations. I'm a prince of the church and I'm not modest about it. You're our best policeman. But did you have to visit the chancellor's schools without giving him notice? He's a good Catholic. Worked hard to get his Ph.D. Wouldn't want to ruin his reputation."

"But it's the children," Isaac said. "They're suffering because of him. We'll never bring the middle class back into the schools with Alejo around. There's a crisis, Cardinal Jim. And Alejo isn't the right lad for the job. He won't anger the mayor. He won't anger you. He waltzes with the bureaucrats and the Party machine. He creates a holding pen for kids who spend a couple of seasons with him and disappear into the ruins."

"But they might disappear no matter what Alejo did. It's not the black and brown pols who've been complaining, Isaac. Only you."

"Because they're fat cats, Cardinal Jim."

"I want you to apologize to Alejo Tomás."

"I can't."

"Isaac, if you create bedlam in the public schools, it could catch fire. And I've my own schools to consider. We need a unified policy, not a police commissioner who goes on shotgun parties and makes war on the City's schools."

"We weren't carrying shotguns, Jim."

"You know what I mean," the cardinal said. "I've defended you, Isaac. I've never interfered. Will you do it for the old vicar? Apologize."

"All right," Isaac muttered. "I'll kiss him on both cheeks if that will make you happy."

The cardinal laughed. "One cheek will do."

And they marched off the terrace in their capes, the vicar of St. Patrick's Cathedral and the invisible policeman, Isaac Sidel. The pols tried to waylay them and kiss the cardinal's ring, but he thrust both hands into the pockets of his black silk coat and brought Isaac to the chancellor. Alejo Tomás was six feet tall. He'd been an amateur boxer and had a tiny spur on his nose. He gave up boxing at sixteen and found a new home in the political precincts of Manhattan and the Bronx. The Bronx machine had subsidized Alejo, paid for part of his tuition at Notre Dame, and he'd become a thug with a Ph.D. Isaac knew he was collecting kickbacks from certain contractors who built and maintained his schools, but that was how business got done in the land of New York, and Alejo was clever enough to cover his tracks. Isaac didn't mind the thievery. It was the politicking with Rebecca Karp and the county clubhouses. He'd turned the schools into one more fiefdom of a rotten machine. A chancellor had to remove himself from the pols and argue his case for the kids. But Tomás was the opposite sort of man.

Alejo had been standing with a bunch of school concessioneers, those hawks who profited from his patronage. But they disbanded when they saw the cardinal coming. "Alejo," the cardinal said. "I've brought an old friend. I think he'd like to have a few words with you."

But the chancellor wasn't in a conciliatory mood. "Next time, Isaac, I'll have guards with automatics waiting for you. We'll see who has more cojones. Don't you ever walk into my schools again, or I'll personally crack your skull."

"Holy Mother. You can't expect the man to apologize after a coronation like that."

"I don't want his apologies, Jim. He's been busting my hump ever since I've gone to the Board of Ed. Fancies himself an educator, when he's an illiterate prick."

"Watch that tongue of yours," the cardinal said, but Jim was enjoying himself. He loved the idea of a boxing match on the roof of the St. Moritz.

"Chancellor," Isaac said. "It was wrong of me. I should have asked your blessing. But tell me, have you installed those computers in your kindergartens yet? Because if you have, I'd like to sign up for the class."

He winked at Cardinal Jim and moved away from the chancellor. But the chancellor clutched Isaac's arm. "I'm not finished with you, Sidel."

"Let go of me, Alejo."

"You want a vendetta, you'll get a vendetta. Speak to Becky Karp. You'll be a commissioner without much of a portfolio pretty soon. You've lost most of your marbles. Your friends have a habit of dying on you . . . remember Manfred Coen?"

Isaac swung at Alejo with his free arm. But the cardinal got in the way and caught the blow. He blanched for a moment and then smiled. But his teeth were clamped together.

"I'm sorry," Isaac said. "Your Eminence, I . . ."

"It's all right, son," the cardinal said. "I was a bit of a boxer myself in the old days. Like Alejo. A bantamweight, would you believe it?"

His lips were still tight and gray flecks appeared on his mouth. Alejo had gone to fetch him a glass of water. And Isaac stood like a dummy. The entire ballroom had seen the police commissioner strike Cardinal O'Bannon in the chest.

12

He sat at a table reserved for Becky's high commissioners. He wanted to run home in his cape and howl at the moon. But there was no moon that night. And his absence would only have angered the mayor, who sat across from Isaac and glowered at him while the governor spoke. The governor was a silly man. He stood on the podium and talked about some city of his dreams, where white and black children would build a dream future in Alejo Tomás' schools.

"And I say to you," the governor said, his handsome inert face leaning into the microphone, "I say to you that we will have a partnership where the color of a man or woman's skin will count for nothing at all. I am committed to excellence, not a secret cabal of advantages. And when our school children of today forage in the next century, let them be hunters after the good, seekers of the just, not lazy, not selfish, not alone. We will give our chancellor whatever he desires to accomplish this mission."

The pols clapped for five minutes. The governor touched

his lips with a handkerchief. The machine was grooming him for president. He had a beautiful wife, a son at Dartmouth and a daughter at Yale, and he could carry a couple of ideas in his head. But he had no humor or real compassion or awareness of what would ever save the City. He could have been born inside a box. He'd been packaged well, and the pols wanted to be certain that he would be loved in Indiana and Idaho, that he didn't have the stink of New York City about him.

He sat down next to the beautiful wife, hands reaching across the table to grip his sleeve for good luck. And then Cardinal Jim got out of his chair and climbed onto the podium. He coughed into his fist. He was still pale from Isaac's blow. He put on his reading glasses, took his little speech out of his pocket, and uncrumpled the page. You could hear the electric pull of the paper. The cardinal wouldn't begin. He stared down at all his parishioners and the pols.

"We're greedy," he said.

And people wondered if the sock in his chest had deranged him a little.

"We're greedy."

The cardinal grabbed the sides of the microphone stand. His hands were red. And under the wings of his cape he looked like some avenging angel who'd come to slaughter the governor's guests. The worm purred in Isaac's belly. And now Isaac knew he'd have a terrific time, despite his humiliation.

"I'm an old man," the cardinal said, "and I don't intend to leave a legacy of doom to the young ones of this town. I'm not a native, you know, but a Chicago boy, weaned in the wildlands, among the poorest of the poor. And a little crook until the brothers at St. Benedict's beat the piss out of me so I could hear the music of my Christian soul. And I wonder, as I stand here, if all of us shouldn't be whipped."

There was a muttering, a kind of laughter, and then a silence fell upon the St. Moritz.

"It's not your treasure I'm after. It's your hearts. And that's where we've all been greedy. Hiring a chancellor and shutting our eyes and thinking all the problems would go away. But our children are stuck on a battlefield, fighting the demons in themselves and the indifference all around them." And the cardinal shut both his eyes, his ruddy face like a porcelain mask as all the color was mysteriously gone. "There's the demon. Indifference. *Our* children aren't in Chancellor Tomás' schools. And so we sit here and eat and ask him to make miracles without offering Alejo our children. We cannot have schools that are charity wards."

The cardinal opened his eyes. "I'm a bachelor. But I do have children in this big parlor . . . most of you are mine. And I'm claiming a vicar's rights. I want you to lend yourselves to Alejo. Give him what he needs, not your fancy pocketbooks, but your sons and your daughters. Remember now, if the schools fall, the City will fall. You'll have a population of broken children that none of us will be able to mend." The cardinal stared into the little islands of faces at the St. Moritz. "Will you help your vicar now?"

He climbed down from the dais and there was a slow thunder of hands and the chanting of "Yes, yes, yes to the vicar. Yes."

It was all flapdoodle. The pols wouldn't deliver their sons and daughters. Alejo's own children went to the cardinal's parochial schools. But at least old Jim had shaken the sons of bitches. And Isaac dug into his tapioca pudding. The Ball was about to begin. The musicians had stood in back of the cardinal like silent crows, and now they tinkered with their instruments. Isaac got up from his table and wandered a bit. He was surprised to see Jerry DiAngelis, his wife, and father-in-law at another table. They sat by themselves. The pols were embarrassed, because they couldn't do business with Jerry at the Governor's Ball. But Jerry had paid for his tickets. He was more of a prince than most of the governor's other guests. And Cardinal Jim knew that. He broke the bloody ice. He walked over to Jerry's table, chatted with the melamed, and then asked Jerry's wife to dance. And suddenly all the pols were saying hello. They were chickenhearted people who could only feel secure in a cardinal's wake.

And Jim was the wily one. He would be on the front page of every single morning paper, dancing with DiAngelis' wife. How could it hurt? It was gallant of the cardinal to escort a Mafia man's wife on the penthouse floor of the St. Moritz. Why should she have to pay for Jerry's sins?

Isaac waited until the pols shook hands with Jerry. And then he sat down between the melamed and the prince.

"Jerry, is that funeral clothes you're wearing?"

"Why?" DiAngelis asked in a blue tuxedo that must have cost him a couple of thousand.

"Your bookkeeper is dead."

"Crabbs? I thought you visited him with my brother."

"I did. But I sent in a back-up after the visit."

"One of your commandos, Isaac?"

"What's the difference?"

"The commando could have killed him."

The melamed covered Isaac's hand and Jerry's hand with his own. "This isn't the place for philosophical discussions. We're at a banquet. Smile. The cardinal is dancing with Jerry's wife. How will it look to the world if we seem gloomy?"

"You're right, Iz," the commissioner said.

"We'll mourn Crabbs tomorrow. Not tonight. Now get up, Isaac," the melamed said. "You sat with us long enough."

And Isaac shoved off in his cape. The cardinal had returned Eileen DiAngelis to Jerry's table. Photographers covered him from every side. No one seemed to bother about Becky Karp while Jim was working the room. He broke from the photographers and sidled next to the PC.

"How was the speech, son?"

"Amazing," Isaac said. "But did you mean it?"

"Every word."

"If the middle class comes marching back, what will happen to the parochial schools?"

"We have more than enough, Isaac. We're filled to the brim. Two-year waiting lists, I'm told. Part of the spill ought to go the chancellor."

"It won't," Isaac said. "I'm sorry I punched you. It was—"

"It's good for the circulation, a sock in the heart. I'm fine. But will you make your peace with Alejo?"

"It's too late, Jim."

"A pity," the cardinal said. "Because I'll have to back him on this. And you're already a bit of a pariah. Watch your flanks, son. Or the sharks will bite your legs off, beginning with Becky Karp. She's turned sour on her favorite Commish."

And he was gone from Isaac, into some other territory of the ballroom, where he danced with a politician's wife, while the rest of his flock, the people who loved him and feared him, glided out of his way.

Isaac felt a hand on his shoulder. He started to growl until he recognized the governor's handsome, unmarked face, the teeth capped to perfection, the eyes with all the sympathy of a fish.

"Isaac, get rid of your Gestapo."

"Gestapo, Governor?"

"Don't play the virgin. I won't tolerate a secret police."

"Who's been telling you bedtime stories, sir?"

"Never mind. I want assurances, Isaac. Can you promise me that you're not harboring your own band of spies?"

"Yes."

"I don't believe you."

"Would you like me to swear on the cardinal's ring?"

"Keep Jim out of it. He already owns half the real estate in town. Isaac, I don't want you to become an embarrassment. I'm considering a run for the presidency. You're aware of that. And if some reporter should ever accuse me of funding a goddamn Gestapo, I'm out of the race."

"I'm clean, Governor."

"Sure," the governor said, turning from Isaac. "Ivanhoes, isn't that what you call them?"

"I wouldn't know, Your Excellency."

But the governor vanished from Isaac to shake whatever hands he could find. And Isaac was left in deep shit. If the governor, who had no inside sources of information, knew about the Ivanhoes, Isaac was lost. Who the hell had ratted on him? LeComte? But the cultural commissar would have had to reveal his own part in creating the Ivanhoes.

Isaac was pondering this when he noticed Schyler Knott. The president of the Christy Mathewson Club had come out of hiding to attend the Ball. The Bomber was with him, as his bodyguard. Harry Lieberman in a tuxedo that could have been a butcher's coat. And Isaac still had the urge to tell him, Harry, you shouldn't have jumped to the Mexican League after the war. You would have had a better chance with the Giants. But it was ancient history, an old wound that would never heal, neither for Isaac nor Harry.

"Hello, Schyler," Isaac said, sounding as mournful as he could.

"You're not funny," Schyler said. "I trusted you and you betrayed us."

"Me? I'm an honorable member of the club. I wouldn't betray the memory of Mathewson and Mel Ott. My whole fucking life was baseball. All I ever wanted to be was a New York Giant." A meanness crept into Isaac. "Harry was a Giant, but Harry jumped."

"We're not talking baseball. And Harry's career is his own business. You brought thugs into our house."

"Never," Isaac said. "I never would."

"I didn't tell a soul about Maurie, Isaac, not a soul, except you . . . no one else could have known he was a member of the club. He always met with our board in secret session. Maurie didn't want to compromise us."

"And you think I did?"

"Yes."

"And you, Schyler, are so fucking pure. We found Mau-

rice's boyfriend. The male nurse. He told us Maurie used the
club as his private bordello."

"Bordello? Would you have said that, Isaac, if the nurse was
a woman and not a man? Where else did Maurie have to
meet? The St. Moritz?"

"All right, if I'm such a bad ass, why the hell are you here?"

"I never miss the Manhattan Ball. The governor is a friend
of mine."

"You didn't happen to utter the word 'Ivanhoe' to His
Excellency, did you?"

"Isaac, I don't remember meeting any Ivanhoes, unless you
mean Tilly Ivanhoe, who pitched for the Reds in Nineteen
seventeen. He's in a sanitarium now . . . excuse me, I'd like
to say hello to the governor."

And Isaac was left with that rawness of another failed
encounter. He looked around and spotted Sal Rubino, master
builder and brains behind the rebellious Rubino captains.
He'd led the fight against Jerry DiAngelis' ascension to the
Rubino throne. His uncles had been killed and Sal blamed
Jerry DiAngelis. He shouldn't have come to the Ball. But he
was reckless, like both DiAngelis brothers. He was dancing
with a lady. Isaac could only see her back. But the worm tore
at him. Margaret Tolstoy was in Sal Rubino's arms. She had a
new protector now. She didn't need the Commish. Her spine
wiggled beneath her silk gown. Her laughter sounded like hot
coal. Sal spun her around and her eyes met Isaac's for a
moment. There was no sadness or sense of surprise. He could
have been any guest at the Governor's Ball.

Isaac retrieved his top hat and winter coat and abandoned
the St. Moritz.

13

He drifted downtown like the lone wolf that he was. He could have stopped any police car and hitched a ride. But he felt like walking, a fool in his cape, with a top hat that was a hundred years old. People stared at him. A woman offered him a dime, thinking he was a beggar who'd come out to haunt the streets of Manhattan in carnival clothes. He took the dime, because it seemed much simpler than having to explain his circumstances. He, Isaac, who'd arrived at the St. Moritz as Mandrake the Magician, socked a cardinal and seen the love of his life in the arms of a Mafia man—not a prince like Jerry, but the president of a concrete company. Sal Rubino.

Isaac was already thinking how he could arrange the hit. It soothed him to imagine the whole scenario. He could steal a gun from the property clerk, put on his putty nose, catch the concrete maker in some coffee shop, pop him behind the ear, and walk out, one-two-three. Who would have ever dreamed it was the police commissioner? But he'd only complicate the civil war between the old Rubino captains and Jerry DiAngelis, and the melamed might get hurt. Still, it was delicious to think about. . . .

Isaac was taking off his tuxedo when the phone started to ring. He picked up the bloody instrument. "Hello."

"You cocksucker."

It was Becky Karp.

"My own prize man, and he runs out on me."

"Had a headache," Isaac said.

"You mean a hard-on. I caught you looking at Sal Rubino's whore. Margaret Tolstoy. Isn't that her name? She's your new cookie. I figured there was another woman. And you fall for a cunt like that."

"I went to school with her, Your Honor."

"Don't you 'Your Honor' me. We're practically engaged."

"Becky, I—"

"Shut up. What kind of moron hits a cardinal? Isaac, do you want to sink my whole administration?"

"It was an accident," Isaac muttered. "I was trying to hit your chancellor."

"That's brilliant," Rebecca said. "A war between the Puerto Ricans and the Jews. The papers would love that. And Alejo would tear your kidneys. He was a boxer. I thought you had some sense. And who gave you permission to leave the table? A fight broke out after you were gone. Between Rubino and Jerry DiAngelis."

"That figures."

"Then why weren't you there to prevent it, Isaac? Isn't that what I pay you for?"

"Rebecca, I'm not a referee. What was the fight about?"

"That bitch. Margaret Tolstoy. That's how I learned who she was. Jerry insulted her. And Sal started climbing on Jerry's back."

"And did your boxer stop the fight?"

"No. It was Jim. The cardinal got between the warring parties and they were both ashamed to fuck with the Powerhouse. But Jim gets all the publicity and I can't even get laid, because my police commissioner is in love with Sal Rubino's mistress."

"We were classmates," Isaac said. "Margaret and . . ."

But the mayor had hung up on Isaac. She'd fume and call again. One phone call wasn't enough for Rebecca. He unclipped his bow tie and toyed with the shirt studs. He took off his shoes and socks. The phone rang and Isaac considered not answering it, but Her Honor would ring the whole bloody night. He could hear an odd chirp on the wire.

"Who is it?" he growled.

"Anastasia. Can I come up?"

Isaac received her in his robe like some aristocrat. She had a little mouse over one eye.

"Did Sal hit you?"

"It's nothing," she said.

"I'll make him wish he'd never heard of the Manhattan Ball."

"It's nothing."

She let her coat drop to the floor, and she stood in her silk gown, with a curious glow in Isaac's darkened rooms, his bear cave on Rivington Street. She began to shiver.

"You're cold," he muttered. "I'll find you a sweater."

"No. I'd like something to drink."

Isaac searched his cabinets and discovered a pear brandy from Poland. His worm didn't take to whiskey, and Isaac didn't keep much alcohol in the house. But he poured a glass for Margaret and himself.

"*Santé,*" she said, touching Isaac's glass with her own.

"You must have been to Paris. My dad lives there. He's a painter. Does portraits of rich Americans. He wanted to be the next Cézanne."

"Yes, I've been to Paris. And Brussels. And Amsterdam."

"Before you were Margaret Tolstoy."

She swallowed her brandy. "I wanted to see you tonight."

"For old times' sake. Isn't that it? One school chum to another."

"I wasn't thinking of old times. I risked my ass to come here, Isaac. Sal didn't want me to leave him."

"Is that how you got your swollen eye?"

"No. It happened at the St. Moritz. Sal didn't think I should have gone over to Jerry's table. But I like the Hebrew teacher. Isadore was always nice to me."

"Sweetheart, did you know that your husband is dead?"

She nibbled on the rim of her glass. "What husband?"

"Stop it, Margaret. This isn't a fucking Chekhov play. The accountant. Crabbs. He was shot in the ear by someone who got awful close to him."

"Someone like me. Isn't that what you're saying?"

"Yes. For starters. You tell me the Nose is trying to kill you. Some mother shows up outside my window with a Mafia shotgun aimed at your head. I took you to a safe house, Margaret. I left you with my own people. And you run away."

"They were getting pretty familiar. I went to pee and one of them comes into the toilet and starts a conversation."

"Who was it?"

"I didn't take the time to ask. I got out of there."

"Well, what did he look like?"

"It was dark, Isaac. He was wearing a holster. I don't know . . ."

"And you ran to Sal Rubino."

"I didn't have much of a choice. Should I have gone to the FBI? Sal was fond of me."

"I know. He took you dancing. He brought you to the Governor's Ball so DiAngelis could eat his heart out."

"I asked him to take me," Margaret said. "I'd never been to a ball like that."

"I could have taken you."

"Yes, but you weren't around." And the Roumanian princess started to laugh.

"What's so funny?"

She cupped a hand over her mouth to contain the laughter. "Your tux," she said.

"It wasn't supposed to be comical."

"But I adored it. That's why I'm here. My own sweet Isaac."

"I'm not all that sweet," Isaac said. He grabbed Margaret's wrists. "There's too much fucking amnesia. Where were you, Margaret, before you married the accountant? And who were you?"

"You're hurting me," she said.

And Isaac was miserable in his own policeman's heart. He couldn't cure himself of Anastasia. He was attached to some bloody hook that brought him home to samovars and black tea. But if she did have a derringer in her handbag, he wouldn't have sent her away. His head bent a trifle. He could feel her nostrils and the heat of her mouth. And finally, after thirty-seven years or so, they kissed. It felt strange, as if Isaac were watching himself in a two-way mirror. Was he kissing Margaret, or the ghost of a little girl? The gown slipped from her shoulders. And Isaac was afraid. She led him by the hand, and he found himself in his own bedroom with Margaret Tolstoy.

It was more like peace than any particular passion. He was grounded in the princess. He had no desire to leave his bed. He came twice, like some big lucky bear. And all the while he watched her face. Her almond eyes turned another color. They went green under the weight of Isaac. Her mouth tasted like tea. No other woman had held him the way Anastasia did. She touched the wool on his chest, one arm circling his back, as if he were an enormous baby.

He shut his eyes to see her better, to imagine her next to him, when he heard a little rustling noise, like an engine that could breathe. Anastasia was already in her clothes. Isaac

stared at the clock on his night stand. It was a minute to five.
And Isaac's windows were dark as some deep well.

"Where are you going?"

"To Sal's place," she said. "I promised him I wouldn't spend
the whole night."

"So he lent you to me. You struck a bargain with Sal
Rubino."

"Isaac, it was the only way I could come."

"What if I kept you with me like a fucking prisoner?"

"He'd send out his crew to knock on your door."

"I could have two riot squads here in ten minutes, with
bulletproof vests. They'd bump Sal home to his cement
company."

"Isaac, I gave him my word."

"Margaret, live with me. I mean it. We already lost
thirty-seven years."

"I can't," she said.

"I don't have another thirty-seven years to wait. I'm already
losing my teeth. I had a hernia operation. I get spots in front
of my eyes. I don't remember half the names of my deputies.
And I have a worm in my gut that's eating me alive."

"You're still a boy," she said, smiling at Isaac. She bent over
to kiss him between the eyes, and he was too forlorn to
handcuff Margaret to his bed.

She floated away from Isaac. The door clicked. And he
knew he'd dream of samovars, even while he was awake.

Part Three

14

Ismail, that's what he called himself. He was a cipher at the Syrian mission to the U.N. A minor-league clerk who stood five feet tall. Isaac pictured his office in a basement somewhere. But the little clerk read most of Syria's traffic. Isaac never asked Ismail to compromise himself, to produce documents, or betray his country. He'd met the little man at a party. And it was curious that a clerk at the Syrian mission should have acquired a passion for baseball. Ismail had collected baseball cards, as Isaac had done. He knew batting averages. He was qualified to join the Christy Mathewson Club, but the Syrians would never have allowed it. He'd unearthed a baseball book when he was a boy in Damascus, and something about the uniforms, the caps, and the wallowing knickers had compelled him for life.

He was lonely in America, and he couldn't relate to the modern teams, because they didn't wear the knickers he recalled from his book. And so he held to his boyhood heroes. He had no wife. His only brother had died in Damascus. He scribbled poetry and helped Isaac whenever he could. The

PC cultivated Ismail as an informant and a friend. They'd have lunch in Chinatown, at little restaurants where the cooks, the owners, and the waiters guarded Isaac's privacy. The Syrian was always grateful. They'd talk about their card collections, how much each card might be worth. Ismail had cards that went back to 1910. He was a much more serious collector than Isaac could ever be. The cards were Ismail's America. His Ty Cobb was worth thousands of dollars. But he'd never part with his collection.

They only discussed business after the meal.

The little man had been able to piece Margaret Tolstoy's life together. He must have gone to some Russian source, but Isaac never asked where Ismail got his information. He never carried documents. He wove whatever story he had in his head.

"Roumanian," Ismail said. "Couldn't find her birthday."

"It's not important, Ismail. She's about my age. But was she born Margaret Tolstoy?"

The Syrian smiled. "Isaac, does Tolstoy sound Roumanian to you? Magda is her name. Magda Antonescu, I think. She was an orphan. But she could have come from rich people. She was living in Paris by Nineteen forty. And she arrived in America around Nineteen forty-three. Without any parents."

"Was she Jewish?" Isaac asked.

"No. There isn't any evidence of that."

"But why come here then? Roumania fought on the Nazi side. Their soldiers occupied Odessa, didn't they? She would have been safe in Paris."

"Perhaps. But she arrived with a group of Roumanian children. They were all parceled out to foster families. Some were lucky, others were not. Magda couldn't seem to find a permanent home. She had a succession of uncles and aunts. She might have been stealing the family silver, who knows?"

"But I met her during the war," Isaac said. "And the people she was with were very refined. They had a samovar."

Ismail laughed at his friend. "If a samovar was a mark of refinement, Isaac, you'd have a million aristocrats in Manhattan alone."

"I don't mean that," Isaac protested. "It was how she behaved. She knew French."

"Naturally."

"It was more than the French, Ismail. She was different. The teachers loved her. We all did. And then she vanished."

"Vanished? No. She returned to Bucharest . . . after the war. Had a long-lost uncle who suddenly claimed her."

"King Carol?"

"Not a king, Isaac. Ferdinand Antonescu. Some financier. Then it all gets a bit cloudy. She was a ballet dancer, an actress. And Uncle Ferdinand dabbled in the black market. He was arrested and shot. The niece fell into disgrace. Lived like a beggar, hand to mouth. She emerges again, the mistress of a Roumanian general. It's all caviar and champagne. The Russians took notice of her. And she's sent to a Soviet kindergarten class."

"Kindergarten?" Isaac mumbled. Margaret's journeys had begun to rattle his head.

"A school for spies. Nothing special. It was strictly low grade. Her masters never really trusted her. She'd been to America. The FBI could have suborned Magda Antonescu."

"She was in junior high, for Christ's sake. Thirteen, fourteen at the most."

"It's been done before."

"I don't believe you."

"Then call it speculation. A theory, Isaac, a hunch. But she graduates from kindergarten. She's a swallow now. You know what a swallow is."

"Yes, Ismail," Isaac muttered. "A whore."

"Her masters provide her with all the documentation she could ever need. She'd lived in America. So the Russkies returned Magda to her 'native ground.' She poses as a

Roumanian refugee, which was near enough to the truth. She has six or seven aliases. And she makes the rounds. Seduces men in Washington, San Francisco, Los Angeles . . . minor diplomats, soldiers, sailors, scientists. I told you. They didn't trust Magda. She brought them little morsels of information, enough to keep her on the payroll. But she was too striking a woman not to be noticed, even if her handlers marched her from place to place. She had a dozen good years. Then the FBI caught on to the mysterious Magda."

"I thought you said they'd recruited her when she was thirteen."

"Just a theory of mine, Isaac. Nothing more. But now the fun begins. The Bureau doesn't arrest Magda. And the Russians aren't really concerned that she's been unmasked. She knows very little about their operations. They'd provide her with some nest where they could photograph Magda and her 'client' in compromising positions, so they could blackmail the poor bastard, or frighten him to death. And now the Bureau decides to use Magda as an informant. The Russians don't even object. They offer her to the FBI as an 'Easter egg'—a very small gift. But on one condition. That the Bureau doesn't set her up in the international market. She can only go after American game. That's perfect for the Bureau. Magda 'dies.' And enter Margaret Tolstoy."

"And who's her handler?"

Ismail drank a cup of green tea.

"Who's her handler?"

"Le Comte, of course."

Isaac slapped his forehead. "God, I'm dumb. Jerry keeps wiggling out of Le Comte's hands. He can't make an indictment stick. Juries have a habit of falling in love with Jerry DiAngelis. So LeComte tosses Margaret Tolstoy into the stew. She shacks up with Jerry's bookkeeper. Sal Rubino is crazy about her. Margaret is like a combat zone. She heats up the civil war. And then, as icing on the cake, she shows up at the Christy Mathewson Club, and I'm dragged into the plot . . . compromised before I even say hello to Margaret."

"She's a beauty, our Margaret," the little man said. "Fifty, and still going strong. Remember, Isaac, Count Dracula was a Roumanian man. And she's Dracula's Daughter. That's what they call her in certain code rooms. She sucks the blood out of the men in her life. I'd be careful around her. She might still be free-lancing for some of her old masters. Don't give too much of yourself away."

Already introduced her to the Ivanhoes, Isaac muttered to himself. He was dying for a cappuccino, not twig tea. He took a baseball card out of his pocket, wrapped in cellophane. It was Goose Goslin, 1921.

Ismail held the card with trembling hands. "Isaac, I couldn't take it. Not in good conscience. It would cripple your own collection."

"Kiddo, you deserve the card."

Isaac got up to pay the bill. It was always a difficult song and dance. The PC was an honored guest, the lord high commissioner. And Isaac would have to answer that the meal itself was an honor, and that the lord high commissioner had to pay for that honor like any other man. The chef himself would come out of the kitchen and scribble signs on a blank white pad. And with such meticulous care, a meal for two might cost Isaac nine dollars and seventy cents.

Ismail went to the toilet and Isaac loped across town to the shirt factory. Something nagged at him, more than Margaret Tolstoy. Ismail seemed to have *too much* information about Dracula's Daughter. He couldn't have been a common cipher at the Syrian mission. And what the hell was a kid from Damascus doing with baseball cards? Isaac seemed surrounded by magicians.

He entered the factory. The Afrikaner was there to greet him.

"Burt, you lied. You said you didn't see Margaret at the factory. But you followed her into the toilet, didn't you?"

"Yes I did."

"What the hell for?"

"I wanted to ask her some bloody questions, and the woman was avoiding me. Isaac, I didn't peek at her underpants. That's not my game. Jesus, you know that."

"Well, we have to move. Because the lady works for LeComte, and she might have a lot more clients than that."

"You're a bloody mind reader. Because I was having the same thoughts."

"I'll expect you to be packed in twenty minutes."

"But we have a whole dormitory of cots. We have bedding, Isaac. A hundred pillows."

"Forget the dormitory. Take all the other gear."

"And what's our new address?"

"We don't have one. It's too risky to have a permanent home. The governor's on to me. Open the safe, Burt. Divvy up whatever's inside. And then wait for me in that white hotel."

"Where the bookkeeper is lying with a bullet in his brain?"

"I'd be willing to swear that the body's been removed. And not by the Catskill police. I think our lads will be okay . . . for a little while. I'll count on your judgement, Burt. If it doesn't smell right, lease another hotel. The mountains are full of them."

"But I'll be arriving with an army, Isaac. Someone's bound to spot us."

"Then you'll have to split up. And when you call me, Burt, say you're Friar Tuck."

"Won't that sound conspicuous to some little secretary?"

"No. She'll think you're a monk."

He hadn't worn his paging device, because Isaac didn't want to be at the mercy of Rebecca Karp. But when he got to headquarters, it wasn't the mayor who was dogging him.

Sweets stood outside Isaac's office with all the gloom of a disinherited man.

"I've been paging you for an hour."

"I had urgent business," Isaac said.

"I don't give a damn. You're our fucking chief. And you owe us your blood twenty-four hours a day."

The First Dep screamed at Isaac in front of all his sergeants and fellow commissioners, and Isaac didn't scream back. "I'm sorry," he said.

"Save your apologies, Mr. Isaac. The Maf's been partying. Jerry's father-in-law was shot."

"Where is he?"

"St. Vincent's. I think he'll pull through."

Sergeant Malone brought Isaac out of One Police Plaza in the old Dodge, with the sirens wailing against traffic. They got to St. Vincent's in seven minutes. Isaac blundered through the hospital, showing the stars on his commissioner's shield. Doctors, nurses, and nuns couldn't hold back the Commish. He found the DiAngelis brothers, Jerry and Nose, outside intensive care, with Eileen DiAngelis. Jerry had six of his own lieutenants guarding the intensive-care unit. The hospital was like an army barrack.

One of the nurses complained. "I'm going to call the police."

"Ma'am," Isaac said. "Forgive the intrusion. I'm Commissioner Isaac Sidel."

"This is outrageous," the nurse said. "These people have no business being here."

She frowned at the gold stars on Isaac's badge and skulked into another ward.

"I told him not to go walking by himself," Jerry muttered. "Jesus, this isn't a country club. They send a kid, some geep with a toy gun to shoot Izzy. Isaac, he looked like a messenger boy. He was riding a bike . . . but this is the end. Sal Rubino, I'm taking out that son of a bitch."

Eileen stood in the corner and started to cry. Isaac looked at the Nose.

"Ah," Teddy Boy said, "you don't touch a melamed. He's sacred. Like Cardinal Jim."

A doctor came out of the unit. "Is Commissioner Sidel here?"

"Yes," Isaac said. "That's me."

"Mr. Wasser would like to see you."

"Doc," Jerry asked, "how is my father-in-law?"

"He'll be fine," the doctor said. "But he wants to talk with Mr. Sidel."

And Isaac passed through the magical door of the intensive-care unit. Men and women were lying in criblike beds, comatose after surgery. But the melamed had his own curtained-off corner. Isaac went inside the curtain. It could have been Ali Baba's tent. The melamed had tubes in his arms, but he was as conscious as Isaac would ever be.

"Izzy," Isaac said. "I'm glad you're alive."

The melamed motioned to Isaac with a finger. And Isaac approached the crib. "Tell you a secret," Izzy whispered. "So am I. But I'm superstitious. I don't like rooms with crosses on every wall."

"It's a Catholic hospital, for God's sake. Be a little kind. Your daughter married a Catholic."

"That's different," the melamed said. "Speak to Jerry, Isaac. Please. If he declares war on Sal, nobody wins."

"I'll take care of Sal Rubino."

"Shh," the melamed said. "You're the chief of police. But promise me, Isaac. You'll talk to Jerry. He's not to move a finger until I'm out of St. Vincent's. They were trying to humiliate us, that's all. So they sent a child on a bicycle."

"I don't agree, Iz. It was clever of Sal. A kid wouldn't arouse suspicion. A kid could come through the lines."

"But he had a peashooter. If I hadn't fallen down, I could have recovered at home. No, no, Isaac. It wasn't meant to be a kill. It was a message. 'Dear Jerry. A little present from your own captains. Happy Valentine.'"

"But we're in January, Iz."

"So what? Sal Rubino likes to celebrate as early as he can. Now get out of here. I'm an old man. I need time to recuperate."

15

He went down to St. Andrews Plaza, where LeComte kept an office in the same building as the U.S. attorney for the Southern District. Isaac had no idea if LeComte was around. The son of a bitch could be off playing golf with the attorney general in the fields of Virginia, or having a late, late breakfast on Capitol Hill. He had a flat in Georgetown and a pied-à-terre in Manhattan that was bigger than Isaac's whole apartment. But LeComte must have canceled his golf game. Isaac found him in his office. His sleeves were rolled up.

Isaac saw the ripple of his forearms. "Working late, aren't you, LeComte?"

The prince regent of the Justice Department didn't bother looking up. "Isaac, I don't remember seeing you in my calendar book."

"That's because your secretary is absentminded. I'm in your book, LeComte. You just never took the time to notice. You're the great magician. You run the whole fucking show. You invented that Alexander Hamilton business. The first

130

Hamilton Fellow, Isaac Sidel. It was a game to get me on the road."

"You're wrong. I'm the last ally you have left. Becky Karp and the governor will throw you to the dogs."

"Yes, the governor. Great man. I wonder who told him about the Ivanhoes."

"I did. You've been sloppy, Isaac. Leaving trails. If I didn't tell him, someone else at Justice would. And I'd have lost my credibility with the Gov. He'll be our next president. You know that. He's so narrowed down, he could never lose an election."

"And Frederic LeComte will be his secretary of state."

"No. I like it here at Justice. It suits my temperament."

"Right. You can be invisible whenever you want. You can run agents like Magda Antonescu."

LeComte rolled down his sleeves. "I'm impressed. You must have had a meet with Farouk in one of your Chinese restaurants."

"What Farouk?"

"Your Syrian connection. We call him King Farouk. Would you like a drink?"

"No thanks. I brought my own bottle of milk."

"For the tapeworm, isn't it? I could recommend a miracle doctor, Isaac. He'd cure you in a month."

"I like the worm," Isaac said. "He's the best companion I ever had."

"Outside Manfred Coen."

"Tell me, LeComte, what's my nickname in FBI circles?"

"We've gotten used to calling you Isaac. You'll always be Isaac to us . . . or Alec."

Isaac's nose started to twitch. Soon the worm would gnaw at him. "Ah, Alec. For Alexander Hamilton. I ought to be flattered. But I'm slow today. What about Magda? I hear a couple of agencies call her Dracula's Daughter."

LeComte was silent. Then he laughed. "Farouk is better than I thought."

Isaac looked out the window. He could see the big red monolith of Police Headquarters, the lights of Wall Street, the dark bow of the Brooklyn Bridge. But he felt wounded, and he pulled on his bottle of milk. "Magda," he muttered. "You sent her to the Christy Mathewson Club."

"No. She was naughty. She did that on her own."

"But you knew about Magda and me . . . that I'd been in love with her all these years."

"I suspected it, once I learned she'd been in your class. And I tried to distance you from Margaret as much as I could."

"Tell me about her uncle Ferdinand."

"The Butcher of Bucharest."

"I don't understand. He was a financier, according to King Farouk."

"Yes, the finance minister of the Roumanian province in Odessa during World War Two. The Roumanians had a dream of their own little country, Transnistria. Ferdinand was the architect of that dream. Odessa was to be the capital. He was a clever tactician, brilliant almost, with his little country by the Black Sea. But he forgot something. Transnistria had no escape routes. It was only an island, Isaac, surrounded by a fucking continent that could never belong to his German brothers. They got to the gates of Moscow, but they could never creep in. So Ferdinand was isolated in his island country. He bled the population. He massacred gypsies and Jews. But he had very quiet evenings. He played chess with one of the local champions. He dawdled with his 'niece,' whom he'd brought out of Roumania. They weren't blood relatives, Isaac. She was called Magda Antonescu, his twelve-year-old concubine."

"You're crazy," Isaac said. "Magda was with me."

"Not until Nineteen forty-four. . . . Ferdinand's country was falling apart, so he smuggled the girl out of Odessa, got her on a hospital train. And with all the diamonds and silver he'd stolen from Jewish merchants, he bribed enough guards to send her into Sweden . . . and onto a mercy ship to America."

"I don't believe you."

"She was in Odessa, Isaac, believe it or not."

"And I suppose the FBI cultivated her when she got here, turned her into a teenage spy. That's Farouk's theory."

"Not a spy, Isaac. But the Bureau did interview her. It was common practice. So Farouk was on the right track."

"And then what happened?"

"Transnistria crumbles completely. The fascists are thrown out of Roumania. Carol's son, King Michael, is now on the Russian side, a comrade of Uncle Joe. Ferdinand disappears. The poor king doesn't even have a chance to hang the Butcher of Bucharest. And Stalin never could grab him."

"Did he run to Argentina, like Adolf Eichmann?"

"No, Isaac. That's the beauty of it. He continues his game of chess. But he discovers a new opening. The Ferdinand Defense. He scurries back to Bucharest under a false name. Starts a little circus."

"And plays the magician, I suppose."

"The magician . . . and the clown. And he sends for Magda after the war, posing as another relative. But it was a dumb idea. We return the little package."

"We?" Isaac said. "You weren't even alive in 'forty-six or 'forty-seven."

"All right. The government, Isaac. Are you satisfied? But the Bureau knows all about Uncle Ferdinand. And the Roumanians also get smart to what's going on. They arrest the circus master. He's brought to trial. He blubbers on the stand. Crimes against the people. All that crap. But his blubbering can't save him. A firing squad blows his head apart."

"But he might have outfoxed the Roumanians in his little circus if he hadn't sent for Magda. Why did he do it?"

"He loved her, silly. He couldn't have lived without Magda Antonescu."

"But she was a little girl, LeComte."

"She wasn't *that* little. And I'm not his judge. The Roumanians arrest Magda. They accuse her of crimes in Ferdinand's country by the sea. They say that Dracula and his Daughter drank Jewish blood. They might have shot her too, if the Russians hadn't whisked her off to Moscow. She lives with a couple of generals or admirals, I don't know. She returns to Roumania as some kind of actress. She appears in films. Then she falls into one crack or another. And with a bit of magic from the KGB, she's in America again. Starts seducing diplomats. But the Bureau wasn't fucking blind. It was the same Orphan Annie, Magda Antonescu. So we turn her around— sorry, Isaac. I'm only a kid at the time. And Magda, she starts feeding her Russian masters poisoned information. She's our own little darling of the Cold War. But I don't think the Russians paid much attention to the babble she was bringing in."

"But they left her in place, didn't they?"

"That's true."

"And she could have been free-lancing at your expense."

"It didn't matter, Isaac. Whatever she got was small. And then I arrived at Justice, the Junior G-man. And I inherited this worn-out whore. I think she slept with five hundred men—officially, that is. I assume she had a private life. But she was still a looker, and I decided to go domestic with Magda Antonescu, alias Margaret Malone, alias Rita Danzig. I tossed her at a couple of gangs in Chicago. We dyed her hair red. She fell in love with one or two of the overlords. She wore a wire. We got nine or ten convictions before we pulled Rita Danzig."

"So you went for the Big Apple. You brought her here."

"Don't rush me, Isaac. I like to tell my own stories. First it was Seattle. Then San Diego. Then St. Louis. And Daytona Beach."

"You should have given her my badge, LeComte, and made her your Hamilton Fellow."

"She didn't need a badge. The big-time thugs were cock-eyed over—"

"Dracula's Daughter."

"She had the touch. Ferdinand must have been a good teacher."

Isaac considered slapping LeComte, shoving his head out the window so he could sniff the weather above St. Andrews Plaza. But it wouldn't have changed his status with the Junior G-man. "Finally you did bring Margaret to New York. Your prosecutors couldn't hold Jerry. The media loves a Mafia man with his own sense of style. He didn't have the education. But he learned to talk like a duke."

"Not on his own, Isaac," LeComte said, his mouth turning into a twist. "He had Isadore."

"An ex-Hebrew school teacher who was also a jailbird. He couldn't have made a duke out of Jerry."

"But he did. Come on, Isaac. Admit. Jerry is nothing without the melamed."

"Maybe he is and maybe he isn't. But you have him sewed up. His brother is your prize informant."

"Isaac, would you count on Teddy Boy? I don't believe half his shit. The melamed might have sent him to me."

"I've thought of that," Isaac said. "Many times. But why does Jerry DiAngelis tick you off?"

"Because the public looks at him and sees some kind of knight. He's a scumbag, Isaac. He's killed people."

"I don't care who he kills as long as he sticks to his own corner. LeComte, are you really grieving for the Rubino brothers? Let him wipe out as many of his soldiers as he wants."

"I'm not talking about soldiers," LeComte said. "He's slapped innocent people who looked at him the wrong way."

"You'd be just as paranoid if you were the chief of a crime family with captains who wanted you dead."

The prince regent held his temples for a moment and sucked air through his nose. "You don't get it, Isaac. For you he's a hero of the streets. The poor kid who worked his way up in America. And it doesn't matter how many throats he had to tear, or shopkeepers he burned out of their businesses."

"You live in Georgetown. You come to Manhattan twice a week. The City doesn't run without DiAngelis. Becky Karp has her billion-dollar budgets. But a school can't get built without a nod from Jerry. He's more honest than half the City's inspectors, and much more direct. When you deal with Jerry, there's no red tape."

"Of course. It's his kingdom, isn't it? He's luckier than Ferdinand Antonescu. He didn't have to invent a phantom country. All he has to do is clip a couple of pennies off the chickens you buy at the supermarket. I'm going to nail him, Isaac, and that melamed. Because it's the old man's brains that keeps him from falling on his ass. And don't you dream of fucking with me. You're a civilian, Isaac. You can't even make an arrest. And I have a lot more soldiers than you do."

"Margaret Tolstoy's the best soldier in town. She marries Jerry's bookkeeper and the bookkeeper turns dead."

"Crabbs?"

"He died in a white hotel. Somebody popped him with a lady's special."

"And you think it was Margaret, you dope. Why should she kill him when she was getting Crabbs to sing?"

"If she's so hot, LeComte, tell her to find Maurie Goodstein. Or maybe you'd like Maurie to sit it out while Dracula's Daughter gobbles up the whole Rubino clan. Because if Maurie surfaces, he'll whip your ass in court. He's done it before."

"Not with a subpoena sitting between his tail. I can tie him to Jerry's deals. I have the schmuck on tape. He's going down. With Jerry and the old man. He's part of the gang. He'll have to turn on Jerry. He doesn't have a choice. That's why he's disappeared . . . now I'm tired, Isaac. How can I help you?"

"You already did."

"Can you explain that? I haven't been to my health club for a week. I get groggy after dark."

"I enjoyed that folk tale about Margaret in Odessa. I'd like to ask her a little more."

"Stay away from her, Isaac."

"Why? Because I might ruin her courtship with Sal Rubino?"

"Stay away."

"I can't, LeComte. I can't."

And Isaac left LeComte's lair at St. Andrews Plaza. The worm roiled so hard in his gut he had to stop and drink all the milk he was carrying. It couldn't satisfy the worm. Police Headquarters was only a hop away. But Isaac trundled in the other direction, past the Roman church, past the Federal Courthouse, and onto Foley Square. There was still Christmas bunting in Thomas Paine Park, lights strung along the trees that some parkman had neglected to take down, probably for want of a ladder. Isaac himself was the January Santa Claus who'd lost the line to his own Department. He would have loved to have been a pamphleteer, like old Tom Paine. But there wasn't much room for Tom anymore. LeComte had written his own *Rights of Man*. It was a fucking book of spies.

The worm ripped at Isaac. He had to rest in Tom Paine's park. Where the hell could he find a bottle of milk?

16

Isaac started plunging in and out of restaurants. He refilled his milk bottle at the Red Dot on Park Row. The milk bottle was almost as famous as Isaac himself. It was like a gas tank he wore on his own person. And the barflies wouldn't stop commending him on his capture of Henry Armstrong Lee. It got more and more embarrassing, but Isaac had to admit that his sitdown with Henry in an abandoned building was probably the last time he'd behaved like a cop. He hadn't used his Ivanhoes. He'd arrived with a SWAT team and Sweets, reporters stationed around him, but the Most Wanted Man in the U.S.A. would surrender to no one but Isaac Sidel. That's the note Henry Lee sent out of the building with a runner of his. And already the reporters had their headlines: High Noon in Harlem Heights.

Isaac handed his gun to Sweets, who began to mourn Isaac while he was still alive. "That's a crazy man in there. We could rush him, Isaac. We have a whole tactical unit."

"I'll be fine."

Was he afraid? Yes. He walked in the rubble, his feet crackling against all the broken bricks. He entered the building through a shattered window and there was Henry Lee hiding in a skirt, blouse, and wig. Isaac revealed his empty holster. "I'm not packing," he said.

"I know."

And Henry started to cry. The sobbing was so terrific that the PC wasn't sure what to do. "Can I help?"

"Hold my hand."

And Isaac clutched the hand of that outlaw, Henry Lee. The sobbing stopped. "Been running from the FBIs," Henry said. "Haven't slept in nineteen days. I'm hungry and I'm cold. You wouldn't have found me, Mr. Isaac, without your Mafia connections."

The outlaw was right. His runner had been selling hash on the street. Word of it got to Jerry DiAngelis. And Jerry dropped the dime on Henry Lee.

Isaac walked out of the building with Henry in his women's clothes, and the PC's existence hadn't been the same ever since. Isaac's face was on the cover of *New York* magazine. "Megacop" they called him. A Dutch television crew arrived to chat with Isaac. They called him *El Grande* in Mexico and Madrid. He was Sidel, *le Superflic*, in *Paris Match*. But Isaac suffered a decline. His hero status separated him from most other men in the Department. He was Isaac the Untouchable. And he drifted toward the Ivanhoes. . . .

He had milk and Russian vodka at his fifth restaurant. The vodka was poison for him. He had a veal chop. He wasn't even aware of the direction he was taking. But somehow he knew that he'd end up in Margaret's company. The worm pulled him with a radar of its own. Isaac entered a steak house in the East Twenties. But he sensed something was wrong. No simple steak house would have had three doormen with walkie-talkies and bulges in their coats that could only have meant shotguns with short barrels. *His* man, Coen, had favored a shotgun. Coen carried his shotgun in a shopping bag. He wouldn't have worn it under his coat, like a bodyguard or button man. These were Sal's soldiers. They didn't mess with the Commish. They whispered into the walkietalkies while Isaac went inside.

She was sitting at a table with Sal. The tables around them were filled with button men. Sal had deepened the civil war. He'd sent a kid on a bike to give the melamed a bloody kiss. And he wasn't taking chances. He surrounded himself with soldiers.

Isaac stumbled from table to table. He'd had too much vodka and milk. But he didn't take his eyes off Dracula's Daughter. She was a babushka tonight. Her hair was swept back into a bun. Her eyes shone like puries in the dim light, those marbles Isaac had treasured as a kid.

It wasn't a Russian restaurant. And he couldn't have his tea from a samovar. He thought of the generals she'd been with, the five hundred johns. Isaac had more than jealousy. It was hate. He wanted to harm this Margaret Tolstoy, even if the worm was in love with her.

He ordered vodka and milk. He had some Mississippi mud pie. His lips were dark with chocolate. "Hey, Magda," he shouted. He knocked on the table with his fist. "How are you, love?"

It was Sal who answered him. "Isaac, we have witnesses. What the fuck do you want?"

"Tell Magda to come to her favorite schoolboy."

"Isaac," Sal said, "are you crazy or what? Who is Magda?"

"He's joking," Margaret said, holding Sal's hand. "I went to school with Isaac . . . for a little while."

"I never knew that."

"Oh, it's a thirty-seven-year-old secret," she said. "Let me say hello."

"Not a chance," Sal said. "I'm not sharing you with the Commish. He has no business being here." Sal stood up, his napkin sticking out of his belt like an obscene flag. "I haven't broken a fucking law."

"Let me go to him, baby, for a minute," Margaret said. "I'll be right back."

"No. He can eat his lousy badge. I'm a citizen. I pay taxes."

Margaret got up and nuzzled Sal's neck. "Baby, I'll be back. I promise."

She started around the table and Sal slapped her with an open fist.

Isaac saw the blood on her mouth and he leapt at Sal. He'd climbed over his table and nearly caught Sal's throat. But one of the soldiers socked Isaac in the head with a sack of dimes. The sack exploded, and the restaurant bloomed with a miraculous blush of silver. But Isaac didn't see the dimes. He'd landed on the floor. And the same soldier seized him by the collar and dragged Isaac into the men's room.

"Aw, don't hurt him, Eddie," Sal said. "He's the Commish."

Sal sat down again, and he was so involved with the glory of the moment, he hadn't remembered that Margaret wasn't there. She'd followed Eddie to the men's room. She opened the door. He was leaning over Isaac, strangling him a little. And Margaret struck him twice behind the ear with the flat of her hand. Eddie's eyes glazed, and he toppled over.

"You are a fool," she said to Isaac, who was coughing from his seat on the floor of the men's room. "Why did you come here?"

"I wanted to learn about Odessa."

There was the narrowest smile on Margaret's lips. And Isaac wondered if she'd crack him too, like she'd done to Eddie.

"You were never afraid of the Nose. It was all an act."

"Isaac, I don't have the time. Sal's little helpers will be here any minute."

"Tell me one thing. Were you in Odessa during the war . . . with Uncle Ferdinand?"

"Yes," she said. "Isaac, there's another entrance. Turn right when you get out of the toilet. You'll find a door."

"Margaret?"

"Good-bye."

She climbed over Eddie, wiped the blood from her mouth, and returned to Sal's table. He was still rejoicing. "Did you see that whack? Eddie told it to Isaac." He turned to Margaret. "Where were you?"

"In the ladies' room, Sal. I had to fix my face. Don't you want me to look decent?"

"Yeah, yeah," he said. "But don't crawl away like that. I get lonely for you, Margaret."

"I know that, baby. I won't leave you again."

He stumbled home, a wild man, with thoughts of how he could destroy Sal Rubino's little army. But it wasn't Sal. He couldn't clear his mind of Margaret Tolstoy. She'd saved him from the muck of a men's room, cracked Rubino's soldier in the head like a bionic gal, Margaret of Roumania, graduate of a Russian kindergarten and LeComte's own little school for spies. Isaac was too sore to bathe. His phone rang. "Fuck it," he said. The ringing would stop and start again. Isaac grabbed the receiver. "Who is it?" he growled.

"Friar Tuck."

The fucking world had gone insane. It was filled with freaks from Sherwood Forest. Isaac hung up on the guy. He plunged his head into a sinkful of water. And then he groaned. Friar Tuck was the recognition name *and* signal he'd given to the Afrikaner, Burton Bortelsman. Now Burt would think that Isaac had been sabotaged in some way and couldn't talk. And God knows when Isaac would hear from his Ivanhoes.

"Come on, Burt, try me, will you?"

Isaac got into his flannel pajamas. They smelled of Margaret Tolstoy and he began to cry. He pictured her as a woman-child in that country Ferdinand Antonescu had ruled in the Ukraine. Antonescu had kidnapped a twelve-year-old girl and sat her down in Odessa. Somebody would have to pay, but Ferdinand was dead. And so was Roumanian Odessa. The phone rang. Isaac kept his wits about him.

"Hello, Friar."

"Don't get kinky."

It was Margaret Tolstoy. She asked Isaac if he was okay. The beast in his belly started to purr. "Margaret, when can I see you?"

"I'm not sure."

"Couldn't you get away from Sal?"

"Isaac, I'm risking my ass already with this call. The man has me on a twenty-four-hour leash."

"But you could break his neck."

She started to laugh. "I gotta go." He heard voices in the background, and the phone went dead. Isaac stepped out of his pajamas and ran water in his kitchen tub. The conversation with Margaret had revived the Commish and he felt like soaking for half an hour. Soon as he sat down in the tub his phone rang.

"Son of a bitch."

He climbed out in his bare feet to answer the phone, wishing it was Margaret calling to tell him she could shake Sal Rubino and come over to Isaac's flat. But it was the First Dep.

"Be downstairs in five minutes. I'm coming to collect you."

Isaac couldn't even get a hello out of Sweets and it was four o'clock in the morning. He dried himself, got dressed. He didn't even have time to yawn. Sweets was waiting for him in one of the Department's green Chevrolets.

"Where are we going?"

"Isaac, get in."

They drove across the Brooklyn Bridge, with the barges below them pulling, pulling into the night. They stopped at a warehouse across from Gravesend. The warehouse belonged to an outfit that fronted for DiAngelis and laundered his money. The melamed arranged most of Jerry's deals, and none of Sweet's task forces could tie DiAngelis directly to the laundering operation. Sweets and Isaac entered the warehouse. A police sergeant was stationed behind the door. He looked like a pixie in his uniform. Isaac's eyes wandered over the pixie's head.

"Ah, shit," he muttered.

A boy was hanging from one of the window bars, the bent spokes of a bicycle tied around his neck. He might have been older, but he looked about twelve. His ears had turned blue, and his tongue filled his mouth.

"Jesus, cut him down," Isaac said.

"I'd like to wait for the pathology people," the First Dep said. "And there could be prints on the wire."

"Then cover his face."

Sweets stood on a chair and tied his handkerchief around the boy's face like a bandanna. Then he climbed down and dismissed the sergeant.

"That's one handsome family you're involved with, Isaac . . . I know it's the brat who got to Isadore, one of Sal Rubino's geeps. And maybe he deserved a spanking, but not this."

"Why are you sure it's Jerry's work? I know the melamed. He wouldn't have sanctioned it."

"But Jerry would. He's not as refined as his father-in-law."

"But it doesn't have Jerry's mark. It's too fancy, Sweets. Too poetic."

"Poetic, huh? His chin wrapped in wire."

"It stinks of Sal Rubino. He hires a kid on a bicycle to pop the old man, and then he offs the kid with bicycle wire, so we think Jerry's involved. And it's a genuine civil war . . . no, this isn't Jerry's work. I don't give a damn what the pathologist tells us."

"What's in it for Sal?"

"Sympathy. When the killing starts, he'll play the fucking martyr. The FBIs will shut Jerry down and Sal will get his uncles' family back. He's the executioner, Sweets."

"Aren't you a little partial, Isaac? You celebrate Christmas with Jerry. And you help the melamed light up his Chanukah bush. Sometimes I think you're closer to them than the Department. You're in trouble, Isaac. You know that. We have an awful lot of shit on tape between you and Jerry. Internal Affairs has a big fat dossier. And Becky's corruptions commissioner keeps whistling whenever he hears your name."

"You mean Michaelson, that little prick? He wants to hop on my head, grab his own future, and become king of Manhattan."

"Isaac, cover your ass. Keep away from the melamed, or I won't be able to help you."

"I don't turn from my friends, Sweets. You know me."

"But you're also the Commish."

"Ah," Isaac said. "I'll remember that."

He was snoring hard, and Margaret crept out from under the covers. Sal had this rotten habit of chewing the blankets in his sleep. His mouth was wet and a kind of crust had formed under his nose. She got dressed, but she didn't put her boots on. She carried them to the door. He wouldn't wake up until noon, when one of his bodyguards would draw the curtains and hand him his *caffelatte* and a slice of Milanese cake and the reports of what his captains had taken in last night. Sal would bitch over every lost penny. He had a cement company, a couple of building crews, but it was his loan-sharking that he cared about. He liked to have money circulating on the street. He would tally the slips of paper himself while he drank the *caffelatte*. And then he'd want to make love. The idea of money aroused him more than Margaret ever did.

She had to get past the bodyguard, Eddie, whom she'd

clipped in the toilet while Isaac lay on the floor of Sal's favorite restaurant. Eddie was convinced that one of Isaac's angels had socked him, an angel like Manfred Coen, but this Manfred was supposed to be dead. Eddie wore a bandage over his ear. He was a little doped up, but Margaret knew she'd never get past him without a couple of feels. He was afraid to invite her into his bed, but he loved to talk to Margaret with his hands.

"Where do you think you're going, bitch?"

"Out for a walk," she said. "I'm not sleepy."

"What about Jerry and the old Jew. Sal wouldn't like it much if they copped you off the street. He'd cry into his coffee."

"The Jew's in the hospital," Margaret said. "And Jerry doesn't like the dark."

"So what?" Eddie said. And he pinned Margaret against the door. She could have ruined his kidneys with a couple of rabbit punches, but she stood still while his hands marched clumsily under her coat and went inside her blouse. "Nice," he said. "Very nice." He closed his eyes for a second as he fondled her breasts.

She whispered into his bandaged ear. "What if I told Sal?"

His yellowish eyes opened. "You wouldn't," he said. "You wouldn't."

"Then get your hands off my tits."

And while he fumbled with her coat, Margaret arrived at the door.

The two bodyguards in the street never even questioned her. They worried about incoming traffic, not Margaret Tolstoy. She walked a couple of blocks and then took a cab uptown to one of LeComte's cribs. He was waiting for her in bed, wearing a robe Margaret herself had gotten for him at Saks: sort of a Christmas present he didn't deserve. But Margaret had to soothe the snake in him.

"Frederic," she said. "I hope you appreciate this. It's getting harder and harder to arrange these little séances. Sal's a light sleeper."

"Fuck Sal."

"I always do."

"I'll bet," LeComte told her.

Margaret undressed slowly, slowly, his snake eyes watching the curves of her flesh. She was fifty and she had to play the *danseuse*. She'd be swindling men until she died in some forgotten grave. LeComte was as big a thief as Sal or Jerry, but his game wasn't gelt. Justice supplied him with whatever capital he needed. LeComte liked to grab at your soul. She was his whore, his soldier, his slave, and his spy. He could deport her in five minutes, or send her floating out into deep space. Because she had no real identity without him. Sometimes she'd wake up without knowing which name she had to wear. Margaret Tolstoy, Margaret Tolstoy, she'd have to repeat to herself. Margaret Tolstoy. But it was better that way. She didn't have to toy with the illusion that she was some kind of being, some walking, talking self. She was a mechanical doll with the gift of skin.

"Tell me about Sal."

"He's terrific in bed."

"And me, Margaret?" His snake eyes closed and opened again.

"You, you're the worst lay in town."

He smiled. "I'm glad to hear that. It means we're like a married couple. What about the crusader himself, Sir Wilfred of Ivanhoe?"

"Who?"

"Isaac. What about Isaac?"

"That's not your business."

"Everything's my business," LeComte said.

"He's like a boy . . . he loves me."

"I know that. But how is he in bed?"

"Gentle. Sweet. He makes me want to cry. He's as lonely as I am."

"Lonely? You have Sal. You had Jerry DiAngelis. You have me. And Isaac has his worm."

"Why did you tell him about Ferdinand?"

"Had to," LeComte said. "He has his Syrian connection. King Farouk. And Farouk told him about your nights and days in Odessa. I couldn't deny it all. He would only have dug further."

"He followed me to the restaurant. He started calling me Magda. I had to get him out of there before Sal got suspicious."

"Fucking Ivanhoe. He'll ruin our gig. I'll have to keep the little man busy for a while. But it's your fault, Margaret. Why did you go to that baseball club?"

"I was curious. Isaac's the only history I have. He's like a lost relative, a cousin who followed me home from school. I wanted to make him, even then. But he was so fucking shy. His hands would tremble the minute he saw me. And I was sleeping with the janitor of the building. And one of my teachers."

"You've always been a busy girl. But what if I took you out of circulation . . . after we fix the Rubino clan? There's been too much exposure. We can't keep dying your hair. The bad boys from Chicago might start to connect with Jerry DiAngelis."

"I'm invisible," she said. "Men only see what they want to see. I could go for another fifty years. But my tits might sag after seventy. You'd have to pump me with hormones. Who can tell? I might grow a third tit?"

"No. We're retiring you, Margaret. It's too risky."

"And then what happens?"

"I'll set you up in a little house on G Street. I'll visit twice a week. I could even marry you. Off the books, of course. But you could still be Mrs. Frederic LeComte."

"I'd look like your momma in another ten years. You're the man who grows younger. That's because you have microchips instead of a heart. You piss lemon soda and you never bleed."

"Should I cut my finger for you, Margaret?"

"Forget it."

And he started to bite her lips.

He fell asleep like a baby after straddling her for twenty minutes. Margaret crouched in the dark, gathering her clothes. She'd get back to Sal before six.

Part Four

17

He couldn't release himself from that image of the bicycle boy's tongue thick in his mouth. The blue eyes of strangulation. And for some crazy reason the boy reminded him of Coen. He'd tossed Manfred into his own war with the Guzmanns, Peruvian pimps who were upsetting Isaac's borough in the years when he considered the whole of New York as his personal country. And Manfred got killed because of him, Manfred who'd been sleeping with Isaac's daughter, Marilyn the Wild. And Isaac inherited the worm, who haunted his body the way Coen haunted his head.

He'd never been religious. But Isaac wished he could enter some little shul, cover his balding skull with a prayer shawl, and sing his way to God. But there was no such shul, except perhaps in the dream world of Transnistria, and Isaac didn't have a magic glass that could bring back Russian Roumania. But he'd have to do something about the kid.

He could feel a man behind him. Isaac was always allergic to shadows that crept along his back. He ducked into a store

153

and came barreling out at Burton Bortelsman. "Damn you, Burt. You shouldn't trail me like that."

"Isaac, I read you the signal, Friar Tuck, and you hung up on me."

"That's because I had things on my mind."

"Well, I thought you might have been hurt. Besides, what's the good of exiling the Ivanhoes to Swan Lake? We can't track the Russians or the Saudis and the French."

"There are more important things than the Russians and the Saudis."

"Like what?"

"Sal Rubino and his little tribe of captains."

The Afrikaner laughed. "You'd like a little wet work on Sal?"

"I'm not an executioner. I'd like to hurt him in his pocketbook, cripple Sal's loan-sharking operation. But it has to be done with finesse. And be careful about Margaret Tolstoy. I don't want her touched."

"I'll be kind to the princess," Burt said. "Did you ever discover her pedigree . . . before she got to Manhattan as Margaret Tolstoy?"

"Didn't I tell you? She's LeComte's prize package. Busting up gangs for him from Florida to Seattle."

"And how did he inherit the package?"

"From the Bureau, via the KGB."

"Interesting," Burt said. "And I suppose with her dark eyes she was some sort of a swallow."

"She had plenty of experiences before she ever got to a KGB kindergarten. She was the child mistress of a crazy man, Ferdinand Antonescu. They had a long honeymoon in Odessa during the war."

"Sounds a bit farfetched. Do you think Moscow embroidered the tale? Careful, Isaac. The princess could still be KGB."

"That's why I sent you to the Catskills in the first place. But never mind Margaret. I want Sal's ass. Nothing rough, Burt.

No beatings. No bombs. Just steal his money however you can. I'd like him to be a pauper by the end of the month."

"Relax. We'll mortgage the man. But our lads need a new base. We can't accomplish much from that white hotel of yours."

"Use one of our warehouses. But when you're done with Sal you'll have to go back to Swan Lake."

"Bloody exile," Burt said, and wandered off. And Isaac walked to One Police Plaza. He could feel a chill on the commissioners' floor, as if he'd already become a pariah. His desk was clean. He had one or two papers to sign. His sergeants and his secretaries were polite, but he could have been inside a leper colony. His trials commissioner had canceled lunch. Sweets was out in the field. And Isaac had the dreaded stink of Internal Affairs about him. He was a PC under suspicion, and whoever got close to Isaac ran the risk of being tainted by him. Becky's people had boxed him out of his own Department. He could have raged, fought back, got himself a bloody lawyer. But he was sick of intrigues. His driver, Sergeant Malone, brought him a sandwich. Malone had this stubborn loyalty of the Irish. He was an old-line cop, a relic from Centre Street, where the Commish had a private gold elevator and functioned under a nest of chandeliers.

"Isaac," Malone said, "there's a lot of Judases in town. And some of them are right on this floor."

"I know."

"I spit on the bastards. I was there when they took Tiger John out of this very room, led him to the hall in handcuffs. It was no proper way to treat the Commish. You can't outrun these jackals, Isaac. What is it you intend to do?"

"Nothing."

"Then flee from here, for Christ's sake."

"I'm not a hider, like Maurie Goodstein."

"It's not Maurie I care about," Malone said. "These lawyers, Isaac, they have their own little league. But you're fair game for any prosecutor who'd like to build himself a reputation. . . . Isaac, I've been with the Department thirty-eight years. I've seen them rise and fall. And you're a falling man."

He went up to the Christys to peek at pictures on the wall. Home Run Baker. Heinie Zimmerman. And the Big Train, Walter Johnson. It was a liturgy he liked to think about. Those little lost gods of baseball. Who would ever worship Heinie Zimmerman after the arrival of Babe Ruth? No one but the Christys themselves.

He sat on a leather chair in the lounge. And while Isaac meditated, the Bomber appeared with his big hands.

"Isaac, come with me."

"I'm tired, Harry. I think I'll rest. It's peaceful here at the club. I can dream of my old favorites. Remember that one-armed bandit the Brownies brought up from the Memphis Chicks in 'forty-five? Pete Gray. Everybody called it a stunt. The Brownies needed a lift, they said. But I saw him, Harry. He moved like a magician. He could catch the ball, slide the glove off his hand, and throw bullets to the infield in one fucking motion."

"Isaac, Schyler wants to see you."

"You mean the president who disappeared from his own club?"

"Cut the comedy. I could smash you one."

"But I'm a guest, Harry, sitting in the lounge, minding my own business. I could complain to the steward of the club."

"I am the steward. I always was."

Isaac got up from his chair and followed the Bomber out of the Christy Mathewson Club. Harry had his own car. And Isaac wondered where the Bomber would take him. "Aren't you going to blindfold me?"

"No. But you can sit on the backseat. This is strictly a chauffeuring job."

Isaac climbed into the car. He could see the hairs on the Bomber's neck, the slightly wilted collar of his old hero who'd jumped to the Mexican League and left the Giants in last place.

"Harry, what was it like? Playing with Veracruz."

The hairs seemed to knot on the Bomber's neck. He wouldn't answer the PC. And Isaac couldn't unravel the Bomber's route. He was driving in a semicircle, passing the very same streets.

"Commissioner," he finally said. "It was baseball and there would have been no room for me on the Giants in 'forty-six. All the team's soldiers were coming back. I would have had a long sleep on the bench."

"Harry, how do you know that?"

The Bomber tilted his head. "Isaac, I was a war baby. Couldn't you tell? So I jumped to Veracruz. It wasn't for the extra cash. There were fires in the bleachers during every game. I couldn't eat the food. I'd get the shits. I found a woman. I married her. I played."

"*El béisbal mexicano.*"

"My eyes went bad. I had a kid with my *mujer*. A girl. She caught the measles. And then she died. I could still hit the long ball. But grounders would go right through my legs. I began crashing into the fences. I wore specs in the outfield. I was an old man at twenty-nine. The *mujer* stayed in Mexico. And I ran home to New York. . . . Isaac, don't fuck my head with your dreams."

"I'm sorry. I loved you in the outfield, that's all."

"Then love me a little less."

"I can't," Isaac said. "It's not in my nature."

The Bomber parked two blocks behind the Christy Mathewson Club. Both of them got out of the car. "You never moved Maurie, did you? He's in some secret closet at the club."

"You'll find out," the Bomber said.

They returned to the Christy Mathewson Club via the roofs. They stood on the club's roof deck for five minutes until the

Bomber felt it was safe. He smoked a cigarette, rocked along the roof's little gutter, and surveyed the streets. Isaac didn't care what the Bomber said about being a grandpa at twenty-nine. He still had the lithe walk of an outfielder in the Mexican League.

He knocked on the roof's narrow door. "Schyler, it's the Bomber and Isaac Sidel."

The door opened. The Bomber disappeared first. And then Isaac descended into the dark. He was the dummy of all time. Isaac should have listened harder to that male nurse. The nurse visited Maurie at the club because that's where Maurie was staying. And all the nonsense about coded pictures on the Christys' wall was a game to throw Isaac off the mark. If Allan Locksley "broke" the Christys' code, it was a code that Schyler wanted him to break. What had the message been? *Crash Landing.* Isaac was the only one who'd crashed.

He found himself in some old forgotten maid's room deep within the well of the roof. Schyler Knott was leaning against the wall. He wore his Christy Mathewson blazer, dark blue, with the golden emblem of a fielder's mitt above his heart.

"Where's Maurie?" Isaac growled.

"In good time, Isaac."

"I took you for granted, Schyler. That was my mistake. And no one really tried to strangle you. You invented that story."

"Not at all. It was true."

"But I didn't breathe a word to anyone about your connection with Maurice."

"Except your silly Ivanhoes . . . but it doesn't matter. I don't think you sent the strangler. That was a Jerry DiAngelis job."

"But Maurie is the only ace DiAngelis has. He can't go to court without him."

"Yes he can. But he'd rather not go to court at all. And he might not have to . . . if Maurie stays underground."

Isaac grinned. "Underground in the Christys' roof."

"I forgot. You're the singing policeman. So goddamn clever.

Maurie *is* underground. This roof is as much a grave as anywhere else."

"Then why did you send for me if I'm such a cow?"

"Isaac, I have the Bomber and a few old men. That's not much of a network. And I wanted you to see Maurice. He's suicidal. If I bring him to a convalescent home, LeComte will find out no matter what name I pick for Maurice. He's frightened of LeComte. He thinks the FBI is listening to his brain waves."

"What can I do?"

"I'm not sure. But you're the only one he isn't paranoid about. And I know the trouble you're in. You might even have less of a future than Maurice. Somehow that consoles me. I don't think you'll sell us out . . . come on. I'll take you to Maurie."

They crept out of that maid's room and into another, which was overheated and had a tiny dormer window covered from the inside with a metal grille. Maurie Goodstein sat in a child's rocking chair, its slats painted red. He wore trousers and an undershirt. He had no shoes. One of the Christys guarded him, an old man in the club's blazer. The old man left the room when Schyler and Isaac arrived.

Maurie didn't rock in his chair. He looked at Isaac and dribbled onto his undershirt. But his lawyer's eyes were as keen as they'd ever been. "They'll crucify you, you poor stupid bastard," he said.

"Happens all the time. My predecessor is sitting in Green Haven."

"Your predecessor was a thief."

"But you would have gotten him off, Maurie."

"Not a chance. You know what they call you at Justice? Ivanhoe. Which means schmuck in their language. You're the crusader man. Always crashing into windmills. Isaac Sidel wants to save the public schools, become the new chancellor. No one gives a shit about the schools. All they do at the Board of Ed is slide memos back and forth. But Ivanhoe wants to get in there. I wish you did. They'd bury you under a wall of paper."

"No they wouldn't," Isaac said. "And Maurie, you care as much about the schools as I do, even if most of your clients are scumbags. Why did you ask for me?"

"Because I'm dying," he said, and he began to rock in his tiny chair. "Isaac, I took from the till. I set up phony companies and accounts for Jerry DiAngelis and walked away with barrels of cash. I arranged hits."

"Was it pressure from Jerry or the melamed?"

"No, no. Once in my life I wanted to be Jesse James. Jewish boy from Park Avenue joins the mob. I'd waltz into court, the matador himself, and between cases I'd snort coke."

"What's that got to do with dying?"

"It's the Bureau. They're rotting my brain. They've got the machinery, Isaac. Tell LeComte to call it off."

"If they know where you are, Maurie, why don't they haul you in and indict your ass?"

"It's easier this way. Less publicity."

"Then why bother to hide?"

"Because I'm Maurie Goodstein. My father was a judge. I'd embarrass the cocksuckers in open court."

"But why would LeComte bother listening to Ivanhoe?"

"He likes you. You're his Hamilton Fellow. You captured Henry Lee."

Maurie rocked faster and faster and started to cry. Schyler had to hold the rocking chair. "It's all right, Maurice."

"I've been constipated for weeks," Maurie said. "I'm too scared to shit. My stools are radioactive. The Bureau can turn them into bombs."

Schyler called back Maurice's guardian and then walked with Isaac deeper into the well and climbed down to the top floor of the club. And suddenly Isaac was in the land of people, with guest rooms and a gallery of photographs on the wall.

"You can't closet him forever," Isaac said. "He'll go out of his mind. Make a deal with LeComte."

"If we went public, DiAngelis would wipe out the Christys, one by one."

"Then what would you like me to do? I'm the Commish. At least for a little while."

"I just wanted you to see him, Isaac, that's all. I think you can solve how to get to the street from here. And I wouldn't try the roof on your own. You might slip. And I'd feel responsible. Good-bye, Isaac."

The PC went down the winding stairs. He still couldn't figure this fucking case. He met the Bomber in the lounge. Perhaps Isaac was wrong about Harry. Veracruz might have been a better place than the Polo Grounds. The Bomber had done his military service in the Mexican League.

Isaac went home. His door was unlocked. He walked in gently, gently, wondering who might have set him up for a kill. He heard noises from the kitchen. Fucking amateurs.

He picked up a piece of vacuum-cleaner pipe from the hall closet. He held the pipe in his hand. Had Sal Rubino's little soldiers come to haunt him? The Commish wasn't going to evaporate without a fight. He entered the kitchen and saw a ghost. It was the bicycle boy, the geep who'd shot the melamed. But he didn't have wire around his neck. He was drinking a glass of milk from Isaac's fridge.

"Hello, grandpa."

Isaac blushed.

18

Captain Cole, that chief of detectives from St. Louis, was standing behind the kitchen door like a wanton bear, digging into a box of Rice Krispies.

"Glad you're enjoying my house, Loren. How the hell did you get in?"

"Sorry, Isaac. I'd have called first, but it ain't regular police business. I had to come on the sly."

"I asked you how you got in. That door is supposed to be pickproof."

"Some locksmith's been handing you a lot of lies."

"Show me your picks," Isaac said.

Loren removed a chamois cloth from his pocket. The cloth held a series of long silver needles, the finest picks Isaac had ever seen.

"I copped them off a second-story man. Are you satisfied?"

"And how's Mr. McCardle?"

"Ask him yourself," Loren said.

"I don't need asking," Kingsley McCardle said. "I'm doing

fine, grandpa. They sure don't take care of police chiefs in New York. This is a dump."

"Then you can stop drinking my milk."

"Aw, he didn't mean nothing. He's excited about being away from St. Louis. He's been living in that children's shelter half his life."

"I thought you were pretty content about leaving him in there."

"I was . . . until last night. We got a court order to give the boy up. One of my own people served the papers. They're figuring to get Kingsley on a manslaughter rap. Not while I'm alive."

"But it doesn't make sense. You hid him all these years. And now the courts wake up and find Kingsley McCardle."

"Don't ponder it, Isaac. It's one of them twists of fate. But I'd like to leave him with you for a while. I have to get back to St. Louis."

Loren winked at the boy, one hand still inside the Rice Krispies. "I'll miss my plane," he said. "Now you be good, Kingsley, and listen to the man."

"I'll get along with grandpa," Kingsley said.

Captain Cole started out the door with the Rice Krispies. Then he turned to Isaac. "Didn't mean to swipe your breakfast cereal."

"That's all right. You'll have something to munch on at the airport."

"And do me a kindness, Isaac. Don't call me at headquarters. I'll be in touch."

It was peculiar having someone live with him in the same house. He'd been a bachelor husband so long, without his daughter and Kathleen. Isaac didn't quite know how to move with Kingsley McCardle around him. But the boy seemed to navigate with his own invisible rudder in Isaac's rooms. He was never in the john when Isaac needed it. He didn't monopolize the fridge. He washed whatever plates he used. He got rid of the garbage. He'd arrived with toothpaste and dental floss in his pocket and a package of twenty-dollar bills.

"Is that some kind of allowance?" Isaac asked.

"No. It's my dowry."

"I don't understand."

"The captain gave it to me for working my butt off in that orphans' asylum."

"Should I open a bank account for you?"

"I don't trust banks," the boy said.

"Suit yourself. But I wouldn't carry all that cash around. Keep it in your room."

"A burglar might come."

"Well, then give the bundle to me. I'll hold it."

"Do you pay interest, grandpa?"

"What the hell for? I'm not borrowing from you."

"Then I'll hold the bundle myself."

"All right," Isaac growled. "But we'll have to find you a school, Mr. McCardle. You're twelve, aren't you?"

"Can't be sure."

"But you told me twelve. That's the one thing I remember from my trip to St. Louis."

"I could be fourteen. Uncle Sol wasn't too reliable about dates."

"Don't you have a birth certificate?"

"Not that I can recollect."

"You don't look fourteen to me. I'd say more like eleven. But we'll have to get you a certificate and another name."

"What's wrong with McCardle?"

"Nothing. But the courts are looking for you. And we wouldn't want to get the captain in trouble, would we?"

"Pshaw," McCardle said. "The captain can fix anything. He's Mr. St. Louis."

"Well, we don't have a Mr. New York. We have cardinals, mayors, and police chiefs."

"That ain't much, grandpa."

Isaac was already fatigued by his new parenthood. He had to get out of the little box they were in and breathe some winter air. McCardle was driving him crazy. Isaac got his chauffeur on the horn. "Sergeant, will you bring my bus?" And Malone was downstairs in ten minutes. Isaac introduced the boy.

"Sergeant Malone, this is my nephew, Kingsley McCardle."

McCardle stared at Isaac. "I thought I wasn't Kingsley anymore?"

"Don't mind him," Isaac muttered to Malone. "My nephew has bad manners."

The sergeant dropped them off at an abandoned stable where the Ivanhoes had established their new shop. McCardle loved the tall windows, the balconies, and the breadth of the stable, which reminded him of a ballpark without bleachers. The boy wasn't much interested in Isaac's men. He climbed up to the balconies and remained there like a wooden Indian.

The Afrikaner noticed him first. He'd been busy plotting the destruction of Sal Rubino when he looked up and saw this strange boy on the lower balcony. "Isaac, is that one of your commissioners?"

"I'll need a birth certificate," Isaac said. "A whole new legend."

"Ah, you brought me an illegal."

"Burt, I don't have the time," Isaac growled.

"All right," the Afrikaner said, reaching for a pad. "Name?"

"Mortimer Sidel."

"Middle initial?"

"None."

"Place of birth?"

"St. Mary's County, Maryland."

"Date of birth?"

"December twenty-fifth, Nineteen hundred and sixty-seven."

"A Christmas baby."

"Why not? I'll need report cards and stuff. Pick some rural school in Maryland no one's heard about. And I'll need death certificates for both his parents. Mother: Eva Gallant. Father: Samuel Sidel. Born and died in Maryland. I'll leave the dates and cause of death to you."

"And when do you want this merchandise?"

"By tomorrow."

"Impossible. I have seals to forge. I can't ruin Sal and attend to this monkey business."

"The boy has to go to school."

"Let him wait over the bloody weekend."

"Monday morning then. First thing."

Isaac started to whistle for McCardle, but the boy was already at his side, as if he could sense Isaac's own calendar and clock. They walked out of the stable and Sergeant Malone took them to Orchard Street. McCardle unfolded a twenty-dollar bill. "Sarge, thanks for the ride."

"You don't have to pay him," Isaac said. "The sergeant works for me."

"There's more to life than wages. And it's my dowry, grandpa, not yours."

Malone looked at the boy. "I appreciate it, Mr. McCardle. But the commissioner's right. I couldn't . . ." He saw that terrible wound in the boy's eye, as if he, Malone, had delivered a slap. "I'll make an exception this time, but promise me that you and the PC will come to dinner."

"No promises," McCardle said, stepping out of the car. "But I'll try."

The sergeant returned to One Police Plaza, and Isaac and the boy went into Abraham's of Orchard Street to buy Kingsley McCardle some school clothes. But a fight started in the store. The boy was interested in blue jeans and neckerchiefs and belts with silver buckles.

"Mr. McCardle, they don't have much room for cowpunch-
ers at St. Paul's."

Isaac planned to hide the boy in one of Cardinal Jim's
parochial schools. He didn't care what kind of waiting list the
school had. He'd pressure Cardinal Jim. He wouldn't lend *his*
boy to those lazy madmen at the Board of Ed, not while Alejo
was still chancellor.

"All right," Isaac said, "blue jeans *and* regular pants and a
jacket."

"I'm not paying for regular pants."

"Then we'll call it a gift from your grandpa."

"*Meshuga,*" Abraham's black assistant said, laughing at the
commissioner with gray sideburns and the grim, gray-looking
boy.

"What's he laughing at?" McCardle asked.

"You and me." And Isaac paid for McCardle's pants.

They left the store with Kingsley carrying his new ward-
robe in a big shopping bag. He paused in the middle of the
street. "Grandpa, someone's been following us."

"I know."

"Following us for a long time. I don't like it."

Kingsley had spotted a man in a London Fog coat and a
Donegal button-down cap.

"He's only doing his job," Isaac said.

"I still don't like it."

Isaac called out to the man. "Sergeant Hayes, will you come
here a minute?"

The man in the button-down cap crossed over to Isaac and
shrugged like a huge, awkward infant. "Commissioner, I'm
sorry . . ."

"Mr. McCardle, this is Sergeant Hayes of Internal Affairs.
He's sort of my shadow . . . when he can find me."

Hayes took off his cap and shook McCardle's hand. Then he
drifted to another block.

"That's better," McCardle said. "Now we can walk in
peace."

❈

Isaac, who was walking along his own doom line, trailed by Justice and Internal Affairs and Becky's corruptions commissioner, liked being McCardle's grandpa, the secret Santa Claus. He could have taken the boy up to the Christys, shown him all the batters and pitchers on the wall, but the Bomber would have interpreted it as a ruse, a means of spying on Maurie and the club. He wondered how much clout he had left. Would the Yankee management invite him and McCardle up to the Stadium on Opening Day to sit in the owner's box and drink champagne? The last time he'd seen Maurie as a sane man was Opening Day, 1981. Maurie had come like a king. Politicians of both parties gripped his hand. Even the governor and Cardinal Jim wanted to have a word with Maurie Goodstein, the mob lawyer.

But Isaac couldn't afford to dream until he turned McCardle into Mortimer Sidel, with report cards and fake parents and a seat in St. Paul's parochial school. They had Peking duck and red-bean ice cream in Chinatown. McCardle rolled the skin and meat of the duck into tiny pancakes, which he devoured. "Beats the shit out of St. Louis," he said. "I'm never going back."

"But you'll miss Stan Musial Day."

"I won't cry."

"And what about Captain Cole?"

"I'll send him a card," Kingsley said. "Grandpa, could you pass me the duck?"

They were sitting at a booth in one of Isaac's hideaways. And when Isaac looked up to offer McCardle some Peking duck, he saw the carcass of his first deputy commissioner. Sweets had slid into the booth, next to the boy, as if he were part of the family.

"I don't think you've met," Isaac muttered. "This is—"

"I know who it is, Isaac. Do us a favor."

"Us?" Isaac asked.

"Yes. I decided to bring a little war party."

And Isaac discovered three of his own detectives standing near the door of the restaurant with uncomfortable grins on their faces.

"Isaac, will you tell the young man to take a little stroll. Perhaps the cook will give him a tour of the kitchen."

"You could act civilized, Sweets, and say hello to the boy."

"I don't have the time, Isaac. I have a department to run. My boss has gone off into Indian country all on his own. He's a renegade now."

"Say hello to the boy."

"Hello, Kingsley," Sweets said, shaking the boy's hand with his own enormous paw.

"Grandpa, whose hand am I shaking?"

"It's all right, Mr. McCardle. This is Carlton Montgomery the Third. We call him Sweets. He's one of my deputy commissioners."

"I wouldn't want a commissioner like that."

Isaac smiled. "Oh, it's not his fault. I've become the great rogue elephant of the Police Department."

McCardle scrutinized Isaac. "Grandpa, you don't look like an elephant to me."

"That's awful kind, Mr. McCardle. But grab a little duck and ice cream and I'll be with you in a minute."

McCardle jumped around Sweets' tall knees like a giant grasshopper, clutching a dish of Peking duck and a bowl of ice cream. And then he was gone.

"Isaac, you're fucking out of your mind. You harbor a fugitive."

"He's a kid, Sweets, can't you see?"

"He happened to kill a man. And he's the property of St. Louis. I don't care if the courts make him a king. But it's not for you to decide."

"Now I understand how you got to me so fast. The Justice Department was singing in your ear. It was LeComte who snitched on the boy, LeComte who got the courts to reopen the boy's file, LeComte who had him followed to Manhattan, LeComte who told you where to find him."

"Blame yourself, Isaac. You've pissed him off. He's moving to indict DiAngelis again and you get in his way. Damn you, did you have to send your Ivanhoes after Sal? Couldn't you keep them in their closet?"

"I told you. I didn't like Rubino strangling that little bicycle boy."

"It wasn't Sal, Isaac. It wasn't Sal. We have two witnesses. It was Jerry's brother, Nose, who put the make on the kid."

"I don't believe it."

"A couple of old warehousemen saw him at the scene, carrying a big duffel bag. I'd bet my life the boy was in that bag."

"Then why the fuck aren't you arresting the Nose?"

"Because the old men are scared shitless. They'd never testify in court."

"Why don't you dig a little and see if your old men are FBI informants?"

"And suppose they are."

"It's a plant, Sweets. LeComte will do anything to nail Jerry. It was Sal who killed the boy. Forget LeComte's magic witnesses."

"But I can't forget Kingsley McCardle. I'm putting him on a plane to St. Louis."

"You'll have to kill me first."

"Isaac . . . you saw the detectives. We could shackle your hands and feet."

"I don't care. You'll have to kill me."

The First Dep began to eat Isaac's ice cream.

"Sweets," Isaac said. "Give me one more day. And I'll surrender Mr. McCardle. I promise. But let me do the arrangements."

"Isaac, you are a rogue elephant. You're capable of putting that boy in deep cover. And we'll never find him."

"Here," Isaac said, clutching a ballpoint pen. "I'll write you a fucking affidavit on the menu. I'll resign tomorrow if I don't deliver the boy. And you can hold my badge."

Sweets looked in Isaac's face. "I don't want your badge." He freed both his kneecaps from the confines of the booth and limped out of the restaurant.

19

L/eComte.

Isaac had been playing Ivanhoe in Alexander Hamilton's clothes. And LeComte was the magician . . . and puppeteer. Justice owned the Commish. LeComte had broken Maurie, had used Margaret Tolstoy as a love doll in the war between the old Rubino captains and Jerry DiAngelis, had manipulated Isaac, sent him into the provinces to sing and dance and talk about Henry Armstrong Lee. But Isaac had discovered America on that trip, had visited orphanages and penal colonies, worked in the fields with convicts under a raw, terrifying sun, his lips parched, his throat burning, but he wouldn't drink water until the convicts were allowed to drink. The jailors were a little scared of Isaac. He'd come to them with the imprimatur of the Justice Department. How could they have known that Isaac himself was like a love doll, LeComte's little geisha boy who performed for whole populations of police chiefs?

And now LeComte had brought Kingsley McCardle into his fucking circus, had jeopardized the boy to get at Ivanhoe,

172

and Ivanhoe didn't like it. He couldn't run to the mayor. He'd been shut out of City Hall. And the governor would have nothing to do with Isaac Sidel. But neither of them would have taken on LeComte. Isaac had to go to the Powerhouse.

He called St. Patrick's Cathedral. But the cardinal was on the road, visiting parishes in the Bronx. "It's urgent," he told the cardinal's secretary, and Isaac's call was switched to Jim's car telephone.

"Ah, it's the hairy boy himself. How are you, Isaac?" the cardinal asked.

"Not good."

"I've been hearing about your troubles . . . from all sorts of people. Isaac, I can't interfere. I have my own sheep to protect."

"I know that, Jim. But I have a child in my custody. He needs help."

"A lad, you say?" The cardinal was as fond of children as Isaac was. They both piloted baseball teams for the Police Athletic League. The cardinal was a cruel, efficient manager. Jim's teams always won. "The lad, what's his name?"

"Kingsley McCardle. An orphan from St. Louis."

"Bring him along then, will you, Isaac? I'm in a rush. Meet me at Fox Street in half an hour."

Isaac didn't want to be late for Cardinal Jim. But he had to slick the boy's hair down and tighten his neckerchief and get Sergeant Malone. The three of them drove across the Willis Avenue Bridge and entered that Indian country of the South Bronx with the sergeant's siren on. The boy gazed out the window like a stricken child. He'd seen the slums of St. Louis. But not mountains of rubble with a church in the middle. Rats played in the rubble. They looked like little crocodiles. He could almost see into their eyes.

Isaac arrived at Fox Street a minute early. The cardinal was waiting in his black Lincoln. The boy had to smile. A big shiny bus like that seemed impractical around all the rats.

"Don't dawdle," Isaac said. "And be polite to Cardinal Jim."

Isaac and the boy got out of the Dodge and climbed into the cardinal's car. Jim was wearing a skullcap and a pectoral cross and a red sash around his middle. He sat smoking a cigarette. There was tobacco on his fingers when he shook the boy's hand. "Ah, it's a rotten habit," he said. "But I can't function without five cigarettes a day."

"Hello, Father," the boy said.

"Kingsley," Isaac muttered, "you're talking to the cardinal."

"He's still a priest, ain't he?" the boy said.

"Isaac, leave him alone. He argues like a Jesuit. I like your Mr. McCardle."

Kingsley McCardle kept staring. He couldn't reconcile that skullcap and the pectoral cross. He wasn't idiotic about religions. But he wondered if the cardinal was a rabbi too. "Father, do you ever think of girls?"

"What kind of question is that?" Isaac said, feeling his chances to enlist the cardinal fall out of his grasp. He should have let McCardle remain in the Dodge.

But Jim ignored Isaac and turned to the boy. "You mean in a carnal fashion?"

"Yes, Father. I do."

"Well," Jim said, devouring half the cigarette while tobacco spilled onto the skirts of his robe. "I wasn't celibate when I was a boy."

"But now, Father?"

"I'm not a eunuch, Mr. McCardle. I dance with the prettiest ladies I can find. That's my deviltry. . . . Isaac, what can I do for the lad?"

"Get him home on the qt."

"I ain't goin'," the boy said. "I like it here."

"Shhh, Mr. McCardle," Jim said. "Isaac, what's preventing you?"

"The courts will pounce all over him. They'll eat him alive. It's LeComte. He's getting back at me by sabotaging Mr. McCardle."

"Well, what's the boy done?"

"Killed his uncle."

"Shite," the cardinal said.

"It was self-defense. The uncle was a brute."

"How old was the boy when it happened?"

"Seven or eight."

The cardinal maneuvered the cigarette in his mouth like a worm with one eye; an enormous piece of ash dangled at its edge. "Isaac, no court in the land would touch a boy who committed a crime at the age of seven."

"But they'll publicize the event. They'll get jurisdiction over Mr. McCardle. And he'll be a ward of St. Louis for life."

"Isaac, I have the Church to consider. And you want me to make an enemy of LeComte. . . . Mr. McCardle, are you a Christian lad?"

"I think so, Father. Uncle never took me to church."

"A bit of a heathen, eh? And you had to protect your own life?"

"It was him or me, Father. Him or me."

"I believe you," Jim said, the ash still jutting from his mouth. He knocked on the partition that separated him from his black chauffeur. "Charles, be a good man and get me the White House, will you?"

Kingsley was suspicious about some guy in a skullcap calling the White House. He heard buttons being punched behind the glass wall. Then a slot opened in the wall and the black chauffeur handed Cardinal Jim a telephone.

"Edith, hello. How's the president? Will you ask him if he can spare a minute for old Jim?"

The cardinal held a hand over the mouthpiece. He started to whisper and the cigarette dropped into his lap. Isaac had to beat at the ashes. "Never mind," the cardinal said. "Isaac, I'll have to tell a couple of fibs."

He took his hand off the mouthpiece. "Hello, Mr. President. I'm fine. . . . I have a celebrity in the car. Isaac

Sidel. . . . Indeed, the Hamilton Fellow. Well, Justice has been hampering him a bit. Seems Isaac met a boy in St. Louis at the city shelter. A darling lad. The commissioner sort of adopted him. From afar, I mean. And somehow the courts have gotten involved. They want to take him out of his home. The lad's an orphan. He likes it where he is. And I was hoping . . . Yes, Mr. President. His name is Kingsley McCardle. . . . Of course. I know you wouldn't want to trample on Justice. . . . Yes, he's right here."

The cardinal motioned to Isaac. "Will you take the bloody phone? The president wants a word with you."

Isaac clutched Jim's car phone like a cumbersome bear. He was a Democrat, reared during the reign of Franklin Delano Roosevelt, and he had no love for a Republican White House. He'd guarded Richard Nixon after his fall from grace, when Nixon had a town house in New York. Isaac hadn't believed in that brouhaha over Watergate. Presidents needed "plumbers," like police commissioners did. But he'd never been on a direct line to the White House.

"Hello," the president said, and the big bear was bewildered. The cardinal had to jab him in the ribs before Isaac could speak.

"Hello, Mr. President."

"We're proud of you, Isaac. My wife and I watched you on television when you caught Henry Lee. It was clever of him to wear a woman's skirts. But you were magnificent."

"Thank you, Mr. President."

His hands were shaking, and Cardinal Jim had to return the phone to his black chauffeur.

"A darling man, the president is, wouldn't you say so?"

"But will he—"

"Isaac, it's done. The lad is safe. Now will you get out of here before the FBI arrests me."

Isaac and Kingsley McCardle climbed out of the car.

"Isaac," the cardinal asked, "how is your pension plan?"

"I'm not sure."

"Hold on to it, son. . . . Good-bye, Mr. McCardle. I'll look you up in St. Louis."

And the Lincoln drove across the rubble of Fox Street.

Kingsley had liked that cardinal in the skullcap, but he worried for his grandpa. Isaac shouldn't have had such a pie-face when he talked to the president.

☩

He felt a bleakness at the airport. The arrangements had been made. The boy was flying United to St. Louis. A car service would meet his plane and return him to the shelter. And the courts would develop amnesia concerning Mr. McCardle. But Isaac didn't really want to let go. He'd learned to admire Kingsley's neckerchief. He loved having breakfast with him, and long, long dinners in Chinatown.

"Smile, grandpa," McCardle said, as both of them waited for the flight. "I'm the one who has to go back to kiddie jail. I'll never graduate."

"Yes you will. The captain promised. He's going to find you a chair at Washington University."

"Pshaw," McCardle said. "I can read menus and baseball scores, but not a book."

"No one can stop you from reading."

"Grandpa, the sentences don't hold in my head."

"I'll ask Loren to locate a tutor."

"Wouldn't work. It's become a habit with me," McCardle said. "You're going to jail, ain't you, grandpa?"

"Not if I can help it."

"But that's what the father was hinting at when he talked about your pension plan."

"Talk is talk," Isaac said.

"Grandpa, we could hide together. I don't have to get on that plane. St. Louis has some streets that nobody wants to remember. We could get there by car."

"It's tempting," Isaac said. "But I can't."

The boy was given his boarding pass. He didn't quite know how to say good-bye. "You could write to me, grandpa, from prison. I'd be proud to get your letters." And then he ran to the gate.

20

Isaac fell into a wicked depression without the boy. It had nothing to do with the beast in his belly. He missed McCardle. The boy had reminded him how lonely he was. He'd played detective too long. He wasn't some medieval knight home from the crusades. Sir Wilfred of Ivanhoe. He was more like a mechanical bear. But even a bear had particular needs. And this bear had a sudden desire for family. He called his daughter in Seattle. Her husband picked up the phone. And Isaac was embarrassed. Because he couldn't recollect the husband's name. She was always moving from man to man. But the bear remembered just in time.

"Hello, Mark," he said. Mark was a public defender, a lawyer of the people. He couldn't have earned enough for them to afford a decent house and a car. The lawyer probably had to walk to work. Marilyn was constantly falling in love with lost causes, like Mark or Manfred Coen. Isaac had been much happier when Blue Eyes was around. Perhaps he had his own affinity for damaged goods.

"Mark, I'd like to speak to Marilyn."

"I'll see what I can do," Mark said. Isaac heard him put down the receiver. He'd developed monstrous ears. Mark was pleading with Marilyn. But Isaac couldn't catch his daughter's voice until he recognized a scream. It was Marilyn the Wild. "Fuck," she said. Mark returned to the line.

"She can't talk right now. She's taking a nap."

"Yes," Isaac repeated. "Taking a nap." She blamed him for Blue Eyes. And Marilyn had Isaac's nature. She could never forgive.

"Congratulations," Mark said.

"What have I done?"

"You put the bank robber away."

"But suppose," Isaac said, like some bitter melamed, "suppose you had been representing Henry Armstrong Lee."

"I only deal with the indigent," Mark said. "Your man busted up people and robbed banks."

"But he was caught with twenty cents in his pocket."

"Isaac, it was a federal case. And I work for the City of Seattle."

Off the fucking hook, Isaac muttered. They always get off the hook. That's how lawyers operate. And it doesn't matter much if their clients are rich or poor. But Maurie was the exception. He would have waived his fee and had the jury crying for the Most Wanted Man in America.

"Mark, will you tell her something? I miss Blue Eyes as much as she does. Good-bye."

He'd have to keep away from orphans. It hurt too much. But Isaac was drawn to sad people. He'd adopted Blue Eyes, promoted him to detective first grade, and then got him killed. But thank God Kingsley McCardle wasn't a cop. And Isaac began to consider that other orphan, Margaret Tolstoy. Ah, he *was* medieval. Because he couldn't stop caring about Dracula's Daughter, even though she'd probably betrayed him. But it was the worm, the worm had unhinged Wilfred of Ivanhoe.

Not his Ivanhoes. Sal was bleeding money from both ears.

His shylocks were losing a lot of cash. Ivanhoes would grab their little satchels right off the street, or enter Sal's countinghouses with handkerchief-masks, like Billy the Kid. Or play the part of Sal's own bagmen and collect from all his clients. There were no car bombs. No shotgun blasts. Just a persistent grinding down of Sal Rubino. The Ivanhoes forged his signature and relieved him of the revenue in his legitimate accounts. Isaac should have gloated, but he couldn't get out of his gloom.

One of the Department's own chaplains, Rabbi Horatio Goode, visited Isaac at his flat. He was much more secular than the other chaplains. Isaac had approved a gun permit for Rabbi Goode, and the chaplain wore his Police Special in a holster near his heart. He'd also been a chaplain in the Marines. He was a cowboy from Oklahoma, as burly as Isaac himself, and he never played the pious man. He was president of the Hands of Esau, the fraternal order of Jewish cops, but Isaac wouldn't attend meetings once he became Commish. He didn't want to set off rivalries between the different orders. He wasn't a Jewish police commissioner, only the Commish.

They had a glass of whiskey together. "Isaac, I think you ought to visit a shrink. I don't mean Department bullshit. I can recommend an excellent man. It will all be confidential, of course."

"Do I look that bad to you, Rabbi?"

"I talked to Cardinal Jim. He agrees. You're drifting, Isaac. Do you know how many appointments you've missed? I'm not sure what you've done. And I couldn't care less."

"Rabbi, I'm an atheist," Isaac said.

"You're still part of my congregation."

"What congregation? You don't have a shul."

"The Department is my shul," the rabbi said.

"I've killed people," Isaac said.

"That goes with the job."

"It hasn't always been for the Department. I've bent the rules."

"That's between you and your Maker. But you ought to talk."

"Rabbi, I read somewhere that Freud analyzed his own daughter. Now what kind of shrink would do that?"

"He was a remarkable person," the rabbi said.

"His own fucking daughter. What could Freud have told her? Darling, we'll forget the Oedipus complex?"

"Electra, Isaac, the Electra complex."

"No, Freud treated her like a man. . . . I have a daughter, Rabbi. She hates my guts. . . . I'll survive without a shrink."

❦

He had no appetite, but he wouldn't neglect the worm. He brought his milk bottle wherever he went. He waited and waited and wasn't surprised when he got a call from Becky's corruptions commissioner. Boris Michaelson. He sucked on the milk for good measure. "Isaac, can you come to my office tomorrow? We have things to discuss."

"I'll look at my calendar," Isaac said. But he had no calendar. "Yes, Boris, I can squeeze you in . . . what time?"

"Say after lunch. Around half-past two."

"Perfect."

Isaac hung up and smiled in the mirror. His appetite returned. Becky had sent her vulture, and now Isaac could fight back. He owed nothing to Her Honor, who'd kept him on as police chief when she arrived at City Hall. She could have sacked him, but Isaac was a popular PC. They'd become lovers of some sort until Isaac found his old schoolmate, Margaret Tolstoy. And then politics fell out the window for Isaac Sidel.

He had bowl after bowl of egg-drop soup in Chinatown. He had Peking duck with plum sauce, even though it bothered him a bit to swallow the duck without Kingsley McCardle. He had shrimp balls with hot peppers. He had General Ming's chicken. He drank plum wine with the chef. He had pistachio ice cream until his belly ached. He'd glutted the worm and Isaac walked home like a drunken tent, his body pitching from side to side.

He slept until noon.

He shaved in the bathtub.

He wore a clean shirt and his best cologne.

He arrived at Michaelson's office on Maiden Lane. It was two twenty-nine. The corruptions commissioner had his "Three Sisters," his own little gang of young prosecutors who'd become notorious in Manhattan. Michaelson had a mandate from the governor *and* Becky Karp to get at the bad guys who worked for the City of New York. And the governor had provided him with three top assistant attorney generals. None of them was as old as thirty. They'd all graduated from Columbia Law and could have earned fortunes in private practice. But they wouldn't leave Boris. They had detectives and auditors and City marshals at their disposal. They could reach into any department, seize whatever books they needed, and preside over the arrest of an errant commissioner. Isaac was high on their list. He was the catch these witches wanted to make.

Their names were Susan Sodaman, Selma Beard, and Trish Van Loon. One of them was married, the other two were engaged, but they didn't contemplate having children until they were thirty-five. And Isaac wondered what a witch's child would look like. But he had to admit. They were the most attractive witches he'd ever seen. Tall, long-legged women, while Michaelson himself was short and fat, with little hairs protruding from his nose. The Three Sisters adored him.

The worm began to eat at Isaac, eat and eat. The Commish sucked on his milk bottle before Michaelson even opened his mouth. The worm was scared of the Three Sisters.

"You're looking pale," Susan Sodaman said. "Would you like to sit?"

"It'll pass," Isaac said. "Now tell me what you want."

"Your resignation," Michaelson said.

And suddenly the worm stopped pulling and was Isaac's ally again. "Boris, did you bring your handcuffs?"

"We don't want to hurt you," Michaelson said. "You're the hero of New York."

"Well, either cuff me, or leave me alone."

"It's not as simple as all that," Michaelson said. And the Three Sisters surrounded Isaac with all their splendid height.

"You've become an embarrassment," Selma said.

"You've put yourself right in the middle of a RICO case," Trish said. The Racketeer-Influenced Corrupt-Organization Act, better known as RICO, was a 1970 law that hadn't been used against the Mafia until LeComte came along. He didn't have to prosecute Jerry DiAngelis for an individual murder, which was always hard to prove. He could weave an entire history together, produce a little fable in open court, and show that DiAngelis was the chief of a family involved in the business of crime. The Feds had gone after DiAngelis and Isaac had gotten in the way.

RICO, Isaac muttered. "You mean Jerry and the melamed?"

Michaelson laughed. "The melamed? That's rich. Isadore Wasser is the brains behind Jerry's half of the Rubino clan. And he's a fucking thief."

"Don't curse," Isaac said. "There's ladies around. And Isadore is a friend of mine."

"That's the problem," Michaelson said. "He's a little too much of a friend. Isaac, we've taped you talking to the old man. We have you on video with DiAngelis outside his rifle club."

"It's a free country," Isaac said.

"Not for a police commissioner it ain't. You've been handing them information, Isaac. I could toss you to the Feds."

"What's stopping you?"

"You're one of us, one of our own."

"Boris, I'd rather belong to Izzy than you."

"Isaac, how much cash do you have in the bank?"

"You tell me."

"Nine hundred dollars and sixty-six cents," Trish said.

"Can you afford to lose your fucking pension? Resign, Isaac, that's the only way out. Internal Affairs has enough on you to fry your ass right within the walls of One Police Plaza. Isaac, give up. Go out with a little glory. We don't want to prosecute. Forget Jerry. You've been sleeping with a Soviet agent who likes to call herself Margaret Tolstoy. And you've been handing out baseball cards to Syria's chief of counterintelligence for the whole American desk."

"Ismail?" Isaac muttered. "He's a clerk."

"His name is Amid Rashid. . . . I think you'd better find yourself a lawyer."

"I have a lawyer. Maurie Goodstein."

"That's a riot," Michaelson said, winking at the Three Sisters. "Maurie's on the moon. He can't afford to show his face. His lawyer-client privilege don't mean shit. Not with RICO on the books. When Jerry goes down, he'll go down too."

"He's still my lawyer," Isaac said.

"I'm glad you like to be represented by a ghost."

"He isn't a ghost," one of the sisters said. "At least not yet."

"And even if he appears, Isaac, and LeComte shows him a little mercy, he's useless to you. Maurie's all coked up. He can't put two sentences together."

"How the hell would you know?" Isaac asked.

"I've talked with him on the phone. Oh yeah, Maurie's been making overtures. I'm his emissary, Isaac. You should have figured that out. I'll have to negotiate for him with LeComte when the time is right. Now be a good boy."

"Fuck you and your Three Sisters," Isaac said. "You didn't call me here for my satisfaction. You'd love to nail me. That's been your dream all along. But it's Becky who's reined you in."

"You're wrong, Isaac. She wants you out. You're worthless to Becky."

"Remember," Isaac said, "she's living in a house of cards. Touch me, and the house could fall."

"We'll take our chances," Michaelson said.

"I'm happy for you."

"Isaac, what about the boy?"

"Which boy?"

"Ah, what's his name again?"

The Three Sisters went into the folders on Michaelson's desk. "Kingsley McCardle," Selma said.

"I get it now. LeComte sang you a song and you put the squeeze on my First Dep."

"But the boy had no business being here."

"I returned him, Boris, didn't I?"

"He's still under deep cover. And I happen to be friendly with a certain judge in St. Louis."

Isaac hopped around the table and grabbed at Michaelson's tie before the Three Sisters slapped at him with their folders and called in one of Isaac's own cops. The cop had to wrestle with the police commissioner, remove his hands from Michaelson's throat.

"Boris, what should we do with this imbecile?" Selma said.

Michaelson coughed. He couldn't speak for a moment. "Get him out of my sight," he finally said.

And Isaac left the corruptions commissioner and his Three Sisters, who had a dark silver look in their eyes. He marched down into the street and walked along the bend of Maiden Lane, past the Federal Reserve Bank, with its dark and light gray stones, its steel doors, and its turret on top. America's own money castle. He was trembling now. He shouldn't have given up the boy. And then he muttered *"Ismail."* What an idiot Isaac had been. The Syrian spy chief and his Jewish connection. And the PC had thought he was befriending a lonely man. The Syrians must have researched Isaac's interest in baseball. And Ismail had prepared his own fucking legend. Damascus could smile at Isaac Sidel. Amid Rashid, alias Ismail, alias King Farouk, had the singing policeman in the palm of his hand.

21

Somehow he couldn't go back to his lair, or find much solace at One Police Plaza. His office was filled with spies. And so he trundled into DiAngelis' territories for a cup of *caffelatte* to clear his head, but before he arrived at his favorite trattoria, he discovered Nose in the street. And something about Jerry's brother seemed peculiar. Nose was stuck in the dream of his own thoughts. Isaac could almost feel the grindings of his brain. And Nose was a man who wasn't paid to think. He delivered beatings for his brother and then tattled to the FBI. But Teddy Boy was mumbling to himself and walked right past the Commish, who sacrificed his *caffelatte* to follow Ted.

It couldn't have been some score, because Nose would have brought his shooters along. He didn't like being alone. Nose couldn't amuse himself. He had to have his *compares* or the company of a woman. That's why he stuck to Eileen DiAngelis, ate her food like the infant of the house, or visited a *puttana*.

Isaac watched the back of his head. Teddy's ears were

188

wiggling. His neck was dirty. He'd been too preoccupied to wash. He got to the northern end of Mulberry Street, stood in front of a house, rubbed his hands to keep them warm, and shouted up at a window. "Silvana, come downstairs."

It wasn't a little song that was meant to die in the winter air. Nose was bellowing like Caruso. "Silvana, come down to me."

Isaac understood. Nose was in love. And this Silvana could only have been his *innamorata*. Isaac felt a sudden sympathy for FBI Informant M 76666. Nose was bats about a woman, like Don Isacco himself.

She came downstairs, his Silvana. Isaac wouldn't have considered her a beauty. Her hips were too wide. Her mouth was smeared with purple paint. She had a mole under one eye. But who was Isaac to judge? He'd fallen for the child mistress of a Roumanian madman, the Butcher of Bucharest. Isaac's *innamorata* had slept with five hundred men.

He almost called out to Ted—It's me, Isaac—when a man came down after Silvana with a hammer in his hand. The guy stood freezing in his undershirt and hissed at Ted.

But Nose wasn't concerned about the hammer. "Get back upstairs, Al. Save your own fucking life."

"She's my woman," Al said.

"That's yesterday's news."

"She's my woman." Al drew close to Ted with the hammer. Ted didn't flinch. And that's when Isaac noticed him draw a little derringer out of his sleeve. A lady's gun. A single-shot. Al stared at the gun and started to shiver. He was crying now. He turned away from Silvana and disappeared into the house.

Isaac's head was blue with hate. He could have jumped on Teddy Boy. But he left him with his *innamorata* on Mulberry Street.

The melamed had been removed from intensive care. He had a private room at the top of St. Vincent's. There were flowers and bonbons on his bedside table. Isaac had brought him one yellow rose.

"Ah, that's kind. A flower from a friend. And I'm fond of yellow."

"It's the color of courtship," Isaac said.

The melamed smiled. "I'm a little too old for that."

"A special courtship. It goes back to the Middle Ages. When two knights would joust in a tournament, their squires would exchange a yellow rose."

"Where did you read that?"

"In a book. When I was a boy."

"So you didn't come here to wish me well."

"No, Izzy. I didn't. I was imagining what it would be like to put a pillow over your face."

"Be my guest. I couldn't stop you," the melamed said.

"You could ring for a nurse."

"Nah, I wouldn't ring. It's not my style."

"It was Nose who killed Jerry's accountant, wasn't it? Nose was his best friend. He brought me to Crabbs, took me home, and then returned to Swan Lake with his little fucking derringer, the derringer he holds in his sleeve, like a magician. It was your idea, Iz. You wanted me to think that Margaret Tolstoy had clipped her husband."

"Isaac, she's a rat for the FBI. We had to do Crabbs. He was getting nervous, and he would have started to sing. It was Margaret's fault."

"But why did you take her in? You didn't have to let her near the Family."

"Have a heart," the melamed said. "You can't learn everything in a day. But she doesn't have much of a future, that girl. We told Sal Rubino all about her."

And for a moment Isaac did have the urge to suffocate the Hebrew school teacher with a pillow. "You told him? Just like that?"

"It was a gift. A belated Hanukkah present."

"I thought you weren't speaking to Sal."

"Oh, we speak from time to time. He's tried to kill me and my son-in-law, but we're still part of the same Family . . . and Isaac, I don't think it was much of a gift. This Margaret of yours did some sloppy work in Chicago, under another name. It would have gotten to Sal, sooner or later."

"Why didn't you finish her yourself?"

"We would have, but you stepped into the picture. She ran to Sal, thinking he could save her neck. Poor girl."

"And the bicycle boy," Isaac said. "That wasn't Sal Rubino."

The melamed peered out of his bedcovers. "I must have heartburn. I'm missing the point."

"The zip who shot you in the street. It was Teddy who strangled him and left him hanging in one of your warehouses, so I'd think it was Sal."

"Isaac, you butted into this mess the minute you took up with Margaret. Now don't call yourself an innocent party. Why shouldn't we return Sal's favor? That boy put a hole in me."

"Come on. He was a kid. Twelve or thirteen at the most."

"Cry for him, Isaac. Run to shul. The boy was a member of Sal's crew."

"It wasn't vengeance," Isaac said. "I know you better than that. It was a strategy to suck me into the war. You shouldn't have hurt that kid. You could have found another way."

"There was no other way," the melamed said. "Do you want your flower back?"

"No, Iz."

⚜

He was the chessplayer now, the tactician, manager of his own phantom Giants. He had to get Margaret Tolstoy away from Sal Rubino. He could have gone to the candy man, LeComte. LeComte would have pulled the plug, withdrawn Margaret from circulation. But how would he have treated Margaret once she was no longer valuable to him? Isaac couldn't afford the risk. He had his Ivanhoes. He could have mounted a kidnapping operation, but he didn't want whole armies moving about. It would have brought too much attention to Margaret and unmasked his own men. And the Ivanhoes were busy ruining Sal. Don Isacco had to laugh at the irony of it all. Sal hadn't strangled the bicycle boy. But he wouldn't have a nickel by the end of the week.

Isaac left his Ivanhoes in place. He wanted a whirlwind around Sal Rubino. It would be easier for him to grab Margaret amid all the confusion. He would move on Sal without an army, become his own rook and bishop, shortstop and second baseman.

He arrived at Sal Rubino's Manhattan address. He announced himself to the doorman, flashed his shield with the five gold stars. The doorman recognized Isaac. His hands were trembling as he connected the intercom. "Mr. Rubino, you have a guest. It's the commissioner, sir. Isaac Sidel."

And Isaac took the elevator to the north penthouse. One of Sal's captains, Eddie Boy, let him in. He had a bandage on his ear. He was grinning like an idiot. It was Ed who had socked Isaac with a sack of dimes, Ed who had tried to strangle him in the toilet of the steak house.

"How are you, Commish? It's a lovely surprise."

The soldier took Isaac all around the flat, from the foyer to the sunken living room to Sal's own den. But Sal wasn't in as kind a mood as his captain.

"You have some fucking nerve," he said.

Isaac played the ignorant son. "What do you mean, Sal?"

"You think I don't know what's been going down? Jerry DiAngelis wouldn't hit my shylocks. So I got the Hebrew teacher on the phone. I like Izzy Wasser. I really do. And his daughter is one handsome lady. Jerry DiAngelis doesn't deserve Eileen."

"Tell it to Jerry," Isaac said.

"I already did. I'd marry Eileen in a minute. . . . Isaac, your scumbags have been hitting up my people. And somebody's gotta pay."

"Why don't you call One Police Plaza and negotiate with the Department's chief counsel?"

"Because the geeps you're using aren't regular cops. They're like kamikaze pilots. Fuckin' suicide squads. They don't scare."

"I don't give a shit about your shylocks," Isaac said. "I want your *comare*."

Sal Rubino smiled. He was wearing a leather jacket with a silk scarf around his neck. He couldn't allow the other dons to entertain the notion that DiAngelis was a better dresser than Sal. "Which *comare* do you mean?"

"I'm only interested in Margaret Tolstoy. I have to question her . . . about a case that doesn't concern you."

"Do you have a warrant, Mr. Isaac, some piece of paper from a judge?"

"I don't need a warrant," Isaac said. "I could arrest her if I want."

"You can't arrest Margaret. You're not a peace officer. You're a lousy, stinking Commish. But I'll be fair, Isaac. I'll let Margaret decide." And he started to scream. "Hey, honey, come here . . . Margaret, I'm talking to you, you bitch. Get your ass into my room."

Margaret appeared in the doorway without the least bit of paint. Her almond eyes wouldn't receive Isaac. Her mouth was pale. She had nothing for the Commish. Not one little finger. He could have been some ancient delivery boy. The worm started purring and stopped.

"Honey," Sal said. "The Commish wants you to go with him. It's your choice."

"I'm staying with you." And she marched out of the den.

"The queen has spoken," Sal said. "You lose."

Eddie arrived with three other soldiers. They were carrying brass knuckles and baseball bats. Eddie himself had a gorgeous Louisville Slugger. Isaac couldn't stop admiring the bat, though his heart was pounding like an insane machine.

"Isaac," Sal said. "You must have lost your marbles. You

don't cripple a man and come into his house. . . . Ed, take him downstairs in the service car."

"Aren't you forgetting a couple of details, Sal? I didn't come unannounced. The doorman let me in."

"So what? He works for me. I own the building, Isaac. My tenants take a vow of silence when they sign the lease."

"But I have your name in my appointment book."

"Bullshit. Isaac, you're all alone."

He got into the service car with Sal's four soldiers. Eddie clutched a lever and the car jumped from floor to floor and descended into the bowels of the building. Isaac felt like he was in the bloody heart of a whale. They hadn't used their knuckles yet. But one of the soldiers prodded him with a bat. They landed in the basement and Eddie opened the elevator door and that's when they started to thump Isaac with all the brass. They pushed him along like a dirty old cow. The knuckles ate into his back. But Eddie had to satisfy himself. He twisted Isaac around and punched him in the face. "That's for what you did to me in Sal's restaurant."

But they wouldn't let Isaac fall. They dug the bats under his arms and carried him along like a coolie, while Isaac swallowed his own blood. Ah, what would he miss the most? Memories of Marilyn as a little girl? Blue Eyes? Margaret Tolstoy? The Bomber shagging fly balls in center field? His friend from St. Louis, Kingsley McCardle? He started to cry.

"Eddie, look, he's pissing in his pants."

"I'm not pissing," Isaac said.

"Then what do you call boohooing in a cellar like a baby?"

"It's my privilege," Isaac said. "It's my right."

They brought him out through the service entrance. A car was waiting for them in the street. The back door opened. A pair of hands clutched at Isaac and tossed him into the cushions. Eddie blinked at the driver.

"Hey, this isn't Otto. What the fuck is going on?"

The car shot away from the curb and Isaac looked up at the mandarin eyes of King Farouk and the Syrian secret service.

"Ismail," Isaac said, his teeth soaked in blood. "Give me back my baseball card."

22

"**G**oose Goslin," Isaac spoke from the depths of Ismail's cushions. "I want the Goose."

"My friend, your mouth is bleeding."

"You're not my friend. You're a phantom. A fucking spook . . . Ismail, did you find me in Moscow's data bank? Is that how you learned I was a card collector?"

"We're not that close to Moscow at the moment. And I can assure you, Isaac, I've been collecting baseball cards all my life . . . here, wipe your mouth."

King Farouk gave Isaac a handkerchief that was half the size of a shawl. Isaac hawked up blood and phlegm into the handkerchief, folded it, and returned it to Farouk. "Thank you," he muttered with a hollow head. His ears still rang from the force of Eddie's blow. His own words were coming up from inside a well, and Isaac was swimming in some crazy water with bullfrogs all around him. Farouk himself was a frog. Isaac closed his eyes and fell into a dream.

He woke up on a couch of many pillows. At first he couldn't find his legs. He panicked until he realized they were under

196

the pillows somewhere. And then he wondered if he was in Damascus, because who could tell what the Syrians were after. The show trial of a Jewish cop? He poked his head out of the pillows but he couldn't see much of a sky beyond the window shades. Then Farouk appeared with a coffeepot and powdered candy called Turkish delight. Isaac ate like a wolf. "Where are we?"

"In a safe house."

"That tells me a lot."

"Does the neighborhood really matter so much?"

"It certainly does if we're in Damascus."

Farouk started to laugh, but he must have thought it was impolite, because he covered his mouth. "You think too highly of me, my friend. We're in Brooklyn. Cobble Hill."

"That figures," Isaac said. "The candy comes from Atlantic Avenue. I've had it before."

"Ah, now you're thinking like a police chief again. The paranoia is gone perhaps?"

"How did you know I'd be coming out of Sal Rubino's cellar? Who tipped you off?"

"Margaret Tolstoy."

"Jesus," Isaac said. "I give up. Is she also a Syrian agent?"

"No. She does favors for us from time to time."

"Like sleeping with men you wanted to blackmail. She was the perfect swallow, wasn't she? Until the FBI borrowed her from the Russians and made her into a scalp hunter. I still can't figure how she got in touch with you so fast."

"On our hot line. Margaret called from the kitchen while you were with Mr. Rubino."

"But Sal's soldiers were all over the place. They would have listened."

"We have our own private language. The soldiers wouldn't have understood a word."

Isaac felt demoralized. Ismail was his Santa Claus. Should Isaac kiss him on both cheeks? "Why does LeComte call you King Farouk?"

"Because the Americans love their precious code names. Isaac, do I look like much of a king? Farouk was a playboy and I'm almost a monk. Egyptians, Syrians, Saudis, we're all the same to Uncle Sam."

"But I'm not Uncle. And I'm not Frederic LeComte. You used me, Ismail."

"Yes. A little. But if I had revealed who I was, would you have chatted with me, Isaac? It was better to remain an anonymous clerk. You needed bits of information, and I gave them to you. I helped you, Isaac, whenever I could."

"And what was the price? You registered me as an informant in your little black book."

"I have no such book," Ismail said. "And you are my friend. I valued that. And I shared my love of baseball with you. How many commissioners collect cards?"

"I wouldn't know."

"I can return the Goose Goslin if you want," Ismail said, like the sad-eyed clerk he was supposed to be.

"Keep it. I'm not an Indian giver. The Goose is yours."

"And I have a surprise . . . if you're not too tired."

"What?"

"Margaret," Ismail whispered, and a woman stepped out of the dark. "I'll leave you both," Ismail said.

Isaac observed her from the pillows. He couldn't see much more than Margaret's silhouette. "You were standing there . . . all this time? You heard our conversation?"

"No," she said. "I just arrived. And I can't stay more than a couple of minutes."

"You're with the Syrians," Isaac said, like a mean-natured boy.

"The Syrians saved your life."

"Come closer, Margaret. I can't see enough of you."

"I'm Anastasia," she said. "I told you that."

"Yeah. You're Anastasia in my dreams. And you're Margaret Tolstoy when you're in Indian country, working for LeComte."

"I'm still Anastasia." And she stepped nearer to Isaac, with the boldness of the girl who'd invaded his junior high.

"I want to know about Ferdinand Antonescu."

"What difference could it make?"

"I want to know."

She smiled at the Commish and her ripeness seemed to shatter the darkness of the room. "It was a hundred lives ago."

"Did you love him?"

"Yes."

"That's all you have to say?"

"Isaac, I met him in Bucharest when I was nine. He was my ballet master."

"Some career he had. Magician. Ballet master. And finance minister of his own country."

"He gave me private lessons. I was poor. I couldn't afford a school. And he was . . . a balletomane."

"And you were his mistress right off the bat."

"Don't soil him, Isaac, please. I fell in love. But that was later."

"How much later? When you were eleven?"

"It doesn't concern you, Isaac. I came to see how you were."

"Tell me about Odessa . . . during the war."

"What's there to tell? We lived in the palace of some forgotten count or prince. A Jewish count, if there ever was such a thing. Czar Nicholas welcomed a couple of Jewish bankers into the nobility, I think."

"And that's how you got obsessed with Anastasia. While you were in that palace."

"No. It was long before that. I loved the idea of a lost princess. Anastasia appealed to me. So I borrowed her name."

"And did the little princess go around Odessa in Ferdinand's official car?"

"Sometimes," she said. "Isaac, you could never imagine. People sold human flesh on the black market. Ferdinand established his own currency. He would print more and more of it, but it was always worthless within a week. We had to steal chickens to survive . . . and we were rich. But Isaac, I don't have the time. Sal took a nap after lunch. He'll wake up and start asking for me."

"Margaret, he knows. That's why I knocked on his door. Are you deaf? He knows you're with LeComte. He'll kill you. You've got to get away from Sal."

"Isaac, I'm going to break him. That's my job. And don't you interfere again."

"Jesus, I'm not getting through. He's talked with the melamed about your career in Chicago as LeComte's little gangbuster. He'll kill you, I said."

"No he won't. You don't understand the first thing about Sal. He enjoys the danger of having me around. That's what turns him on. He loves me, Isaac."

"So do I."

"But you're not one of my tricks."

"Yes I am," Isaac said. "Yes I am."

"Don't ruin it for me, Isaac. I want to take him down."

"Margaret, does LeComte give you some kind of commission for every scalp you bring in?"

"No," she said. "It's the work. I'm good at it. And if you go near Sal, you'll get me killed."

The worm pulled at Isaac in Margaret's presence. But it wouldn't purr.

"I'm sorry," she said, "for what Sal did to your face."

"It wasn't Sal. It was his captain, the one with the dirty-yellow eyes."

"Oh, Eddie. I never liked him."

And her silhouette jumped about the room. She was Sal's moll. And why did he have to think of samovars? Now he understood the worm's maneuvers. The beast was mourning Margaret.

"Anastasia, did you love me a little when I was a boy?"

"No. Yes. No."

He saw the full crop of her hair, the little scar under her lip that was like a gorgeous caterpillar in the gloomy light.

"Isaac, I'd been with Ferdinand. I'd lived with him as his wife. And you were some fresh kid. I'm not sure if I loved you. But I remembered those dark eyes of yours. That means something."

He sat one entire night in the Syrian safe house. His mouth was still bruised. Ismail couldn't keep him company. Isaac had other baby-sitters. And it wasn't much fun, though they fed him that powdered candy. They weren't collectors. They knew nothing about baseball. And he had little desire to talk shop with a bunch of Syrian bandits. He bathed, swabbed the inside of his mouth with a salt solution, and left the safe house. He rode the subway out of Brooklyn, searched for phantoms behind his back, shadow men from the Internal Affairs Division, and went uptown to the stable where his Ivanhoes were.

The street was a little too quiet.

Isaac entered the stable. The morning light beat upon the balconies. He could have been in some holy manger. But there was no straw around, no horses and donkeys, no three wise, magical men.

The Ivanhoes had fled without a trace.

There was nothing that could suggest a command post for Isaac's own police, not a pencil or the scuff marks of a shoe or a coded message on a wall, the simple signs that Burton Bortelsman might have left. Nothing for Isaac.

He was a bad penny, a broken shoe. Even the worm had started to snore.

Part Five

23

He didn't have to wait for the house to fall. His sergeants got him on the phone that very afternoon. Isaac was almost grateful. He was wanted on the fourteenth floor. He went to One Police Plaza wearing a baggy coat and a suit that he'd bought out of a secondhand bin. The collar of his shirt was cracked. His tie had a couple of egg stains. His belt had come off his own father's pants. He picked his socks carefully. They had the same color. The heels of his shoes were practically gone. But he had his milk bottle.

He said hello to the sergeants and his secretaries and sat at his desk. No one visited him or came in to water the plants. The quiet around Isaac was like the eve of an electrical storm. The air breathed its own blue color.

And then the pounding started. Soft at first, as if it had arrived from another planet, and Isaac was only the innocent observer of a doom that didn't belong to him.

He was sitting where Teddy Roosevelt had once sat, that stouthearted man with a mustache, rooting out corruption wherever he went, wandering into the old Tombs to bring out

205

a convict who happened to belong to Connecticut, not New York; and sometimes he'd stand in the yard and exercise with the convicts themselves, because Commissioner Ted believed that a man who exercised must have some moral worth. The desk was an oak affair with such deep drawers that Isaac could have stuffed his whole experience into them and all the shirts he'd ever had. But they weren't deep enough for him to hide. And the noises were getting louder and louder until Isaac thought the walls would melt from the heat of all the bodies outside his room. They wouldn't offer him the last little dignity of announcing who the hell they were. He deserved that. He was the Commish, like Teddy Roosevelt had been, long before Isaac.

They barreled into his office, a mob of women and men, with Boris Michaelson as their leader. The corruptions commissioner had arrived with his Three Sisters and half the reporters in Manhattan. There wasn't enough room for them all. They destroyed Isaac's plants. But not even Michaelson could pronounce the magic words. He was a bit of a prosecutor, not a policeman. They had to wait for Deputy Chief Inspector Morris McCall, head of Internal Affairs. And Morris was at the back of that little circus. He was taking his time.

There was no pleasure in McCall's eyes. He wasn't really part of the mob. He was only the arresting officer. He'd been in Isaac's graduating class at the Police Academy. He was an old-line cop, ferocious and polite. He believed in protocol.

"Begging your pardon, Commissioner, but you're under arrest."

Isaac was booked at the precinct on Ericsson Place, like Tiger John. Two PCs in a row had been marched out of their domain in handcuffs, like common criminals. Reporters snarled in his face. "Anything to tell us, Isaac?"

"Talk to Michaelson. He's an eloquent man."

And while Isaac was being printed and photographed,

Becky Karp appeared on the five o'clock news. McCall allowed Isaac to watch Becky on the precinct's tiny television set. The reception was poor and Becky Karp had to compete with ghosts of herself. "It's a sad day," she said. "We've all been so fond of Commissioner Sidel. He's still innocent in my eyes. But I would never block an investigation."

"Your Honor, will you fire him?" a reporter asked.

"Not a chance. But I'll have to suspend him without pay."

And Isaac was trundled off to the Criminal Courts Building at 100 Centre Street. He sat in the holding pen with black prostitutes and their pimps, Latino drug dealers, men who might have jumped bail and were back for another sitdown with the judge, a madwoman who talked to Jesus. Isaac seemed like the only Anglo in town, and no one was really sure of his roots. The mayor was hoping to humble Isaac, teach him a lesson. But Isaac wasn't forlorn in the holding pen. It was much quieter than the emergency ward at Bellevue.

He was called upstairs to the arraignment room, which was like a big, dirty library without books, and was charged with two counts of "bribe receiving in the second degree." Isaac had used his office to become involved in a criminal enterprise, a family of crime. There was a bit of a tangle at the bench. The judge had asked where Isaac's counsel was, and Isaac mentioned Maurie's name. The judge smiled. He was fond of Isaac. He was also some kind of a king at Manhattan Criminal Court. "Isaac, you can't be represented by an invisible man."

"He'll show in good time," Isaac said. "Meanwhile, Your Honor, I'm communing with Maurie and taking care of myself."

The judge offered to postpone the arraignment, but Isaac said no.

"Then the court will have to get you a counselor until Mr. Goodstein decides to come."

There was a grab bag of legal aid lawyers lurking in court. They looked almost as broken as Isaac.

"Mr. Swanberg," the judge said to one of these broken men. "I'm assigning you to Mr. Sidel. There will be a fifteen-minute recess."

"Recess, recess," Isaac muttered with a crack in his mouth. He knew Owen Swanberg, who bled money out of prostitutes and crazy old women.

Isaac stood in the corner with Swanberg. "Owen, fuck you." And he returned to the bench.

Swanberg pulled on his ratty tie. "For the record, Your Honor, my client refuses to confer with me."

The judge could have been Roy Bean in the badlands of Manhattan. He made the law, and he was losing his patience. "I can whistle your client off to Bellevue if you like and request a psychiatric exam."

Isaac muttered in Owen's ear. "Your Honor, may we have a few more minutes?" Swanberg asked.

"But no more tricks."

And Isaac waltzed back into the corner with Owen Swanberg. "Owen, if you don't do exactly what I tell you, I'll bust your balls every day of the week. I'll get affidavits from all the old ladies you swindled out of cash. And if I can't find them, Owen, I'll invent a few."

"I don't understand," Swanberg said.

"I need a rest."

"I don't understand."

"Just shut up and bring me home."

They were like a comedy team, Swanberg and Sidel.

"Well, how does your client plead to the charges?"

"Not guilty," Swanberg said.

"Let the court note that Isaac Sidel has been a good policeman," the judge said. "And I'd like to release him on his own cognizance if Ms. Beard doesn't mind."

The Three Sisters huddled with Boris.

"No objections, Your Honor," Selma Beard said. Boris

didn't want Isaac to sit in jail. It would make a martyr out of the Commish and might hurt Becky's chances at the polls.

Isaac muttered again in Owen's ear. "Your Honor, my client cannot accept the court's generosity. The charges are grave. He might bump into criminals on the street and—"

"Mr. Swanberg," the judge said.

"He could have an irresistible urge."

"Mr. Swanberg." The judge was angry now. Isaac had mocked his office. And Isaac wasn't king of this court. "Then your client will have to come back. I'm not setting bail tonight."

Isaac slept in the basement. He found a cockroach in his pants.

The judge was still angry in the morning. He stared at Owen and Isaac and set bail at sixty thousand dollars. "I hope that will keep your client from bumping into too many criminals."

⚜

Isaac was brought downstairs and put on a bus to Riker's Island. He was one more piece of garbage, him with the swollen mouth, handcuffed and chained to a bench. He sat among all the prostitutes and petty thieves and imbeciles who couldn't make bail. But Isaac was some borderline case. He looked like a bum, but the bondsmen upstairs at Criminal Court would have secured Isaac's bail if only he'd winked at them. But Isaac wouldn't wink. He wanted a little jail time. A burglar sitting next to Isaac on the bus scowled at him. "What the fuck is a white man doing on our bus?"

The black corrections officer who was in the "shotgun seat" told the burglar to shut his face. The officer moved closer to Isaac. He had a little gold star in his ear, like some lost prince of Riker's Island. He was the tallest man on the bus. "Commissioner, I heard you talk once. About the projects in Brooklyn and the Bronx. You know all the shit that's going down. But you shouldn't have gone after Henry Lee. He was

our last hero, man. He was telling it to Uncle. He didn't care
about no banks. He supported every church in Harlem. He
visited hospitals and the old folks' home. That's why he wore
them skirts. He needed a good disguise."

"What's your name, son?"

"Isaac, like you," the officer said.

"Well, Isaac, if I hadn't gone in after Henry, my associates
would have shot him dead."

He was put in the isolation ward at the House of Detention.
He lived among a society of fallen public servants, child
molesters, and stool pigeons waiting for their trials, men who
wouldn't have stood much of a chance among the general
population of prisoners. And so they took their meals alone in
a little dining room and had a tiny yard to play in. But they
had to pass another cellblock to get to their yard. And the
prisoners would hiss at them or hurl light bulbs at their heads.

The child molesters clung to Isaac. He had to hold their
hands like infants. The rogue cops and deputy commissioners
would bunch at the end of this ragtail line. But it was Isaac
who got most of the flack. The Rastafarians and black Muslims
would murmur, "Henry Lee, Henry Lee." Isaac stared into
their eyes, as if his own psyche was entering their cells, and
the Muslims grew to admire him. But they wouldn't stop
murmuring "Henry Lee."

One of them broke into the isolation ward and started to
strangle a child molester, and it was Isaac who had to lift the
Muslim off the molester's back. "Are you the monkey man?"
the Muslim asked.

"No. I'm just Isaac Sidel." And to show his good faith he
helped smuggle this Muslim out of the ward. "Thanks for the
visit. But if you come again, I'll break your fucking skull."

And a kind of truce was declared. The lads from the
isolation ward could go to their playpen, and all they had to
endure was some hissing and songs about Henry Lee.

The warden visited Isaac in his cell. His name was Salinger. He'd been a policeman once, a member of the Hands of Esau, that order of Jewish cops.

"They crucified you," he said. "Michaelson arrests you in front of your own men and brings you to Criminal Court like a fucking animal."

"It's politics, Warden. Rebecca wants to embarrass me."

"Without an indictment?"

"She'll get her indictment. The Three Sisters are probably sitting with Michaelson's grand jury right this minute."

"It's Mickey Mouse time. Michaelson will have to cut you loose."

"We'll see," Isaac said. "The corruptions commissioner is a clever boy."

The warden took a little plum cake out of his pocket and shared it with Isaac. "Anything I can do, just ask." And then he disappeared.

Isaac wasn't lonely. He imagined whole progenies of baseball players out of the past. Socks Seibold. Bubbles Hargrave. Braggo Roth. Cotton Tierney. Sheriff Blake. Flint Rhem. General Crowder. And the Goose. Baseball had become Isaac's America. It had "naturalized" a boy from the Lower East Side. And the names themselves were like a river Isaac could journey on. He had his own Mississippi at Riker's Island. With Bubbles Hargrave and Braggo Roth.

A guard knocked on Isaac's door. "Telephone call."

Isaac received the call in a special booth that had been built for the isolation ward. It was made of Plexiglas and looked like some curious time bubble, a contoured womb.

"Hello, grandpa."

Isaac shivered and cried in the bubble. It tore at him that his first phone call at Riker's should be from a boy in a brother institution.

"How are you, Mr. McCardle? I guess you must have heard the news."

"Grandpa, I'm not so sure you can take care of yourself."

"I think you're right. I functioned better when you were around."

"I could come and live with you again."

"They wouldn't let you into Riker's. I'm a prisoner, Mr. McCardle."

"I'm a prisoner too," the boy said.

"No you're not. That's a children's shelter you're at."

"It's a jail, grandpa. Just like yours."

"Kingsley," Isaac asked, "are you studying for college?"

"I'd never get in."

And the line went dead on Isaac. He stood in the bubble until a guard retrieved him and returned Isaac to his cell.

There was a furor that afternoon. The cardinal had come to Riker's. He wore his red beanie. The Rastafarians had never seen such a prince of the Church. And even the Muslims showed their respect. "Morning, Cardinal."

"Good morning to you."

Jim smiled as he stepped along the narrow bridge between the different tiers of cells. Warden Salinger had offered to accompany him, but the cardinal didn't want the chief screw on his ride across Riker's. He got to the isolation ward and sat down with Isaac in the visitors' room while a little gang of blue-eyed boys stuck close to Isaac.

"Who are these comely lads?" the cardinal asked.

"Child molesters," Isaac said.

"Jesus Christ. You'll give me a heart attack one of these days." And the cardinal took out a pack of cigarettes. "Can we have a little privacy?"

"Of course," Isaac said, and turned to the leader of the gang, a young Latino with the bluest eyes of them all. "Macho, will you go to the checkerboards, *por favor?*" But Macho kneeled down and whispered in Isaac's ear.

"Jim, Macho would like to kiss your cardinal's ring."

The cardinal's own blue eyes began to twist in his head.

"Isaac, I can't allow it. He's a bloody pervert . . . attacked a child, didn't he?"

"He hasn't been convicted yet. He's waiting trial, like the rest of us."

"I can't," the cardinal said.

And Macho went away with the other blue-eyed boys.

The cardinal lit his cigarette with faltering hands and blew ribbons of smoke around Isaac's ears. "He subpoenaed me, the little shit."

"Michaelson?"

"Michaelson, indeed. I had to meet with his Three Sisters."

"I'm sorry, Jim."

"It's not your fault," the cardinal said. "He's playing Oliver Cromwell. I'll excommunicate the man."

"He isn't Catholic."

"I'll get a dispensation from the pope," the cardinal said with a wink. "He's bumping around in the dark, asking me questions about your finances. They'll never indict you."

"Yes they will. The grand jury will give the Sisters whatever they want."

"You should have been more careful. You were reckless, Isaac. Who's your lawyer?"

"Maurie Goodstein."

The cardinal coughed out a little ball of smoke. "You're insane. I can't ask our own lad to represent you. Wouldn't be kosher. He's with the archdiocese. But I can have his law partner look into your affairs."

"Thank you, Jim. But I'll go with Maurice."

"Is it suicide you're thinking of? LeComte will subpoena him the second he shows his face."

"I'll take my chances."

"At least let me make a few calls, so I can come up with a bond that will get you out of this hole. Mind, the Church can't be involved directly. But I have a couple of friends."

"I like it here," Isaac said.

"It's madness. Sitting with child molesters . . . Isaac, I won't be able to visit you again."

The grand jury returned a true bill on Isaac's fifth day in the ward. The Three Sisters wove a little history of Isaac as a rotten police chief *and* a soldier of crime. He was the pirate of One Police Plaza.

There was a rejoicing in the other cellblocks. And Isaac thought that the Muslims and the Rastafarians were celebrating his own fall from grace. But it wasn't Isaac they were celebrating. It was Henry Armstrong Lee. He'd escaped from the federal penitentiary at Leavenworth, Kansas, on the afternoon of Don Isacco's indictment. It never should have happened. The pen was situated inside a military compound. But Henry Lee had stepped out of Fort Leavenworth in women's clothes. It was the first prison break at the fort in seventeen years.

And there was so much singing, so much carrying on at Riker's, that the warden had to suspend yard privileges and take away the prisoners' ice cream. It would have caused a riot on another afternoon. But the Muslims and the Rastafarians forgot about dinner. They had Henry Lee on their minds. The Rastafarians prayed to their own Jesus, Haile Selasse, the Lion of Judah, for Henry's safe return to Harlem. He couldn't function anywhere else. Harlem was his blood country. Harlem was where he lived. And for the second time in his life Henry Armstrong Lee was America's Most Wanted Man.

And it was into this madhouse of rejoicing that Isaac's daughter came. Marilyn the Wild had flown in from Seattle to see her dad. Isaac was scared to death. He didn't want to confront his daughter. He'd found some peace in the isolation ward. But he shuffled into the same room where he'd met Cardinal Jim.

"We sold the house," she said. That was her hello to Father Isaac. But she didn't seem worn after eight or nine husbands.

She had her mother's Irish temper and Isaac's own stubborn ways. The worm clawed Isaac's belly and then curled into a fist, hiding from the ghost of Blue Eyes, Manfred Coen.

"How's your husband?" Isaac asked. "How's Mark?"

"We sold the house."

"Aren't you happy in Seattle?"

"Don't talk like an idiot. Just tell me which bondsman to go to. I'm sort of rusty."

"You don't need a bondsman. I'm staying where I am."

"Yes, my father the jailbird. It suits your complexion. You never liked the sun. But you'll get tired of it. I know you, Isaac. It's another part for you to play. So let's end this little drama and tell me what to do. Or should I go to the chief rabbi at One Police Plaza?"

"Marilyn, you don't understand. I could have made bail. I don't want it."

"Good. Then I can get my house back. And we have nothing to discuss."

"Marilyn."

"Good-bye, Isaac, good-bye."

The blood was boiling up in Marilyn. But he didn't dare touch her, hold her. She would have screamed.

"Baby," he said.

That one word halted Marilyn the Wild. She turned on Isaac with such fury that he thought he'd drown in the dry air together with his worm.

"Don't you ever call me that."

"Sorry," he said.

"Sorry for what?"

"Coen."

She slapped his face and Isaac was glad there was no iron grille between them. The warden had removed it. He had a celebrity in the house, the first Alexander Hamilton Fellow.

Isaac nearly grinned. If he couldn't get a kiss from his daughter, a slap would have to do.

"If you say 'Coen' again, I'll kill you, Daddy dear."

"I thought I could save him."

"He loved you, Isaac. And you shuffled him around like one more pawn."

"I'm a policeman, for Christ's sake. He grew up with that gang of pimps. I had to throw him into the pot. . . . I didn't mean for him to die."

"Yes you did. You couldn't bear it, Daddy dear, that I was crazy about Coen." She started to cry. "God, he was so sweet . . . and so dumb. He never even noticed how you were using him. We were orphans, Manfred and me. That's why I liked him so much."

"You're no orphan," Isaac said.

But Marilyn was gone.

24

He wasn't sworn in at the Blue Room of Rebecca's City Hall. He would have dreaded that. All the mayor's clowns patting him on the shoulder. There were no ceremonies for Sweets. He was only the Acting Commish. He wore Isaac's badge, sat at Isaac's desk, delivered lectures at the Harlem Ecumenical Council and B'nai B'rith. He was wanted on talk shows five nights a week. Pretty ladies powdered his face. He was introduced as the first black police commissioner the NYPD ever had. And it didn't matter how many times Sweets said he was only minding the store until Isaac came back.

"Commissioner Montgomery, Isaac isn't coming back."

"Don't let him fool you," Sweets had to declare. "He's like the Count of Monte Cristo. Isaac always comes back."

He couldn't see his children. He couldn't make love to his wife. Carlton Montgomery III had become a public creature. And now Sweets understood why Isaac had behaved like a gypsy in this room, why he'd gone off the edge of the earth and created the Ivanhoes when he had his own Intelligence

Division that could have monitored the Russians and the Iranian mission. Isaac had to find some fucking way to get back out into the field.

Sweets settled disputes between the chief of detectives and the chief of patrol. He addressed the brotherhood of black policemen and the Shamrock Society of Irish cops. The Irishers had been taking sick leave and wouldn't go to work while their "prince" was banished to Riker's Island. They invoked the name of Brian Boru, the first high king of Ireland, and Isaac was only a Yid whose granddad had come out of London, if Sweets remembered right. The Hands of Esau wouldn't even prepare a statement about Isaac's condition. The Polish and Italians were quiet. But the most conservative of all the societies had suddenly become a radical wing.

Rebecca wanted to punish the Shamrocks. "Get rid of them. Dock their pay." But she didn't understand her own Police Department. If the Irish walked, the structure would start to crumble. A fourth of the precincts would become ghost towns. And Carlton Montgomery III wasn't going to fight Brian Boru.

He met with the Shamrocks, assured them that he didn't covet Isaac's job. And one by one the Irishers came back to work. Even Isaac's driver, Sergeant Malone, returned. And he chauffeured Sweets from one banquet or church or synagogue or television studio to the next. The sergeant drove him to a mosque in Bushwick where Sweets had to swear that his Intelligence Division hadn't tried to infiltrate the Nation of Islam. And then he had to run home to his Intelligence chief and see if it was true.

"Inspector Hines, keep out of that fucking mosque."

"There's been talk that the bastards are making bombs."

"I don't believe it. And if you have any hard information, hand it to the FBI."

Hines beat the heel of one shoe with a little stick. "Isaac said I shouldn't get too chummy with the Bureau. They could turn around and slap us on the head."

"That's not a problem. You can always slap them right back."

It wasn't Hines' fault. The job was filled with minefields. The magic rabbis and all their Brooklyn bodyguards who had disliked Sweets when he was First Dep began inviting him to the darkest corners of their synagogues where they cooked food and lent him a prayer shawl, while the bloods in Williamsburg and Crown Heights grew suspicious of the Acting PC. You couldn't win. And for a moment Sweets wished he had his own corporation of Ivanhoes who could disappear at will.

Sergeants jumped when he arrived on the fourteenth floor. He couldn't have little chats with deputy chiefs. Every twist of his mouth was interpreted, taken as a sign. No one would criticize him. His plants were watered religiously. He was all alone.

And when LeComte called from Georgetown, asked him for a meet, it was the Acting PC who picked the time and the place. Sweets didn't want him around the building. It was LeComte who had hastened Isaac's fall, encouraged him to develop new "countries" outside the ken of the Police Department. There couldn't have been any Ivanhoes without LeComte.

⚜

They met at a wine cellar near Gold Street. It was a haven for young brokers who were romancing their secretaries. But Sweets had come before the five-o'clock rush. He'd secured a booth for himself and LeComte, who arrived from D.C. on the midafternoon shuttle. LeComte had narrow shoulders and a cockatoo's colorful crest. He wore a shirt with pink and blue stripes. He had little ears. His mouth was like a rip across his face. He had a cellist's hands. He'd never have been able to strangle a man.

"Has Rebecca been treating you right?" he asked, clutching a goblet of wine with those hands of his.

"I avoid Rebecca whenever I can."

"Well, she'll come calling close to the primaries. You're the hotshot in town."

"Really?" Sweets said. "Next thing I know you'll name me the new Hamilton Fellow."

LeComte laughed, and his chest started to quake. Sweets felt like grabbing LeComte and flinging him across the wine cellar.

"Isaac's tenure is for the whole year," LeComte said.

"Does that include jail time?"

"I'm not sure. I haven't prepared the rule book on Hamilton Fellows."

"The only rule book, LeComte, is what's inside your fucking head . . . you abandoned Isaac. You sold him out to Oliver Cromwell and his Three Sisters. Michaelson wouldn't go to the toilet without asking your permission."

"That's not true," LeComte said in the dark of the wine cellar. The waiter had brought them apples and cheese. And Carlton Montgomery III, who'd been raised around nannies and black governesses, watched LeComte cut an apple into four perfect quadrants. Not even Carlton's dad had that kind of precision at the dining room table. Who the hell was this man from Justice, this Mormon who rose out of Salt Lake City to ride herd over Manhattan? "I didn't want him to indict," LeComte said, eating one of the quadrants. "But Michaelson has big plans for himself."

"Stop it," Sweets said. "You could have killed the whole indictment idea."

"And have it look like I'm tampering with the City's top investigation team? . . . I had to give him Isaac."

"It still doesn't make sense. Isaac knows Internal Affairs is shadowing him. He could have gone to Poplar Street and jerked McCall around until IAD is shitting bullets and Isaac is in the clear. But he allows the investigations to continue. He doesn't bother McCall. He wears handcuffs instead, makes fun of the judge who's arraigning him, and rides out to Riker's."

"Isaac willed it on himself."

"No," Sweets said. "It's another one of his capers. Like the time he moved into the Guzmanns' candy store and pretended he was on the take. He lost his shield—"

"And Manfred Coen. And the Guzmanns gave him that worm."

"I don't care. It's another caper. Isaac can't survive without a lick of Indian country. That's how he deals. He lives inside the elephant's ass. I'd never have understood . . . until I became Acting PC. I'd rather have the heart of darkness than this. All I am, LeComte, is Rebecca's armpit, a public relations man."

"Did you get a call from the Three Sisters?"

"Hell no. I'd destroy Michaelson's grand jury room if Selma Beard ever monkeyed with me."

"Selma could use you on the stand. But she knows you're loyal to Isaac. You'd make a bad witness."

"Is that why I came to Gold Street? To discuss the merits of Isaac's case?"

LeComte swallowed the second quandrant. "Try a piece of apple. It's delicious."

"How can I help you, LeComte?"

"By pulling your tigers off Jerry DiAngelis and Sal Rubino. I don't want some red-hot detective getting in my way. I've got Jerry and Sal. All I have to do is squeeze a little harder and they'll self-destruct. Half of Sal's soldiers are already brain dead. And with the Hebrew teacher in the hospital, Jerry's kind of hopeless."

"I'll back off," Sweets said. "But pull that broad."

LeComte finished the third and fourth quadrants. Sweets had never watched such delicate eating in all his life.

"What broad?"

"LeComte, if you're going to bullshit me, I'll have to close shop."

"Ah," LeComte said. "Isaac's old classmate. Margaret Tolstoy."

"No. Magda Antonescu. I don't want Russian agents running around in Mafia country."

"She's not a Russian agent. The woman happens to work for me."

"Fine. But if she's captured or killed, I'll be caught in a shitstorm. And you'll run a thousand miles from Magda. Pull her, LeComte."

"She's valuable," LeComte said. "Give me a couple of months."

"I want her off the street."

"Did you look at her reports? She's my best scalp hunter. The woman doesn't miss. . . . I could go to Rebecca, Sweets. She won't back you on this one."

"Then I'll tell her to eat the badge I'm wearing for Isaac Sidel."

"I'll pull Margaret . . . soon."

"And she can't testify in open court. We'll all end up in the Lubyanka."

"She won't testify. I promise."

"And what if Michaelson should subpoena her?"

"He won't."

"The Three Sisters might want Isaac's old girlfriend on the stand."

"Then we'll have her disappear," LeComte said.

"Just like that?"

"Just like that."

"Well," Sweets said, getting up from his apples and wine. "I might be able to dance with Justice . . . until something better comes along. By the way, LeComte, what do you intend to do about Henry Lee?"

"Catch the son of a bitch."

"I mean, you didn't have much luck the last time . . . without Isaac. And it doesn't look good for Justice, having the number one bank robber in the world escaping from a goddamn federal fort."

"We have leads," LeComte said. "The Bureau will grab his tail."

"I hope so," Sweets said. "Because I'm scared shit of Henry Lee."

And he marched out of the wine cellar, leaving Justice to pay the bill.

25

It was a life like any life, being a citizen of Riker's. Don Isacco had grown fond of the isolation ward. He preferred it to the commissioners' floor. He could retire here, howl for his pension, get extra ice cream for the child molesters. Macho, who was nineteen, had never learned to read. And Isaac composed an alphabet book, scratching out little stories that he had Macho memorize. He never asked the blue-eyed boy what he had done. It wasn't kosher to talk about one's own case. And Isaac wouldn't use his imagination. In two weeks' time he'd turned Macho into a spectacular speller. In a month Macho was building paragraphs. Isaac was proud of his pupil. But all the little cushions he'd prepared, the habits of a man among outcasts like himself, failed him the moment Margaret arrived in the ward.

It was as if she were some marvel who'd floated through the gates. Her visit was as disturbing as Marilyn the Wild's, and twice as magical, because Margaret was like a piece of family furniture that had been lost to Isaac. And he was wounded all over again. The vacation had ended for Don Isacco. Riker's was only another howling in his head. The isolation ward had drifted to infinity and Isaac was left with Margaret Tolstoy.

"The guards here are jokers," she said. "They kept touching my tits."

"It's nothing," Isaac said like a sleepwalker. "A body search."

"That wasn't a body search. It was more like rape. But . . ."

"I know, Sal Rubino's snoring and you can't stay. He might get up any minute and ask about his Margaret."

"Isaac, shhhh. I heard Sal talking to his captain."

"You mean ol' Yellow Eyes."

"The two of them were arranging a hit. They have a soldier in this lousy jail. They called him the Big Blue. They said, 'We'll have the Big Blue jump on Isaac. The Blue will put out his lights.' Why the hell are you laughing?"

"A blue is a black man. The Big Blue could be anybody at Riker's."

"Then find him, Isaac, because he won't go away. Sal was talking dollars, a lot of dollars."

Isaac clutched her sleeve. "You're half the family I've got. I missed you, and I never even called out your name. Didn't ask myself, 'Where's the Odessa girl?'"

"Isaac, don't get crazy on me."

"I am crazy," Isaac said. "I always was. My mother collected rags. My kid brother is in and out of alimony jail. My father ran to France."

"That's got nothing to do with Sal Rubino's hitter. Isaac, you have a price on your head."

"Then I must be an important man."

"I warned you, Isaac. It's out of my hands."

She started to go, but Isaac spun her around, Dracula's teenage bride.

"I could keep you here," he said. "Plenty of souls have been lost in Riker's Island. I could waltz you under the bench."

"And what would you accomplish? You'd look into my eyes and see I wasn't there. You'd be making love to some kind of corpse. I died in Odessa, Commissioner Sidel."

Isaac released her from his grip. "I'm not a commissioner anymore."

He wasn't scared of the Big Blue. He welcomed the idea of meeting his executioner. Don Isacco would bite off both his ears. He wondered if the Blue would bribe a guard and sneak into the isolation ward. The Big Blue had Rubino money behind him. Isaac slept with a sharpened fork inside his sleeve. But the Big Blue never came and Isaac fell into his old routines. He revived Macho's alphabet book. Even baseball slipped from his mind. He'd lost that river of names. Isaac would dream of the cities he'd visited as a Hamilton Fellow. Not the scenic routes other police chiefs offered him. But the barrio of East L.A. The shantytowns along the Rio Grande. And while he was dreaming, a note was slipped into Isaac's cell.

> DEAR COMMISSIONER,
> I WANT THAT SHORT EYES AS MY BABE.
> I'LL KILL YOU IF I DON'T GET MACHO.
> —A FRIEND

Isaac smiled. The Big Blue had come to him with a note, realizing that Don Isacco would never give up Macho and would have to meet with the man. Isaac scribbled on the back of the note: "Dear Friend. Fuck yourself."

He gave it to one of the Rastafarians and forgot about the whole affair. And then the Big Blue smuggled a second note under Isaac's door.

> IT'S TIME TO TALK.

But Isaac didn't know where or when. He sharpened the prongs of that fork that he kept in his sleeve. He had his own trident now, like some water god away from the sea. He slept with one eye open, but the Big Blue wouldn't come for Isaac until Isaac started to dream. He felt a hand clamped over his mouth. Convicts dressed as screws lifted Isaac off his bunk and carried him out of the isolation ward. He didn't resist. He clutched the trident in his sleeve. He was bounced from cellblock to cellblock, and he could hear these convict-screws laughing at him. A police chief didn't amount to much at Riker's. He was one burly white man among a tribe of Latinos and blacks. It wasn't Rebecca's planet anymore. It wasn't Maiden Lane, with Boris Michaleson's Three Sisters. The sisters here wore mustaches and had biceps like ostrich eggs.

Isaac was dropped in some recreation room that should have been off limits to prison people. But his kidnappers had the run of the room. Their captain had a shaved head, like Marvin Hagler, the middleweight champion of the world. He had little bumps along his skull, like craters.

"Are you Sal Rubino's man, the Big Blue?"

The captain started to laugh, and soon the whole pack of them were howling at Isaac. They had tears in their eyes.

"He's dead, brother. He had an awful accident. Electrocuted himself in the machine shop . . . we don't like black button men. Hell, I saved your life. Don't you recognize me, little brother? I'm your black angel."

Isaac looked again. He was always clever at reading faces. But his powers had deserted him until a kind of sadness came into the captain's eyes.

"Henry Armstrong Lee," Isaac said. "Without the wig."

"I'm awful proud of you, little brother."

"Henry, why are you here?"

"Can you think of a better place for a black man who's being hunted by all that white trash? I always have my R and R at Riker's. I come and go."

"Like Mandrake the Magician."

"Don't insult me, brother. He was more white trash. He kept a slave."

And Isaac wouldn't argue the merits of Mandrake with Henry Armstrong Lee.

"I want your chicken," Henry said.

"Chicken? I don't get it."

"Short Eyes. The Macho man. I want him to be my babe."

"Then it wasn't Sal's assassin who sent me the note."

The bank robber smiled. "It was Mr. Henry Lee."

"I can't give him up to you."

"Why not, little brother? Is he your babe?"

"I've been teaching him how to read. Henry, he's a fucking kid."

"Should I tell you what he's done out on the street, that kid of yours?"

"I don't want to know."

"Should I tell you about all the black children he touched? Little brother, get smart. Give him to me."

"I can't," Isaac said. "I can't."

And Henry Lee scowled at Isaac. "I could cut your heart out and no one would ever miss your white ass."

"I still wouldn't give him up. I'd haunt you for the rest of your fucking life."

The bank robber scratched his lip. "Guess I'll have to look for another babe."

⚜

After he was returned to his ward, Isaac said, "Oh, shit." He forgot to congratulate Henry Lee for being the first man to break out of Leavenworth in seventeen years. Cops and corrections people didn't know a bloody thing about jails. The institutions they ran were phantoms of themselves. Riker's wasn't what the warden saw. The screws were children who guarded grown men. And Isaac was like an interloper in this hotel. He didn't belong here. He was on loan from the outside world, a luxury that Riker's could swallow whenever it wanted to. In the end Macho would become somebody's babe no matter how many alphabet books Isaac prepared. That was the law of Riker's Island.

He got a call from Eileen DiAngelis, the melamed's daughter. Izzy Wasser had had a stroke. The left side of his body was paralyzed. But he wanted to see Isaac.

"Eileen, I can't walk. I'm . . ."

"He says he's willing to pay your bill. Not a bond. The whole bail."

"That isn't necessary."

Isaac went to see the warden.

"You'll have to wear handcuffs every minute you're away," Warden Salinger said. "And you'll have to sign a note that you promise to return in six hours."

"I'll sign whatever the fuck you want."

"That isn't the correct attitude, Commissioner. I could get in trouble. You'll have to keep a log that lists each and every stop."

"Salinger, for Christ's sake. I'm going to visit a dying man."

"I'm familiar with that dying man," the warden said. "He's a member of a certain Mafia family. Do you realize the trouble Michaelson could make? If you conduct any business, Isaac, I'll shove you into solitary."

The "bride" who accompanied him was the same young black corrections officer who rode with Isaac on the bus to Riker's, the boy with the gold star in his ear, whose name was also Isaac.

"I can get you some pussy," black Isaac said.

"Not on this trip."

Black Isaac drove him to St. Vincent's Hospital in a tiny van that doubled as a laundry wagon.

Isaac went up in the elevator with his hands behind his back. People kept staring at the cuffs. One old lady recognized him. "You're always in my prayers," she said, and stepped out of the car.

Isaac entered the melamed's room while black Isaac stood at the door. Izzy sat like gray stone in his pajamas. He didn't tremble. He didn't move. He hadn't lost the power of speech, but his face was all twisted from the stroke. And when he talked, Eileen had to wipe the spittle from his mouth.

"Go," he told her. "I have things to discuss with the convict."

Eileen joined black Isaac.

"You're a fool," the melamed said, "to make such a spectacle of yourself. I never liked martyrs. You could have served yourself better on the street."

"How? It's too fucking political being the Commish."

"Then you should have resigned."

"And do what? You can't take a downward step in this career. There are always alligators to bite your ass. You're creating enemies all the time."

"Then sit, Isaac, sit in jail. I wanted to apologize. You were our friend, and I shouldn't have broken your trust. But Isaac, I had to use every advantage. Jerry's not much of a planner. And Ted . . ."

"He loves to spy."

"That's the picture."

"But how can I help you, Iz?"

"Take care of Eileen."

"I can't run an escort service from Riker's Island."

"Isaac, I've set aside sixty thousand dollars. Promise me. If Jerry is hurt, you'll accept that money as bail. And you'll move her to Boca Raton. Isaac, I have one daughter, one girl."

"I promise," Isaac said.

"Now get the hell away from me. Such a stupid man." The melamed was crying from one side of his face.

"I told you not to worry," Isaac said. "I'll take care of Eileen."

"But you're the bigger baby. . . . I'll miss you, Isaac."

Isaac whistled through his teeth. "You're not gone yet."

"But I know. I'll miss you when I'm dead. A commissioner who dresses like a bum. Get out of here."

Isaac had an hour to kill. Black Isaac drove him to One Police
Plaza. He had no identity here. He'd fallen between the
cracks. He was a prisoner who'd once been the PC. He had to
get a pass like any glom to get upstairs. "Please tell Commissioner Montgomery I'd like a word with him, if he can spare
the time."

The guard leered at Isaac's handcuffs. "I'm not sure the PC
is in the building."

"APC," Isaac said. "Mr. Montgomery is the Acting Commish."

Isaac rode up to the fourteenth floor with black Isaac, who'd
never been around so many police inspectors. No one said a
word about the handcuffs. His former sergeants and secretaries wouldn't even look Isaac in the face. He was the outcast of
Riker's Island. Only Sweets seemed genuinely glad to see
Isaac, and Sweets had enough rank not to feel ashamed. He
hugged Isaac, who didn't even have the use of his own hands.

"Aw, shit," Sweets said. "Isaac, will you get me out of this
hole, and take your desk back."

"I'm on vacation."

"Can I buy you dinner?"

"No. The warden will shout bloody murder if I'm not back
in his sink. But will you do me a favor, Sweets? I'm worried
about Margaret Tolstoy."

Sweets' bonhomie began to go. He looked like an Acting
Commish. "I can't help you, Isaac. The woman belongs to
LeComte."

"But you could—"

"Isaac, the case is closed. She's FBI business."

"But that fucking Sal will get her killed."

"Then use the telephone. Ask LeComte to lift her."

"I can't call LeComte. You know that."

Sweets stared out the window.

And Don Isacco returned to Riker's Island. He couldn't

even remember the streets. He belonged with child molesters.

Magda, Margaret, Minnie the Moo.

She had more masks than the Phantom of the Opera, who was nothing but a skull with bits of flesh to dry on. And the Phantom wasn't an informant for the FBI. She'd been to the Paris Opera when she was a girl. It was during the Occupation, and the Germans were interested in High Kultur. Ferdinand's little Jewish tailor on the avenue Pierre de Serbie had designed a uniform for him, because not even the German High Command could tell what he was supposed to wear. Officially he was the finance minister of Russian Roumania. But Ferdinand loved to dress like a general or a duke. And Margaret couldn't recall if the pants were brown or blue. But he had gold buttons on his chest, and the buttons smelled of burnt almonds. It could have been because of the tailor, a stubborn little man with thick fingers who had temper tantrums all the time. The Germans wouldn't dare touch Ferdinand's Jewish tailor, because Ferdinand was essential to their plans. The tailor's name was Karl. He looked like Ludwig van Beethoven, or one of the Seven Dwarfs.

He dressed little Magda too. And she hated all the fittings where he would hover over her with needles in his mouth. And she could smell those burnt almonds on his tongue. The almonds had come from huge honey cakes that he kept in his shop. He was much too busy for breakfast or lunch. He would tear off a hunk of cake between fittings and chew and chew and chew. Margaret wondered where all the needles went, but she never asked Grumpy the tailor.

She was always introduced as Ferdinand's niece and protégé. Generals danced with her. Countesses admired her clothes. And when Ferdinand brought her to the Opera, he would always wrap her in his cape, so that she could lunge out from under him like some mysterious creature. And she'd start to patter in French and look up at the chandeliers and try to guess where the Phantom was with his acid-eaten face.

"Margaret, where have you been?"

"Out," she said, looking past Eddie's yellow eyes and into Sal Rubino's pumpkin head. His head was always swollen after a long sleep.

"Baby, I can't sleep without you."

"You were doing fine."

She'd risked LeComte's whole operation by running out to Riker's. She'd worn wires in her underpants, buried microphones in flowerpots, marched Sal and his yellow-eyed bandit near FBI surveillance trucks. She'd slept with Jerry DiAngelis, taunted Sal's soldiers, and would have slept with the melamed too, but he wasn't interested in her wares. She'd set each branch of the Rubinos against the other and had them fighting like mad dogs. She'd put on a mask like the Phantom of the Opera and robbed Jerry's runners, all in the name of the FBI. Sal knew about her past, but he needed his Margaret at night. He hated to sleep alone. And the fantasy in his own heart and head was that he could contain her, defuse Margaret Tolstoy, and convert her to his own cause. He always had the option of shoving her into a sack, and that's why Margaret had to dance around him, but this time she might have danced too far, reached outside the borders of his own crazy love.

"But where did you go, Margaret?"

"Shopping," she said.

And some kind of menace opened in Sal's sleepy eyes. "I don't see any packages, hon."

"I couldn't find anything I liked."

"Did you know that the Blue is dead? Some niggers clipped him a couple nights ago."

"What Blue?"

"Come on, Margaret. *Our* Big Blue." And he cracked her across the face. She fell against his captain, who seized her by the hair.

Eddie had an idiotic grin. "You shouldn't have gone to Riker's, sweetheart."

"Did you finger our Blue?" Sal said. And he cracked her again. Her head tilted back from the blow. And she had to swallow her own blood while Eddie dug a knee into her groin and wouldn't relinquish her hair. Sal began to waver a bit. "The FBI is one thing. Fuck LeComte. I couldn't care less if you're on his team. But Isaac? You're in love with the Jew boy. . . . Didn't I treat you right?"

Margaret nodded her head as much as she could with the captain's fist in her hair.

"The fuck tried to destroy me and all my people . . . and you run to him at Riker's? Ed, should we whack the bitch, put out her lights?"

"Definitely."

And Sal started to strut in his pajamas. "My own man agrees." Then he turned glum. "Margaret, do you love me, Margaret?"

But she couldn't think with all that blood in her mouth. She closed her eyes and felt Sal's knuckles in her face. Then she stopped hurting. She was no longer there in that room with Sal and Ed. She was the phantom of her own little opera. The princess of a new country at twelve. Ferdinand had his palace that he'd stolen from Finkelshtein, the Jewish count. And Margaret had all of Bessarabia to rule. She had halvah and honey, and the Reichskommissar of the Ukraine took her on a picnic in the mountains, where she saw partisans and Jews hanging from the trees. *It's nothing, my dear,* he said. *They are Urmenschen. They don't exist.*

I'm an Urmensch, I'm an Urmensch, she sang to herself while the Reichskommissar stroked her calf. And then she had no more honey. The halvah was gone. Ferdinand's own little army began to pillage. And when there was nothing more to take, his soldiers deserted him. He was left with twenty policemen in blue pants. The policemen had to patrol Bessarabia and lands along the river Bug. She sat in the palace and listened to her stomach growl. There were no more pillowcases, and Ferdinand made love to her on blankets that hadn't been cleaned in months. Odessa had become a haunted town. Wild dogs reigned in the streets. They attacked sick horses.

Find me a Jew to eat, her prince would shout. And Margaret asked if he'd forgotten his little tailor. *Fuck the tailor. He's probably dead by now.*

The policemen returned with a prize. They'd discovered an idiot boy wandering in the local asylum. They beat him senseless with their own muddy boots. They butchered him in front of Margaret's eyes. They tore at his flesh. She wept and wept, but she ate the boy when it was time to eat. The policemen went off and found other prizes. And Margaret taught herself to club a boy like a wild turkey.

Captain Eddie had let go of her hair.

"Sal's talking to you. Are you deaf?"

That's how she'd come to Isaac, the little murderess who could babble French. And what was it about him that could still move her? The way he'd follow her like one more idiot without an asylum. She adored the holes in his pants, the silly uncombed hair.

"You deaf?"

And Margaret opened her eyes. Sal was bawling. "Baby, I'll give you one more chance. You promise not to leave me again?"

"Promise," she said.

"And you'll never go near Isaac?"

"Never."

He turned to Eddie. "What should I do?"

"Let me have her, boss. She's a rotten bitch."

Sal cracked her once more for good measure.

"Do you love me, Margaret?"

The blood mingled with the noises she made.

"Do you love me, Margaret?"

She was mute.

"Ice her," Sal said. "I don't give a shit." And he shambled in his pajamas to a different room.

Eddie grinned.

She whirled around with blood on her tongue and struck him under his Adam's apple with her own little fist. Eddie wanted to cough. He looked like a startled animal with those yellowish eyes. Margaret found a kitchen knife and cut his throat. Her arm danced out like a surgeon or a princess of Odessa, waiting to eat the flesh of little boys.

26

Isaac wandered into the other cellblocks. There was no Big Blue to bother him. He began teaching courses to the inmates. He wouldn't lecture on penal codes. He talked philosophy and science. He would clip articles from journals and mention the arrow of time. "There's a scientist at Oxford or Cambridge who lives in a wheelchair and believes that if the universe ever started to contract, time would flow in the other direction, and the cradle itself would become our grave. We'd be growing younger by the minute."

The screws had no tolerance for Isaac's speculations. The Rasties thought he was profaning the Lion of Judah. The Latinos figured he was cracked, like some *cucaracha* that had lived too long. But the Muslims listened to Isaac. They argued with him that Allah had created the world, not some scientist in a wheelchair. And what was a man's worth if he grew into a baby and forgot all about God?

Isaac didn't have an answer. He returned to his own ward. Someone was waiting for him. Maurice had come out of his little jail in the roofs of the Christy Mathewson Club. His nose was running, and he trembled as he sat near the steam pipe.

"You're nibbling cocaine, aren't you?"

"I can't help it, Isaac. I've been hiding too long."

Isaac grabbed him by the collar. "Well, you come back without a runny nose."

"I might never get there," Maurie said.

"What happened? Did LeComte give you the green light? He doesn't need you now that the melamed is permanently damaged. He's not so interested in Jerry DiAngelis. What kind of deal did you make?"

"Not a deal," Maurie mumbled. "He sent down a kite that I wouldn't get hurt if I took care of you in court."

"He must have known where you were. Did he arrive at the club one afternoon?"

"Yes."

"Have a drink at the bar?"

"Yes."

"And whistled your name?"

"Yes."

"I thought so. Now get out of here, Maurie, and clean up your fucking act."

He couldn't stop shivering. He'd established his own little law library in Isaac's cell and the visitors' room. The isolation ward had become a feast of papers, files, and books. "I'm no good," he'd moan. "It's been a year, Isaac, a whole year since I've been inside a courtroom."

"Then put on some dark glasses and go down to State Supreme Court. Snoop as much as you want, but don't die on me, Maurie."

"I'm no good."

Isaac began to throttle him in front of the child molesters. "I'll kill you, Maurie. I mean it."

"You could find another lawyer."

"There are no other lawyers. There's only you."

"But I can't face Michaelson's fucking Three Sisters."

"You'll eat them up," Isaac said.

"They're a powerhouse."

"So am I."

"Then tell me, lover, how come you're wearing prison pants and Michaelson is sitting on his fanny at Maiden Lane?"

"I like it here."

"That doesn't help our case."

Maurie rocked along in his little library, muttering at Isaac and the child molesters, who got in his way. Sometimes he'd forget to go home and Maurie would camp out with his law books, sleep on a cot that Isaac borrowed from Salinger himself. The screws delivered coffee and pizza pies. He began offering advice. He set up a little law clinic in the isolation ward. He learned that Macho had been falsely accused. Some overambitious assistant D.A. had brought Macho in to take the heat off a couple of black neighborhoods in the Bronx.

"He's retarded, Isaac, can't you tell? They never even read him his rights. He was wandering in the streets when they picked him up."

Maurie shaved, went to the Bronx, and got the district attorney's office to drop the charges. Maurie was declared the miracle man of Riker's. But Macho didn't want to leave his friends. He'd been making progress with Isaac's alphabet books.

Isaac growled at Maurie. "Damn you," he said. "The fucking cure is worse than the crime. Where's the kid gonna go? They'll pick him up all over again and he'll fall right back into the same clock."

"Fine. But what happens after you split?"

"We'll worry about that later," Isaac said.

And Macho became one more *invisibilito* at Riker's. But Maurie's reputation didn't suffer.

"Hey, miracle man," the Muslims called out from their cellblocks, "what you gonna do for me?"

The screws would bring him extra shirts and started to shuttle Maurie from Riker's to this court and that. The warden complained to Isaac.

"This is highly irregular, you know."

"But it's good business. The inmates have a champion. Don't take away their hope. Even if it's one more fucking illusion."

"You're too philosophical for me, Commissioner Sidel. I have to deal with politics."

"Salinger," Isaac said, "Maurie is the best politics you'll ever have."

⚜

The counselor's confidence was coming back. He dressed in clean shirts, visited his boyfriends, attended Republican and Democratic balls. He arrived one afternoon in a tux. "I saw Michaelson last night. He was looking glum. He never intended to have you sit so long. I think I can get you out of Riker's."

"But no strings, Maurie."

"I promise."

He returned from Maiden Lane with a heaviness around his shoulders. "It's the Three Sisters. They're a bad influence on Boris. They won't let him rip up the indictment. They have this dumb idea that they can win in court. They've been reaching, Isaac, reaching far as they can get."

Maurice lived inside his tuxedo. He neglected to wash. He would go back and forth between Riker's and Maiden Lane, back and forth, as the Three Sisters assembled their case against Isaac Sidel. Maurie read the depositions and police reports, counted off the witnesses those Sisters had, and pondered the evidence.

He was shivering again.

"For God's sake, Maurie, what's the matter?"

"They subpoenaed your bank accounts."

"Big deal. If they find more than a thousand dollars, they're welcome to it."

"And your safety-deposit box."

"Have a heart, Maurie. I need a place to store my birth certificate, don't I?"

"But the Bank of North China?"

"Chinatown is near Headquarters. And I know the bank manager. He sponsors a baseball club for the Police Athletic League."

"Isaac, they went into the vault. The Three Sisters, two City marshals, and their own locksmith. They discovered six hundred thousand dollars in your box, all in hundred-dollar bills."

"That's crazy," Isaac said, stepping over Maurice's little sea of law books. "It's a plant."

"Isaac, we'd better start bargaining with them."

"No. Who are their witnesses?"

"Well, there's McCall."

"They'd have to go with the chief of Internal Affairs. But McCall isn't out to sink me."

"They have you on camera, Isaac, visiting Jerry DiAngelis and the melamed. Don't you get it? They'll say it was DiAngelis who gave you the six hundred thou . . . who is Burton Bortelsman? He's also on the list. Oh, God. Is he the head of your secret service? Isaac, the government got to him. Give up."

"Who else?" Isaac muttered. "Who else?"

"Teddy DiAngelis."

"The FBI wouldn't lend him to the Sisters. He's their star rat."

"But if they're not going after Jerry, they don't need him anymore."

"Maurice, it doesn't make sense. LeComte lets you out of the bag and then gives Teddy Boy to the Sisters." Isaac's whole head went dark. His sideburns froze to his face. "Maurie, did you deal me away? Are you my fucking Judas?"

Maurice met the fury in Isaac's eyes. "If I was going to play Judas," he said, "it wouldn't be at Riker's Island."

And so Isaac prepared to celebrate his own doom. Six hundred thousand dollars. Teddy would pin him to that bundle, and Burt would only have to talk like an Afrikaner in the witness box and that would be the end of Isaac. But he couldn't figure LeComte. What was Justice getting out of this other than Isaac's scalp? Was it revenge for having been the Hamilton Fellow who went away?

He wouldn't shave before court appearances. The judge was a Bronx Democrat who rose on the bench until he arrived at State Supreme Court. He'd never cared for Isaac's shenanigans. His name was Richard Dorn. He was an enormous man whose corpulence seemed to reign in any room he was in. It took weeks to select a jury. Isaac would sit at the defense table while Maurie, who looked as ragged as he did, would duel with Michaelson's Three Sisters over the fate of prospective jurors. Isaac never even watched a juror's face, but he was fascinated with the Sisters, who seemed to work the court like one long-legged spider. Their bodies moved in tandem. They had a flow, a lyrical line, that Isaac hadn't seen before. They never argued. They had a certain clairvoyance, a collective desire to do Isaac in. Now he understood why Maurie was reluctant to go against Boris' girls. It was like battling a merciless, single-minded army.

"Isaac," Maurice said in the middle of jury selection. "I think we ought to deal."

"Fuck the Three Sisters."

"You'll be doing heavy time."

"Then I'll sit with Tiger John in Green Haven and play chess."

"Tiger John is too dumb to play chess. He's the silliest police commissioner we ever had."

"But he was as loyal as a saint," Isaac said. "Go on, Maurice. Pick your jury."

And meanwhile Justice Dorn looked at Isaac with all the weight his body would allow. Isaac knew where Dorn's sympathies were. With the Three Sisters.

❀

The trial began after another month. Isaac would wash in the early morning, put on his bum's clothes, and some screw would lead him out of the isolation ward in handcuffs. He was chained to the bus that took him over the Riker's Island Bridge to Dorn's castle at State Supreme Court. Reporters would try to grab at him when he got off the bus.

"Isaac, give us a line, will ya?"

"I like Susan Sodaman's legs."

And the correction officers would herd him into the building with whoever else had been on board. He might have coffee and cake in the holding pen. People stared at him. He was Don Isacco. One more Commish 'who had joined the mob. Everybody at the castle seemed to know about Isaac's gelt. It was clever of him to use a Chinese bank. The Pink Commish wasn't even patriotic. During his long sits in the holding pen, Isaac wouldn't consider his case. His mind would drift back to the Margaret he remembered, and his thirty years with the NYPD had been a rootless, uneventful dream. He wasn't Dick Tracy. He was a boy in the bleachers, in love with a little dark lady from the other side of the moon.

One of the castle criers called his name. He was delivered in his handcuffs to a tiny conference room, where Maurie waited for him in a shirt that was almost as filthy as Isaac's. The counselor's nose was running again.

"You son of a bitch. You promised me that you wouldn't snort cocaine at my trial."

"Isaac, I'm scared . . . we could ask for a postponement."

"Maurie," Isaac said. "I'll meet you at the defense table."

And that's how Isaac's trial began.

He was ushered into the courtroom. It was a full house. All the spectator seats were taken. The sketch artists sat with their pads. The journalists snickered among themselves and packed little sandwiches into their mouths. And the bisons, old men and women who made it their business to attend jury trials, traveling from one court to the next, monopolized most of the seats. It was like going to a circus. And Isaac was their clown of the month. He recognized Jerry and Eileen DiAngelis among the rabble. They'd brought the melamed out of his hospital bed. His face was still twisted from the stroke. But he had more dignity than the bisons. He wore a blanket around his shoulders. He was handsome in his white hair.

The bailiff marked the arrival of the judge with his own scream. "Hear ye, hear ye! Supreme Court of New York County now in session. The Honorable Richard Dorn presiding. All rise." Justice Dorn appeared from his chambers with his considerable bulk and climbed the little stairs to his bench like a ballroom dancer. It was bad for Isaac, because this judge could control a court with a single shiver of his body. But even Isaac had to admit: God, can that fat man glide.

Dorn smiled at the Three Sisters. He had his own clerk wheel in their evidence cart. He ignored Michaelson and Maurie while he bantered with the Sisters. "I knew your dad," he said to Trish Van Loon. He complimented Susan Sodaman on the dress she was wearing. He winked at Selma Beard.

Maurie began to broil. "Your Honor, this isn't the Russian Tea Room. My client can't get a fair shake when you're enamored of the prosecution team. It's bad enough that Mr. Michaelson has me outnumbered three to one. But what significance does Miss Sodaman's dress have to this case?"

Isaac groaned. His counselor was burying him before Selma Beard had opened her mouth. He tried to grab Maurie's sleeve, but Maurie pulled away and started to bang on the defense table. "This is prejudicial, Your Honor, and I want it to stop."

The fat man peered down from his bench like an innocent owl. "Starting early, aren't you, Goodstein?"

"*Mr.* Goodstein," Maurie said. "I have to start early, or you'll give this case to the prosecution, and I can go to bed."

"One more outburst, Goodstein, and I'll hold you in contempt."

Maurie genuflected to the judge. "Most respectfully, Your Honor, I beg the court's pardon."

"Counselor, will you please approach the bench."

Maurie abandoned his table in the well of the courtroom and stood at "side-bar," that portion of the bench that was hidden from the jury's eyes. He and the judge whispered back and forth and then Maurie returned to the table.

"Maurie," Isaac said, "you're killing us."

"No I'm not. It's like riding a mean horse. You have to stay in the saddle, or you'll get kicked in the head."

Selma Beard's opening statement didn't surprise Isaac. She stood near the jury box, leaned on the rail, and painted Isaac as an evil man. "The prosecution will show that Mr. Sidel deliberately and maliciously used the power of his office to obtain favors for himself, that he accepted bribes . . ." And while she sang her little song the other Sisters moved their shoulders to the rhythm of her words. The jurors seemed mesmerized. Boris Michaelson had the best show in town. ". . . and is an associate of a certain crime family headed by the DiAngelis brothers."

Maurie rose up from the defense table. "Objection! The DiAngelis brothers are not on trial in this court. And Ms. Beard is gluing my client to some mythical crime family."

"Sustained," the fat man said.

"Your Honor," Selma said. "Mr. Sidel is our first police commissioner who is a member of the mob."

Maurice began to roar. "Is this a carnival, Your Honor? Because if it is, I can take my pants down and amuse the jury. I can juggle names. I can conjure up the ghost of Al Capone."

"Goodstein," the judge said. "I'm warning you. Behave yourself. And Ms. Beard, you will refrain from using such epithets as 'member of the mob.'"

"But I will prove beyond a reasonable doubt that—"

"Please don't contradict me," the judge said, wagging his jowls.

And Selma Beard sang again with the help of her particular chorus. All Three Sisters curled their eyes to look at Isaac with such contempt that he wanted to disappear under the table.

And then it was Maurie's time. He held the indictment in his hand like some classical scholar dreaming of Plato. He had an angelic smile. His mouth grew thin. "Ladies and gentlemen of the jury, forgive me, but this indictment is a piece of dreck. Worse. It's a fairy tale. It's made for children. My client is the best police commissioner the Department has ever had."

Susan Sodaman began to titter. And suddenly Maurice had lost his audience. Spectators and jury observed Michaelson's three little girls. No counselor could compete with them. They were dream sisters who'd driven their way into the unconscious will of the court.

Isaac's spittle turned dark. Macho was pulled out of his hands. The Bronx district attorney had discovered where he was and delivered a writ, removing Macho from Riker's. The boy was scared. His blue eyes seemed to narrow into tiny circles. His whole body began to twist. A vulture might have been inside the boy. And Isaac had no warrants that could save him.

Within a week Macho was trampled to death by a gang of vigilantes from the Bronx. Isaac called the acting police commissioner. "I want your best people on the case. The boy was innocent."

"How do you know?"

"I lived with him for seven months."

"And now you're a maven on child molesters. Isaac, it was the Hunts Point projects. He was found with a twelve-year-old kid. They were both undressed."

"It means nothing. He was retarded, Sweets. I want those vigilantes investigated. Bring in a captain from Intelligence if you have to."

"Isaac, baby, don't you remember? You dismantled half the Division. You had your Ivanhoes. I'm not putting Intelligence on this case."

"Sweets."

"What? Should I spring you for twenty-four hours and have you head up the investigation? Isaac, it's Indian country. What are you going to do with all the rubble? You'll be sifting for evidence half your life. You have your own problems. Concentrate on the Three Sisters. They're worse than any vigilantes from the South Bronx."

But Isaac wasn't satisfied. He called Sharkey, the Bronx D.A.

"You piece of shit, couldn't you forget about the boy?"

"Darling, it was your counselor who dug him out of the anthill. Maurie embarrassed us. Telling my lads it was a false arrest. So do us a favor and go fuck yourself."

Isaac arrived in court with a dark blue beard. His skin was mottled. He could have walked through a firestorm. He began eating his own knuckles during the prosecution's little parade of witnesses. His fingers bled. He woke out of his black sleep when McCall of Internal Affairs was put on the stand.

Isaac had picked him for the job. He knew McCall would never use IAD to seek revenge. McCall didn't like the game of politics.

It was Trish Van Loon who examined him. Neither the

248 • JEROME CHARYN

spectators nor the journalists nor the sketch artists could stop looking at her long legs.

"Can you tell the jury, Chief McCall, why you started investigating your own police commissioner? Isn't it a rare occurrence?"

"It certainly is," McCall said.

"Did someone drop a dime on the defendant, snitch on Isaac Sidel?"

"Objection!" Maurie said. "The prosecutor is leading her witness by the tail. I don't like the word 'snitch.'"

"Overruled," the judge said. "I'll allow it. But if you don't mind, Ms. Van Loon, could you be a little less colorful in your remarks . . . as a personal favor to the court?"

"Yes, Your Honor. Chief McCall, can you tell us who first brought your attention to Mr. Sidel's possible misdeeds?"

"Several officers from the Department. They were on surveillance. And they kept seeing the commissioner—I mean, Mr. Sidel—in the company of Jerry DiAngelis and his father-in-law, Izzy Wasser, also known as the melamed."

"Objection!" Maurie said. "Being seen in another man's company is still not a crime in the State of New York."

"Overruled," the fat man said. "Continue, please."

"And there were other allegations. That Mr. Sidel had sidestepped the Intelligence Division to start his own intelligence team."

"And did this intelligence team have a name?"

"Yes. The Ivanhoes."

"And a chief?"

"Yes. A man called Bortelsman, but I could never find him."

"And what use did Mr. Sidel make of his Ivanhoe Division?"

"It's hard to say. But there have been allegations that the Ivanhoes interfered in Jerry DiAngelis' war against Sal Rubino and the old Rubino captains."

"Interfered? On whose side?"

"Jerry's."

"Your witness, counselor," Trish said, and returned to the prosecution table.

Maurie wasn't Trish Van Loon. He didn't have the same lilt to his voice or Trish's long legs. His nose was running, and he had to keep a handkerchief in his fist.

"Chief McCall, in all your surveillance of Isaac Sidel, did you uncover one single crime that he had committed?"

"No."

"We've heard a lot about Ivanhoes, but did you ever see one?"

"No."

"Talk to one?"

"No."

"Thank you, Chief McCall."

The court broke for lunch. Isaac had some pickles and pastrami sandwiches with Maurice in one of the conference rooms. Maurie had no appetite. Isaac devoured two sandwiches with his dark blue face, while Maurie brooded over a pickle.

"Burton's next. He'll kill us."

"I'm not so sure," Isaac said.

"How can we deny the existence of Ivanhoes with Burton right there?"

"Eat," Isaac said.

Burt looked more like a convict than a witness for the prosecution. The Three Sisters had been hiding him in some hotel. His suit was as shabby as Isaac's. His mouth seemed filled with white paste. Ah, Burt, Isaac muttered to himself. And this time Susan Sodaman led him through her little circus. He talked about his days as a homicide captain in Capetown, and his flight from South Africa for having murdered a man. He was already a fulsome character. Even the bisons eyed him with disgust.

"Now tell us what you did for Isaac Sidel?"

"I was head of the Secret Branch."

"Secret Branch?"

"Yes, mum. The Ivanhoes."

"Ah, the Ivanhoes. The Ivanhoes."

And Susan Sodaman brought him through the dance of what the Ivanhoes did.

"Well, mum, strictly speaking, we sort of watched over the world. In New York, of course. We never traveled. If the Saudis were up to some trick, we would defuse it."

"Like a counterintelligence team."

"I would say so. Yes."

"Did you ever kill a man?"

"While I was with Isaac? No."

"Would you, Mr. Bortelsman, if Isaac had asked?"

"Objection!" Maurie said.

"Sustained."

"Bitch," Maurie muttered to Isaac. "She can't get away with crap like that."

"Calm yourself. She's being rather gentle with Burt."

"'Course she is. He's her fucking witness."

"And what was your last assignment for Mr. Sidel?" Susan Sodaman asked.

"To destabilize Sal Rubino. And we would have if the plug hadn't been pulled."

Susan Sodaman smiled as she passed the defense table.

Isaac had to clutch Maurie's pants. "Go slowly with him, counselor."

"What do you mean? I'll break his back."

"Burt's been signaling to me while he was on the stand."

"Signaling?"

"With his ears. It's a gimmick we adopted as Ivanhoes. He wants to help. Lead him a little, Maurie. Slow. Very slow. Ask him how he was paid."

And Maurie approached the witness box. "Mr. Bortelsman,

would you tell the court what kind of salary you had as an Ivanhoe? How were you paid?"

"In dollars," Burt said.

"Without a receipt?"

"Naturally. We were the Secret Branch."

"And who paid you?"

"The boss."

"Can you identify him, please? Is he in this courtroom?"

"Yes. He's sitting at your table. Mr. Sidel."

"And he lugged cash around once a week like some Santa Claus."

"Yes. He was our Father Christmas. But he didn't exactly lug the cash. He put it in our strongbox. And we would take whatever we needed."

"You'd dip into the pot, just like that."

"It was informal. Very informal."

"And you had no one to keep the books."

"Wouldn't make much sense to have a bookkeeper in our Branch. There was never any paperwork, you see."

"How many Ivanhoes did you have?"

"From five to fifteen. Depending on the cash flow."

"And where are they now?"

"Couldn't say, counselor. They've kind of scattered . . . like the Branch itself."

"And so you're the last of the Ivanhoes."

"Yes."

"And do you have any proof at all that the other Ivanhoes existed?"

"Not exactly."

"You did have an office."

"Yes. But we were moving all the time."

"And if I asked you for an address?"

"Wouldn't do much good. We'd strip a place, pick it clean, every time we moved."

"So there wouldn't be any evidence of these particular domiciles."

"None at all."

"But you did mention a strongbox."

"I dismantled it and threw the pieces into the Hudson River."

"And so what you're really saying, Mr. Bortelsman, is that you have no proof of the Ivanhoes other than your very own person."

"Objection!" Selma Beard said. "Your Honor, Mr. Goodstein is putting words into the witness's mouth."

"Sustained."

"All right," Maurie said. "All right. Mr. Bortelsman, may I call you Burt?"

"Yes. Certainly, sir."

"Can you give me one reason why I should believe you that the Ivanhoes ever existed at all?"

Now it was up to the Nose. He sweated in the witness box. His brother and sister-in-law and the melamed were in the audience. He was Michaelson's number one rat. The court artists sketched his miserable face. The journalists laughed at Teddy Boy. The bisons made indecent remarks. The judge had to bang his wooden hammer several times. The clatter of wood upon wood beat in Isaac's ears. The bailiff screamed, "Quiet in the court." But people wouldn't listen to the bailiff. They were having too good a time. Justice Dorn rose from his chair and walked that little "mile" in back of the bench. You could feel the anger in his jowls. That enormous body left its own peculiar wake. The bench had become a rocking boat. "I will clear the room if we can't have some peace. I won't tolerate disrespect." But his pronouncement wasn't necessary. His very bulk had silenced the spectators. He sat down.

And that's when Cardinal Jim entered the courtroom in his red beanie. It was as if the prosecutor's case had fallen into some godless ruin. The Three Sisters began to unravel.

They'd lost their internal rhyme. All you saw at their table was a clutter of arms and legs.

The cardinal had come for Isaac. He was like his own walking cathedral. The bisons scrambled with each other to offer him a place in one of their pews. "Thank ya, thank ya," he said. Even Justice Dorn was confused. He tried to curtsy with his bulk. "Good to see you, Your Grace." But his belly caught behind the bench and it took him a while to wiggle free. "I mean, Your Eminence."

"Ah, don't bother about me," Jim said. "Any title will do." But the damage had been done. The appearance of Jim served to discredit the witness and make him one more invisible man. Teddy was chewing his sleeves when Selma Beard began. What Nose had to say was predictable enough. *He* had given Isaac the six hundred thousand dollars.

"We bought him. Isaac was our man. He did whatever he was told. When we needed a favor, my brother would tell me, 'Go to the Commish.'"

"And what about the honorable Isadore Wasser?"

"Iz was really close to Isaac. I watched them play chess. Isaac would have done anything for the old man."

"Mr. DiAngelis, can you recall one specific favor?"

"Sure, we hired him to fuck with Sal Rubino's boys. . . ." He looked up at the owl on the bench. "Sorry, your Honor." Then he returned to Selma Beard. "We paid him to mess up Sal. Isaac went in with his bambinos." He pursed his lips. "The Ivanhoes."

"And what price did you settle on?"

"I'm not sure. We lost our bookkeeper. But it had to be over a hundred K. Isaac was a greedy guy."

"And how long has your family been associated with Isaac Sidel?"

"I'd have to guess. I'm not so terrific with dates. But he's always been thick with the old man. Figure nine, ten years."

"Your witness," Selma said, bowing to Maurie and Isaac.

"No questions," Maurie said.

Isaac clutched the tails of his counselor's coat. "You're gonna let him lie like that?"

"It's much more damaging this way."

"Maurie, ask him one or two questions, will you?"

"Isaac," Maurie whispered, "shut the fuck up."

Teddy wouldn't budge. He sat in the witness box like some aphasic boy, lost in his own America. He never looked at Jerry or Eileen or the melamed. He twiddled his fingers and watched the shadows on the wall.

"Mr. DiAngelis," the judge said. "You may go now."

"Yes, Father," Teddy said in all that confusion of faces.

And Maurie winked at Isaac. "That's why I didn't subject him to a cross. The more you hit him, the more sympathetic he becomes."

Teddy disappeared through a side door. And Isaac sat at the defense table. He wasn't even angry at the poor son of a bitch. Nose would never survive without Eileen's suppers.

That was the case against Isaac Sidel. Burt, Teddy Boy, and policemen like McCall, and one of the City marshals who broke into Isaac's box and discovered six hundred thousand dollars.

"I want to take the stand," Isaac told his lawyer.

"They'll burn you on the Ivanhoe business."

"I want to take the stand."

"Then I quit," Maurie said. "It's suicide. Find someone else to sit with you at the sentencing."

"All right. Who have we got?"

"Peter Wang."

"You've been building and building, and all we've got is the manager of a bank? Is he my character witness? Is Peter Wang going to tell how we coached a bunch of kids in our own Little League?"

"He's enough," Maurie said.

And Isaac went to court. He sat with his dark, dark mien at

the defense table. The sketch artists began calling him Bluebeard. He looked like a pirate in all the papers. Isaac didn't care. He watched Peter Wang climb the witness stand. "Tiny" was over six feet tall. His parents had come from Hunan Province, which raised whole colonies of giants. He didn't have the officious look of a bank manager but the oxlike torso and piano legs of Babe Ruth. Maurie was right. The Sisters would have a hard time shaking Tiny Wang.

Maurie didn't dance around. He went right to the Sisters' evidence cart. State Exhibit 17-B, the six hundred thousand that was kept overnight in plastic bags inside the vaults of the castle's own property clerk. The bailiff himself wheeled the cart across the well and handed Tiny the two bags.

"Mr. Wang," Maurie said, "is this the money that was removed from the defendant's safety-deposit box at your bank?"

"As far as I can tell. Yes."

"Would you examine the evidence, please. Don't be bashful. Just dig in."

Tiny opened one of the plastic bags and pulled out a handful of money.

"What are the denominations, Mr. Wang?"

"They're all hundred-dollar bills."

"And the dates?"

"Well, they vary . . . Nineteen sixty-nine. Nineteen seventy-six."

Maurice's rump began to bulge. He always worked best with his ass sticking out. It was his own tribal instinct. "Dig in again."

"Objection," said Selma Beard. "I don't get the point of this little sideshow. The money was logged in a long time ago."

"Your Honor," Maurie said. "Indulge me. One minute more."

"But get on with it," the owl said.

"Now, Mr. Wang, will you read off the dates on these bills?"

"Series Nineteen seventy-seven . . . series Nineteen seventy-six."

"And can you enlighten us, Mr. Wang, tell us the last time Mr. Sidel visited your vault?"

"June eleven, Nineteen hundred and seventy-three."

"How can you be so sure of that date?"

"We're not like other banks. We keep a careful record of all entry slips. They're photocopied and filed away on microfilm. And we don't have an entry for Mr. Sidel after June eleven of that year."

"Objection!" Selma said. "Your Honor, Mr. Goodstein has produced no such evidence in this court. Where is the magic microfilm?"

The other two Sisters began to whisper in her ear. "Your Honor, I'll withdraw that objection. I think Mr. Wang ought to have the privilege of hanging himself *and* Mr. Goodstein's client."

"Your Honor," Tiny said. "I can produce the microfilm today . . . tomorrow."

"It won't be necessary," Selma said. "I believe you."

"Your witness," Maurie said.

And Trish Van Loon, she of the long legs, got up to cross-examine Tiny Wang. The Sisters seemed to have found their rhyme again; they were that one magnificent spider. Michaelson sat at his table with an enormous grin.

"Mr. Wang," Trish said, "how long have you known the defendant Isaac Sidel?"

"Long time," Tiny said. "Twenty years."

"And would you consider him a friend?"

"Yes. We're rivals in the same league."

"Rivals? I thought you were friends."

"Yes. But we manage different teams for P.A.L."

"Ah, the Police Athletic League. Then you manage a bank *and* a baseball team."

"I prefer the baseball team," Tiny said, and Trish laughed

along with the journalists and the owl on the bench. She let
the laughter die.

"And Mr. Sidel was a friend before he ever became a client
at your bank."

"Yes."

"Can you tell us about some of your other clients?"

"List is too long," Tiny said.

"I'll help you. Does Isadore Wasser keep an account at your
bank?"

"Objection," Maurie said. "That's irrelevant."

"No. I'll allow it," the judge said.

"Mr. Wasser has an account. But it's very small."

"I didn't ask you that, Mr. Wang."

"He plays mah-jongg in Chinatown. He needs a little
pocket money. So he comes to the bank."

"That's a delightful story, Mr. Wang. But I'm not interested
in the details."

"Objection!" Maurie said. "Ms. Van Loon is gagging my
witness."

"Mr. Wang, you may answer if you wish."

"Nothing to answer," Tiny said. "He plays mah-jongg. He's
forgetful. He needs cash."

"You're the provider, Mr. Wang, aren't you? Just like you
helped provide Isaac Sidel. Can you explain to us how the
defendant has all this miracle money?"

"I cannot explain."

"Did a pixie go into his vault?"

"A pixie perhaps, but not another human being."

"Isn't it possible that you yourself were Mr. Wasser's front?"

"I don't understand."

"Did you take money from Mr. Wasser and put it into the
defendant's box?"

"No. It's not possible. It is a double-key lock. Only Mr.
Sidel has the second key."

"But he could have given it to you."

"Maurie," Isaac whispered. "Stop her, will you?"

"No. She didn't do her fucking homework. Let her talk."

"Come, come," Trish said. "Mr. Sidel could have let you borrow his key . . . so that his name would not be on any slip."

"I would not take his key."

"But we only have your word for it. And a mysterious pile of money. How did it get there, Mr. Wang? How did it get there?"

"I don't know."

"You weren't always a bank manager, were you? Can you tell us what you did before you inherited your seat at the North China Bank?"

Tiny mumbled something.

"Louder," she said. "I can't hear you."

"I was with the FBI. Special-agent-in-charge of the Philadelphia field office . . . until I retired."

Trish looked at Tiny, and the spectators looked at her. The jury seemed like two rows of crippled children.

"Told you," Maurie said. "The bitch didn't do her homework."

27

He arrived on the four-teenth floor in a new black leather coat that had been hanging from a merchant's fire escape on Orchard Street. He didn't bargain. He depleted his bank account to buy the coat. He looked like a Gestapo agent. His beard was still blue. People trembled when they saw the jailbird. His sergeants wanted to congratulate him, but they didn't dare. He wasn't supposed to have come back from that grave at Riker's Island. He was upsetting the order of things, and this Department thrived on some secret internal order amid the chaos. The sergeants had gotten used to Sweets and now they had a Commish they'd wanted to forget. He wouldn't play the diplomat.

He rang for his old First Dep.

Sweets arrived with Isaac's badge. "Glad to see you, boss. I was getting worried. I didn't want to die in your chair."

"Hunts Point," Isaac said without a hello.

He pulled a dozen detectives out of the five boroughs and formed a special "turbulence team." Some of them had Manfred Coen's sad blue eyes. They wore black leather coats like the PC. They moved around after midnight. Isaac descended upon Hunts Point, looking for the vigilantes who had murdered Macho, his own retarded boy. He saw frightened people hovering in dirty halls. He saw rats the size of dogs, and dogs that looked like Moby Dick with a tail and big teeth. There was rubble all around him. Children tramped across the rubble like hundred-year-old men. Isaac didn't have the heart to interrogate them. He shot a few wild dogs and returned to Manhattan.

He went to Sal Rubino's steak house with his leather-coated army. Sal was eating pasta primavera with the vice presidents of his cement company and their wives. He sang bits of Puccini with his fork in the air and delivered dirty jokes while he squeezed the thigh of one particular wife. He was in the best of moods. There were no more Ivanhoes to disturb his numbers machine. The melamed was out of commission. Nose had revealed himself as a government rat. And Jerry DiAngelis had to retreat within the walls of his rifle club to stay alive. Sal was now the prince and high priest of all the dons. The other Families kissed his cheek and called him *cardinale*. But he still missed Margaret Tolstoy. It was funny how a *puttana* could get under your skin. She was the FBI's biggest ballbreaker. She'd destroyed mob captains and soldiers all over the country. And when he'd tried to get rid of her, she'd killed his own captain in the end.

Sal looked up from the table and saw a blue-headed man in a black leather coat. But Sal was the cardinal and he didn't have to stop eating for any cop. "*Buon giorno*, Isaac," he said. "How do you like the fresh air? Better than Riker's, eh? Come, have some pasta with my people. The steaks are on the grill. No more arguments, Isaac. I'll intro—"

And that's when he caught himself tumbling out of his chair. Isaac was on top of him, smothering Sal with his leather coat. And Sal felt a pain that he'd never had before. It was like a shark was chewing on his head. He started to howl.

"Mama." The crazy Commish was biting his ear. And then the biting stopped.

"Sal, next time you start to kill a man, you'd better succeed."

⚜

There wasn't a word in the papers. But the whole town knew. Don Isacco had declared war on the mob. He'd wrestled with Sal Rubino after midnight, bitten off a piece of his ear. All the Irish sergeants were singing lullabies. "Brian Boru is back. We have our king." And Isaac had a visitor on the fourteenth floor. It was Boris Michaelson. He'd moved out of Maiden Lane.

"Did Becky squeeze you, Boris? Did she say that you'd bungled the job with all your little attorney generals? Couldn't even bury Isaac and you had the best prosecution team in town. How are the Three Sisters?"

"They resigned. I've brought them into my practice. I'm representing Sal Rubino now. I have a court order, Isaac. If you ever go near Sal again, I'll slap an injunction on you so fast you'll be back at Riker's before you can blink."

"I appreciate your interest, Boris. Say hello to the girls for me. And get the hell out of my office."

"I will," Michaelson said. "You're a lucky son of a bitch. You and your Chinese bank. How did you manage it? Was that Ivanhoe money in the vault?"

"Ask Burt. Burton ought to know. He was your star witness. And what about Peter Wang? Your girls fucked up. Their shooflies must have figured he was one more Chinaman without a past."

"It was a mistake, that's all. Our computers got him mixed up with another Peter Wang, a former shoe salesman."

"Boris, you're full of shit. You just never dreamed that Tiny could ever have been with the FBI. Maurie was right. The girls didn't do their homework."

Boris left, but Isaac didn't have any peace. Henry Armstrong put on his women's clothes again and robbed a pair of banks back-to-back in Queens. He scribbled a note to the *Daily News*. "Dear Editor, Greetings from The Most Wanted Man. Tell the FBI that they'll never take me. Your Friend, Henry Armstrong Lee."

The Most Wanted Man in America robbed another two banks. He had his own "column" now in the *News*. "Bank robbing is my business. I pay quarterly taxes to Uncle Sam. But I don't leave a return address."

Meanwhile Isaac sat behind Teddy Roosevelt's desk and waited for Henry to surface again. It was an FBI informant at Riker's who ratted on Henry Lee. And Isaac was one of the last men to arrive at the bombed-out hill in Harlem where the Bureau and Isaac's own Emergency Service Unit had surrounded the bank robber. The FBI was working directly with ESU. They had fucking elephant guns with sniperscopes that could see into a cave. They had Daniel Boone, the Department's robot that could knock a door down and punch a brick wall to pieces. Daniel Boone was four feet high. He stood on caterpillar tracks. He had clawlike arms. The video cameras laced to him were almost like a head.

"I don't want Daniel Boone," Isaac told Chief Whitman, the commander of ESU.

"But he has an arsenal in there," Whitman said. "And he won't talk to us. He's threatening to kill whoever comes into his sights. It has to be Daniel Boone."

"I'm going over the hump," Isaac said. "Alone."

"Sir," Whitman said. "I can't let you do that. You're a civilian. And I'm in charge of this unit."

"Are you going to arrest me, Whitman?"

"You can bust me, send me to the Bronx, but I'm responsible for your safety."

"That's the problem. It's safer on the other side of the hump."

And Isaac climbed over the hill in his leather coat. He was marching in some no-man's-land. His feet sank into the mud.

He saw a rat's head, and he prayed that Henry Lee would recognize him in all the leather he had on. He didn't dare shout his name, because he couldn't tell how reliable the echoes were. Isaac made no sudden moves. He marched. He felt like he was crossing a baseball field. Ah, if only he could have been a center fielder, like Harry Lieberman. He would have galloped around in long dark socks. And he'd never have gone to the Mexican League.

He arrived at a block of abandoned buildings. Henry Lee had his own fort. He could have been on the roofs somewhere or down in the sinkhole. Isaac had to trust his own intuition. He hauled his ass through a window as he'd done the last time with Henry Lee. The bank robber was sitting on the floor with a bandolier of ammunition and a couple of M16s. He was shivering in his women's clothes. But he didn't have a wig. He wore a kerchief around his head.

"Little brother, did you bring me any beer or soda pop?"

Isaac gritted his teeth. "I didn't see any groceries in the field."

"Well, come and sit," Henry said. And Isaac sat next to the bank robber.

"Why didn't you stay at Riker's where you had a good deal?"

"I keep telling you, little brother. Harlem is my home."

"But couldn't you have found better quarters? I mean, you robbed four fucking banks."

"I give it all away," Henry said. "I can't hold on to money. What happened to Macho?"

"He got stomped to death in Hunts Point."

"That was Short Eyes? I heard about it on the radio. He was trying to get it down with a twelve-year-old kid and the neighbors caught him."

"Neighbors? A posse, you mean. And what evidence did they have? It was all circumstantial. It wouldn't have held up in court."

"Courts don't mean shit at Hunts Point. You need an education."

"Then give me one."

The bank robber started to laugh. He used the kerchief to wipe his eyes. "I ain't got the time for classes. The Man wants my body, wants my bones."

They both heard an odd, cranking noise, like a mammoth toy on an anthill. Henry grabbed his rifles. "They're coming, little brother. You'd better split. You're just one more white boy who's been to Riker's. They'll mess you up."

The noise grew louder and louder. "Don't worry," Isaac said. "It's Daniel. He belongs to the emergency team."

"I believe you. But who the fuck is Daniel?"

"Our robot. He chews doors."

They crawled to one of the windows. Daniel Boone was riding in the mud. The robot's caterpillar tracks kept climbing hills until Daniel approached the house that Henry and Isaac were in.

"I ain't doing time again in Kansas."

"Come on," Isaac said. "You're Henry Lee. Who could ever hold you in the can?"

They walked out of the building while Daniel Boone began to demolish the walls. Isaac shielded the bank robber with the skirts of his leather coat in case some sharpshooter had funny ideas about Henry Lee. They started crossing the field together. Henry Lee clung to Isaac's coat.

Chief Whitman met them in the middle of the mud.

"Go on," Isaac shouted at the chief. "Arrest the man. And read him his rights."

He was summoned to the Blue Room at City Hall. Isaac could have told Becky Karp to scratch herself, but there would have been a big stink. The mayor was presenting him with a medal. He was the only man alive who had ever captured Henry Armstrong Lee, captured him twice. He arrived in his Gestapo coat and wouldn't take it off. Bottles of pink champagne were waiting for him in the Blue Room. Reporters surrounded Isaac. His blue head appeared in front of television cameras. He had a garden of microphones under his chin.

"Commissioner, was it dangerous out there in Indian country with Henry Armstrong Lee?"

"No," Isaac said. "He was a lamb."

Becky whisked him away from the microphones. "You'll spoil the whole shebang. Why did you come in that thug's coat of yours? I can't pin a medal on such a coat. And you ought to shave, buddy. I don't like my commissioners wearing beards. It sets a bad example. And do me a favor, Isaac. Don't give interviews, huh? I'll do all the talking . . . what's the matter?"

"You shouldn't have sent Michaelson and his Three Sisters after me."

"Did I have a choice? You were meddling in Mafia affairs. I couldn't gag the corruptions commissioner. It was his party."

"Bullshit," Isaac said. "He'd never have moved without your consent."

"Isaac, I have the primaries to consider. You stopped being a policeman when you stepped inside your own secret mirror."

"Then why are you giving me a medal?"

"Because you were cleared. And you captured that pest."

"I didn't capture him. I just wanted to keep Henry alive. But eat your heart out, Rebecca. I might decide to run against you in the primaries."

She deserted Isaac and climbed the platform to her microphone. The room was caught in a blaze of light. She held the Peter Minuit medal in her hand. It was a tiny slug of gold with Minuit's face on the surface and the City's seal. Isaac had to smile, because it was Minuit who'd cheated the Indians out of Manhattan Island. He was the City's first pirate.

Isaac wouldn't listen to Becky's babble. She could praise him until the sky crashed into the Blue Room. But he had to go and get his medal or the whole City government would have stopped. "We love you, Commissioner," she said to the cameras. "You're a son of New York." And she did finally pin the medal onto Isaac's coat. "Cocksucker," she sang in his ear. And she begged the reporters not to bother Isaac.

"The man's been through some ordeal."

Isaac mingled with the guests. He drank champagne with Cardinal Jim. "Mazel tov," the cardinal said.

"Thank you, Jim. You took a chance when you showed up at my trial. I might have been convicted and . . ."

"Boyo, it was nothing, nothing at all."

The cardinal had to waltz away from Isaac to hold a little press conference with Rebecca Karp. And in the wake of Jim's red beanie Isaac saw LeComte. The cultural commissar was chatting with Maurie Goodstein. The pols wouldn't leave Maurie alone. They kept tugging at him. Maurie had returned to civilization, and the town wanted to be in his good graces again. Maurie was terrific collateral. None of the pols knew when they might need him in court. They lured him into a corner, and Isaac had LeComte to himself.

"Where's Margaret?"

"I love your medal, Isaac. Now you have two heavy hitters on your side. Hamilton and Peter Minuit."

"Where's Margaret?"

"I sold her to the Syrians."

"Sold her? She's not a bloody cow."

"She's worse," LeComte said. "A homicidal lady. Had to get rid of her, Isaac. There were too many corpses lying around."

"Jesus, you're a lovely man. I'm glad I stole Henry Lee from you and your boys at the Bureau."

"Isaac, you only walked in the mud. We have Henry Lee. I don't begrudge you the headlines. You're our Hamilton Fellow. That's why I'm here. I want you on the road again."

"A jailbird like me?"

"You're twice as valuable. You beat the rap. You made Rebecca look foolish. She picked on her own policeman."

"Is that what it's all about? You'd like some Republican sitting where Rebecca sits."

"I'd rather have you."

"Then why did you lend Teddy DiAngelis to the Three Sisters? He was your ace."

"I had to give them something, or people might have said it was a cover-up. And I was having some thoughts about letting you sink. Serious thoughts. You are a pain in the ass. But you can thank the Powerhouse."

"What the hell does that mean?"

"Cardinal Jim. He pressured me."

"I still don't get it."

"He didn't want a black police commissioner. He would have lost his pull with the Department. The Irish love you, Isaac. They're already dying out. But they'd have disappeared completely with a black Commish."

"So it's all fucking politics, isn't it?"

"No. The cardinal's fond of you. That was the clincher."

And Isaac walked out of his own celebration at City Hall.

He went to Rivington Street. He dug out his entire collection of baseball cards, all the stock he had. From George Sisler, 1915, to Joe DiMaggio, 1936, and Harry Lieberman, 1942.

He met with King Farouk.

"Ismail, I'll give you everything. But get Margaret Tolstoy out of Damascus. I don't want her dying there. I won't see her. I won't talk to her. I promise. But get her out."

Isaac didn't care if Farouk was Syria's chief of counterintelligence. He still had the manner and the refinement of a clerk.

"Even if I could help you, and I can't," Farouk said, "I could never take your Harry Lieberman. I know how much you love that card . . . you shouldn't tempt me. I'm a fanatic. Please, put your cards away."

"And what about Margaret?"

"I have no voice in that matter. I didn't deal her away from LeComte."

"But is she in Damascus?"

"Probably. Probably not. Never trust an intelligence chief. We all behave like little brokers. I wanted to attend your trial, but I thought it might compromise you if word of it ever got out. I did have one of my own men in the courtroom. It was curious, your trial, like a tale from Scheherazade."

"It wasn't so curious," Isaac said. "Burt was LeComte's man. From the beginning."

"Yes," Farouk said. "I would imagine so. But the six hundred thousand dollars?"

"Burt must have done business for LeComte on the side. Drugs. Bond swindles. Bank robberies. Who knows?"

"And the bank manager?"

"Tiny? I guess he was also LeComte's man."

"Ah, now you're beginning to think like a spy. Isaac, go back to the fixer."

"LeComte?"

"He's the only one who can lead you to Margaret Tolstoy, even if she is in Damascus. But I have one question." And Farouk's eyes began to flutter. "How much are you asking for Joe DiMaggio, Nineteen hundred and thirty-six?"

⚜

He waylaid LeComte outside his Manhattan pied-à-terre.

"All right," he said. "I'll deal."

LeComte looked at him. "What the hell are you talking about?"

"I said I'll deal. I'll go on the road. I'll be your Hamilton Fellow. But I want one meet with Margaret Tolstoy."

"That's impossible. The Syrians have her."

"One meet, LeComte. It doesn't have to last very long. I want to see her face."

"Do you know how many strings I'd have to pull? Can you appreciate the logistics of it?"

"One meet."

"But I'm not saying where or when. It might take a month.
Two months. A year. I can't promise."

Isaac brooded on his way home. He missed the deep,
rounded bowl of a Catskill sky. He thought and thought about
his white hotel on Swan Lake. And he began to have a funny
feeling. He got his chauffeur out of bed. "Sergeant, crank up
the bus. I'll need you in half an hour."

"Where are we going, Chief?"

"Never mind."

They drove across the Washington Bridge. Isaac could
sense his own ruination in the wind behind his ears. The
sergeant got him to the borders of that white hotel.

"Wait here," Isaac said.

"I don't like it. Will you borrow my gun?"

"Wait here."

And Isaac clambered up the hill to the hotel's front porch.
He couldn't find a light in any window. None of his own men
would have been fool enough to advertise themselves with
little squares of light.

He'd come on a hunch, that's all. A policeman's holiday. He
entered that darkened cave of the Hotel Gardenia.

A voice boomed between the walls. "Stop right there."

Don Isacco smiled. "Burt, is this how LeComte takes care
of his men?"

"I'm not with Justice. I never was. LeComte borrowed me
for a little while. I told you he'd fuck us. You wouldn't listen.
You gave him the Ivanhoes."

"I wouldn't do that."

"Are you carrying a grudge?" the Afrikaner asked.

"Against you, Burt?"

"You know what I bloody well mean."

"Where are the other lads? With you?"

"Don't be silly. We've been discarded, boss. LeComte took

Allen Locksley and got rid of the rest, gave them tickets to Timbuktu."

"But you're my commandant."

"That's a laugh," Burt said. "He was going to deport me, Isaac."

"You don't have to explain. But how did you get all that cash into my box?"

"Simple. I took your key. You were always absentminded."

"And the six hundred thousand?"

"That was money we swiped from Sal. I moved it from our vaults to Tiny's bank. LeComte was setting up the Three Sisters. Little Maurice was so high on coke, LeComte had to lead him by the hand. LeComte inspired your whole defense. It was like a war game. Put the Hamilton Fellow in jeopardy and then build him a pair of wings so he can fly out of Boris Michaelson's cage. He's a stupid man, Michaelson is. Now LeComte has the Gov and Becky Karp kissing his backside twice a day. And I saved a nice fat stocking for myself."

"Then why didn't you run to Lisbon or the Canaries?"

"Been waiting," Burt said.

"For what?"

"You, my dear. I'm your liege man. You have to release me."

"I can't," Isaac said. "I want to resurrect the Ivanhoes."

"Should I fart now or later?"

"I'm serious."

"Then I might consider putting a hole in your neck."

"It wouldn't do much good. You'd still belong to me."

And Isaac walked out of the white hotel. He hummed to himself on the way down from the hill. "Brian Boru," the sergeant muttered. "Walks into the blackest house, sits with the Devil, and comes out singing. Brian Boru."

28

The Hamilton Fellow had five days to pack. It was as if he'd dreamt Riker's Island, dreamt his trial. The one bit of reality was Henry Armstrong Lee. That was his particular pearl. But he wouldn't lecture on Henry Lee. He talked baseball in Detroit. "The war was on. America missed DiMaggio. But the Giants had a wartime sub who could hit and field like Joltin' Joe. Harry Lieberman. The Bomber. Every air-raid warden in Manhattan had his picture on the wall. Fans mobbed him at the Polo Grounds. The Giants had to unlock a secret gate for Harry, or he'd never have gotten in. But who remembers the Bomber now?"

There was silence in the auditorium. The police chiefs thought Isaac had malaria and was reliving some old wound. And then the questions came.

"Commissioner Sidel, what does this man the Bomber have to do with crime prevention?"

"Everything. He's a sign of our collective amnesia. How can you have crime prevention without history and a sense of the past?"

The police chiefs whistled to themselves, called Isaac a sly dog who could weave baseball into the war against crime.

He stopped in Albuquerque. He stopped in Phoenix and Tucson, talking, talking about the Bomber. And then in Oklahoma City he spotted a man who had his own blue beard. It was Teddy DiAngelis. He trundled up to Isaac like a corpse at high noon. His eyes were black buttons in his head. His mouth was a penciled line. He couldn't even sweat in the middle of a heat wave. LeComte must have been hiding him here in the witness protection program.

"Isaac, the Sisters said I would go to jail. I got scared. Michaelson gave me a script. I memorized it. . . . I heard about your lecture in the newspapers. I had to come. Isaac, I wouldn't forget the Bomber. I remember all his home runs."

"If LeComte put you in witness protection, you're not supposed to surface like this."

"Fuck witness protection. It's not a life. I'm in the same line of work. I whacked out two people since I got to Oklahoma."

"Jesus, don't tell me that. I'm a cop."

"I called Eileen. She said I was a rat bastard son of a bitch."

Teddy started to blubber with his big blue head. Isaac was the last bit of family he had on the whole crumpled face of America. He took out a pencil and licked the point. "I'll give you my address. We could eat some ribs together and—"

"Don't even talk about it, Teddy. You're a submarine, a ghost, a guy in deep slumber."

Isaac left the auditorium. He cursed LeComte. But he was still the Hamilton Fellow. He arrived in St. Louis that afternoon. He went straight to the children's shelter. He had no authority to meet with McCardle, but he lied. "I'm on a mission for the Justice Department."

"We have our rules," the head nurse told him. She was as muscular as Isaac, but she didn't have mean eyes. She was protecting McCardle. St. Louis wasn't on Isaac's itinerary. LeComte hadn't invited him back to this village of the old crusader king.

"Well, you get Loren Cole on the line," Isaac said. "He's chief of detectives in this town."

"I know that. I'll give you five minutes with Mr. McCardle."

Isaac wasn't even allowed into the hearth of the children's shelter. He had to wait near the door like some bloody dog.

"Hello, grandpa."

Kingsley had the same brown jumpsuit that he'd worn the last time in St. Louis. And Isaac explored the dark design of his face—the tiny, mottled ears, the bitten nose—and he felt cheated: the kid was a fucking old man.

"Sorry," Isaac said. "My schedule is tight. Or we could have gone to a Cardinal game."

"I've been grounded," McCardle said. "Can't leave the premises."

"I still have some pull."

"But it wouldn't be democratic," McCardle said.

"Since when are you such a man of the people?"

"I always was, grandpa."

The nurse hovered over them, pointing to the clock on the wall.

"Ma'am," Isaac said. "Couldn't we have a little privacy?"

And the nurse disappeared into some corner of the jail.

"Grandpa, your head is all blue."

" 'S nothing," Isaac said. "Riker's Island disease. Couldn't I get you something? Like a baseball card on 'Country' Slaughter?"

"I wouldn't know what to do with it, grandpa. Some kid would steal the card and I'd have to break his head. And then where would I be? I have to go. I'm glad you got out of jail."

And McCardle went behind a door in his brown jumpsuit, like a convict who could never graduate. Isaac's blue head was boiling. He'd been tricked by the crusader king.

Loren Cole was outside the shelter, sitting in a police car. Isaac skirted past him. "Isaac?" Loren said.

"Fuck you."

"Will you get into the vehicle, please?"

"Make me."

Loren drove alongside Isaac.

"I should have guessed it," Isaac muttered. "Giving me all this bull about McCardle. How some court was going to sentence a nine-year-old kid unless you pulled him out of circulation. He's not a kid, is he?"

"No," Loren said.

"He just happens to look like a runt. How old is McCardle? Twenty-five?"

"I'm not sure," Loren said.

"Jesus Christ. A distant cousin of yours? Part of the clan? Ain't that so?"

"He's my nephew. My dead sister's boy."

"Did you ever stop and think, Loren, that a prison sentence might be better than this? He's stuck here for life."

"He wouldn't have survived in the slammer," Loren said. "The niggers would have treated him like turtle soup . . . now will you get in? I have to drive you to the airport. The Justice Department's been hollering at me all afternoon. People are expecting you in Salt Lake City."

Isaac swam in the Great Salt Lake. He'd never have believed the buoyancy. He floated for half a mile without a rubber tube or a raft. He was much more civilized with the police chiefs. He went to their private shooting range. He fired a Colt Commander at a wooden rabbit that hopped like a maddening ball along a metal track. Isaac broke the rabbit's tail. . . .

It was June and Isaac wore his leather coat in L.A. He bought a giant peach at the Farmers Market. He marched around, looking like a Nazi policeman who'd escaped from a television pilot. He spoke at the Beverly Hilton. He didn't mention the Bomber once. He sang for his supper like a good little boy. There was a group of mystery writers in the audience that wanted to know about his months at Riker's.

"Mr. Sidel," their leader asked, "how did you get along with the prison population?"

"No problems."

"But you were in an isolation ward, weren't you?"

"In theory, yes. But I mingled. I had access to the other cellblocks."

"Is it true that Riker's was one of Henry Lee's hideouts?"

Isaac wondered if the poor bastard was a district attorney on the side. He wasn't going to give Henry's routes away.

"It's possible. A house of detention is like any hotel. Henry might have checked in. But I wouldn't know."

Isaac was staying at the Chateau Marmont. From his room in the rafters he could look down into that bungalow colony called West Hollywood, with its endless beads of light. His phone rang. It was two in the morning.

"Grandpa, I should have been more polite."

"Kingsley, did you pull my telephone number out of a hat?"

"Loren gave it to me."

Isaac still couldn't think of McCardle as a lad of twenty-five or thirty. "Who's the grandpa?" he asked. "Me or you?"

McCardle laughed. "I've been fourteen so long, I can't remember what it's like to have a birthday . . . shit, nurse is comin'. Gotta blow. But be careful."

"What the hell for? I'm a goddamn lecturer, Mr. McCardle. All I do is talk and talk."

"My back is itchin'. And it means something. Good-bye."

Isaac stayed near the window. He heard footsteps outside his door. The Hamilton Fellow didn't have to get involved in mysteries. And he wouldn't wear a gun. He opened the door and could see a man in a felt hat at the far end of the hall.

"Hey, you look familiar," Isaac said. "Have you been to any of my lectures?"

But the man's face was obscured. He had a winter coat that was as incongruous in California as Isaac himself.

"Want to come inside?" Isaac asked, reaching for a lamp, but the guy in the felt hat started to run. Isaac locked his door.

He didn't sleep. He got to the airport at seven and had a pathetic bagel at one of the counters. And for the first time in months Isaac was conscious of his worm. The beast hadn't bothered him much at Riker's. It ate all the prison food. It never grabbed at him during the trial. And now at L.A. International it decided to roil. It sucked at Isaac with its hundred heads. He could feel his insides snake to the worm's electric rhythms. Isaac had to sit.

A blue head floated toward him. It was unmistakable. Teddy DiAngelis had come out of Oklahoma City. LeComte had him on a curious schedule. The submarine had surfaced twice. He didn't smile. He approached Isaac and extended his sleeve. And that's when Isaac saw the silver barrel of his single-shot, that derringer he could produce like hocus-pocus. And now it made sense. Nose had been stalking Isaac. He'd appeared at Isaac's lecture to wind his fucking clock. But Isaac wouldn't dally in Oklahoma with Ted. He'd run to St. Louis on a whim to see the ex-boy, Kingsley McCardle. And Nose had missed his chance.

"Go on," Isaac growled. "Do your stuff."

The derringer shot back into Teddy's sleeve. Isaac had startled him. His button eyes exploded with crazy points of light. He looked like a blind man in the middle of a hurricane when someone sidled up to Ted and struck him with a blackjack hidden in a nylon sock. Nose fell into Isaac's arms. The guy with the blackjack wore a felt hat. He reached into Nose's sleeve, pulled out the derringer, and put it into his own pocket.

"Margaret," Isaac muttered. "You can take off that bloody hat."

"No," she said. "I'd rather look like a man. It's safer that way."

"You were never in Damascus. LeComte didn't sell you to the Syrians."

"Who would believe a fairy tale like that?"

"Only an imbecile," Isaac said. "He just shifted you to another part of the forest."

Her hair was bunched under her hat and her breasts were invisible with the coat she wore. Ah, Isaac forgot. Margaret had been an actress most of her life. He wondered what identity the Bureau had given her now. Her eyes had lost that almond color. Her mouth was redder than Isaac had recalled. Was she Rita from Detroit? Or Carolina Carole?

"It wasn't LeComte who sent you."

"No. I was in New Orleans. I heard two men talking at a poker game. They laughed every time they mentioned your name."

"Were they melameds, like Izzy Wasser?"

"You are an imbecile. They belonged to Sal Rubino."

"Nose is in witness protection and he works for Sal?"

"Why not? Who else will have him? Isaac, you'd better do something about the Rubinos."

"I will. But how did you find where I was?"

"I bribed a clerk at Justice. It wasn't hard. All your wanderings are in the public record."

"Anastasia?"

"I'm not Anastasia anymore."

"Ah, the little girl with the hole in her sock is gone. And I suppose I ought to forget the samovar. But I can't, Anastasia."

"Shut up," she said.

"Margaret," Isaac said with Nose still in his arms. "Margaret. Haven't you been LeComte's little swallow long enough?"

"It doesn't really matter who my masters are. Haven't you figured that yet? You're too serious, Commissioner Sidel. You always were."

"Yeah," Isaac said, "but couldn't you stay with me?"

"I'd disappoint you, Isaac. I was never much of a housewife, even when I was twelve. And I can't go back to Manhattan. So shut up. I'll be late for New Orleans." She pointed to Ted. "What about the sharpshooter?"

"I'll spank him when he wakes up."

Margaret disappeared and Isaac sat with that huge homicidal baby. He had plenty of time. He didn't bother about the plane he had to catch. There were no pinch hitters in Isaac's universe. Whatever audience there was would have to wait.

⚜

She sat on the plane with her new red hair. The man next to her tried to flirt with Margaret. He was a Cajun lawyer from Magazine Street. He wore a toupee and was twenty years younger than Margaret.

"I can get you a Hollywood contract," he said. "Just like that."

"I'm a grandma," Margaret told him.

"Makes no difference to me. You have a boyfriend, doll?"

"Yes, his name is Isaac. And he swallows people for a living."

"But he isn't on the plane. It's just you and me, cher."

"And my grandchildren," Margaret said, thinking about that schoolboy she'd left behind in L.A., with his sideburns and big brown eyes. It was the longest romance in history. She laughed at the image of herself as the reluctant bride of Isaac Sidel. The lawyer let his hand drop like a silver rodent onto her lap. "Just you and me, cher." Margaret bent his thumb back until he had to bite his lip to keep from howling.

"Are you happy, cher?" she said, and gave the lawyer back his thumb. He hopped into the seat behind Margaret. "Will you take me to Galatoire's? Can we have a little dirty rice and pompano while you reach into my pants? . . . Next time don't disturb a grandma."

But she started to cry, because she'd eaten her own children, orphans who'd wandered out of some asylum in that Odessa under Little Angel Street. Margaret wished she were a child of the Catacombs, a night animal who'd never spilled into the sunny, outside world.

The Leonardo brothers, young lords of Dauphine Street, met her flight. She'd told them she had a sick cousin in L.A., or she couldn't have gotten out of their little parish to search for Isaac Sidel. Emile was thirty-six. Martin was thirty-five. They wore felt hats and sharkskin coats that curled around their bodies like a bat's wings. They'd both fallen in love with Margaret at a party on Royal Street. They looked like chipmunks with balding heads. They controlled prostitution in the Quarter with two other crime families. But they hadn't wanted Margaret for one of their cribs. She was their own particular lady. She could speak French with all the Creole maids. She knew how to order tea and turtle soup in half a dozen languages. And she could make them delirious in bed.

The brothers had given her necklaces and engagement rings, but they hadn't solved the riddle of how they could marry her and still remain friends.

"Was it warm in Los Angeles, Red?"

"Yes," Margaret told the brothers, but she could feel that edge of irritation in Emile's voice: they hadn't believed her story about the cousin. They brought her to their club on Dauphine Street, they had a meal together, and Martin stayed with her that night. She shut her eyes and thought of Isaac while Martin snored with his holster inside his pajamas. The illusion of ordinary life only made her more suspicious. They couldn't even look into Margaret's eyes. She woke up the second night with metal on her skin. Martin had given her another bracelet. But there was sadness to the brothers' deception. They could kill and lure the innocent into some miserable warehouse, but they couldn't really lie to Margaret. Their hands trembled. Emile developed a tick.

"We have some business, Red," Martin told her on the third night. "Like to come?"

"Of course," she said.

And they drove her to a sausage factory near Bayou St. John. She entered the factory with Emile and Martin. She could smell blood and peppers on the walls. The floor was coated with some ancient gelatin, and Margaret almost slipped.

280 • JEROME CHARYN

"Careful, Red."

Men in brown uniforms kept coming in and out of the factory; Margaret couldn't tell if it was an old butchers' reunion. Then she saw Sal Rubino in a summer hat. "Hello, hon," he said.

The brothers kept staring at the walls.

Sal smiled. "You look sensational with red hair." Men came in and out of the factory. "The Feds giving you a bonus for nailing Martin and Emile?"

The brothers began to shuffle their feet.

"How dumb can the Bureau get? New Orleans is almost like my own backyard. These kids are cousins of mine. I wouldn't let them drown, Margaret. I wouldn't let them drown."

"Ah, Sal," Martin said. "Couldn't we hurt her just a little?"

"No," Sal said. "She's a fucking menace. Only the worst FBI bitch would agree to marry two men."

"It's not official," Emile said. "We both gave her rings, that's all. She didn't make any promises."

"Jesus," Sal said. "The woman's selling you to the United States and you defend her?"

"I wasn't defending her," Emile said. "I only wanted to give the facts."

"Well, she's going down. Where's your shooter, Emile?"

"I wouldn't come without my shooter," Emile said.

"I want both of you to hit her between the eyes."

Martin and Emile removed their guns from the elaborate leather cradles they wore. Their hands were steady now. And Margaret was almost glad. She didn't have to maneuver between the brothers and Sal. She could go to that Odessa under the ground.

A pair of men in brown uniforms approached. They were carrying shopping bags. Were they looking for fresh sausages in this charnel house? The shopping bags fell to the floor. They were holding Mossberg Persuaders in their arms.

Emile recognized Jerry DiAngelis. "How are you, padrone?"

"He's not your padrone," Sal said. "He's a piece of shit."

"Who's the other guy?"

"The police commissioner of New York."

"What's he doing with Jerry?"

"Don't you get it, Emile? They're a team . . . pull on the
bitch, for Christ's sake."

"Not with a commissioner around," Martin said.

"Are you blind? Jerry has his Persuader. Pull on them,
before they wipe us out."

"We're citizens of New Orleans," Martin said. "No PC
would ever pull on us in our own fucking parish."

"He's in love with your woman and he hates my guts."

Margaret tried to warn them, but she knew it was hopeless
for Martin and Emile. They'd never understand Isaac Sidel.
She wasn't even sure if she could understand that crazy
Commish. "Martin," she said, "Emile, put your shooters on
the floor and get the hell out of here."

"It's not your business, Red," Martin told her. The brothers
aimed at Isaac and Jerry, and Margaret heard five or six
explosions that shook the roof of the sausage factory and
splintered the walls. Martin, Emile, and Sal Rubino lay
among the splinters. Another man arrived. It was Isaac's
Ivanhoe, the one with the bald head. Burt. He took both
shotguns and walked out of the factory.

She looked at Martin and Emile on the floor. "They really
liked me."

"Cut it out," Jerry said. "The Commish saved your life."

"And what are you doing here? Your own people tried to
kill me half a dozen times."

"That was different," Jerry said. "I couldn't let Isaac walk
into this shit pile all alone. My father-in-law would never
forgive me."

"And what's LeComte going to say?"

"LeComte didn't back you up. We did."

"You're so charitable," Margaret said. "You saw an easy way to get rid of Sal. That's why you're here."

"I'd be dumb not to protect my own interests, wouldn't I?"

"And you," she said to Isaac, he of the dark eyes, who hadn't uttered a word in this catacomb. "Didn't I tell you not to follow me?"

Isaac gripped her hand. And he marched her out of the factory with Jerry DiAngelis. She'd never reach that underground Odessa with Isaac Sidel.

"I won't live with you."

"Shhh," Isaac said. "I have to be in Dallas." And like some kind of husband, he was still holding her hand.